P9-AFW-018

SIMON & SCHUSTER CHILDREN'S PUBLISHING
ADVANCE READER'S COPY

TITLE: Better Must Come

AUTHOR: Desmond Hall

IMPRINT: Caitlyn Dlouhy Books/Atheneum BFYR

ON-SALE DATE: 05/07/2024

ISBN: 9781534460744

FORMAT: hardcover

PRICE: $19.99

AGES: 14 up

PAGES: 336

Please send any review or mention of this book to
ChildrensPublicity@simonandschuster.com.

Aladdin • Atheneum Books for Young Readers
Beach Lane Books • Beyond Words • Boynton Bookworks
Caitlyn Dlouhy Books • Denene Millner Books
Libros para niños • Little Simon • Margaret K. McElderry Books
MTV Books • Paula Wiseman Books • Salaam Reads
Simon & Schuster Books for Young Readers
Simon Pulse • Simon Spotlight

BETTER MUST COME

Also by desmond hall

Your Corner Dark

BETTER

desmond hall

MUST

COME

Ⓐ **A Caitlyn Dlouhy Book**
atheneum
New York London Toronto Sydney New Delhi

An imprint of Simon & Schuster Children's Publishing Division

1230 Avenue of the Americas, New York, New York 10020

Text © 2024 by Desmond Hall

Jacket illustration © 2024 by Krystal Quiles

Jacket design by Sonia Chaghatzbanian

Simon & Schuster: Celebrating 100 Years of Publishing in 2024

For information about special discounts for bulk purchases, please contact Simon & Schuster Special Sales at 1-866-506-1949 or business@simonandschuster.com.

The Simon & Schuster Speakers Bureau can bring authors to your live event. For more information or to book an event, contact the Simon & Schuster Speakers Bureau at 1-866-248-3049 or visit our website at www.simonspeakers.com.

Interior design by Irene Metaxatos

The text for this book was set in ITC Slimbach Std.

Manufactured in the United States of America

First Edition

10 9 8 7 6 5 4 3 2 1

Library of Congress Cataloging-in-Publication Data

Names: Hall, Desmond, author.

Title: Better must come / Desmond Hall.

Description: First edition. | New York : Atheneum Books for Young Readers, 2024. | "A Caitlyn Dlouhy Book." | Audience: Ages 14 up. | Audience: Grades 10–12. | Summary: Two teenagers, Deja a "barrel girl" and Gabriel a gang member desperate to get out, become inextricably involved in a complex web of tragedy and danger when Deja finds herself with $500,000 of drug money that Gabriel is tasked with collecting.

Identifiers: LCCN 2023031485 (print) | LCCN 2023031486 (ebook) | ISBN 9781534460744 (hardcover) | ISBN 9781534460768 (ebook)

Subjects: CYAC: Friendship—Fiction. | Gangs—Fiction | Lost and found possessions—Fiction. | Jamaica—Fiction. | BISAC: YOUNG ADULT FICTION / Thrillers & Suspense / Crime | YOUNG ADULT FICTION / Social Themes / Friendship | LCGFT: Thrillers (Fiction) | Novels.

Classification: LCC PZ7.1.H272 Be 2024 (print) | LCC PZ7.1.H272 (ebook) | DDC [Fic]—dc23

LC record available at https://lccn.loc.gov/2023031485

LC ebook record available at https://lccn.loc.gov/2023031486

To my sister, Carole,
my favorite "Barrel Girl."
See you in the next life.

BETTER MUST COME

*Q*ueen, Uncle Glen's sea-scarred, twenty-foot fishing boat, daubed in the sweet stench of fish and gasoline, tore through waves of turquoise toward Springtown Harbour's floating dock at way too fast a speed. But Deja stood serenely behind the wheel, troubled only by inventory. Exactly how many bars of Irish Spring soap did she have left back at home? That was where her focus was. Her mother had included some in the barrel she'd sent from the United States. If Deja could figure out how many she and her siblings had used up so far, she could tell her mother exactly how many to pack in her next shipment of stuff they couldn't buy on the island. Then there'd be more room for other things.

That was when the boat's two engines started sounding like one.

Deja immediately slowed the boat down. Uncle Glen lunged from the casting foredeck toward the casting rear deck, where his friend, and fellow fisherman, Mr. Wallace stood. The sound of Uncle's boots made Deja think of fat flounders jumping out of the water and into the boat. The two men hunched over one engine, their heads rocking side to side.

"Backside!" Mr. Wallace shouted his favorite non-curse curse word. "Engine done."

Uncle Glen gripped his chin. "Seems so."

Two engines made docking easy. One was trickier. Much trickier, especially since the boat hadn't been centered for one engine. Deja licked her sea-salty lips, eager for the chance to prove herself, hoping her uncle wouldn't insist on taking the wheel.

With the morning winds whipping every which way, this had gotten real. She quickly adjusted the LED spotlight to shine on the slip up ahead.

Mr. Wallace joined Deja at the helm, waving his skinny arms. "Turn di boat, Deja, and head fi di west side dock. Di current no so strong pon that side."

"No, mon, di fish market no right over deh." Uncle Glen flicked a hand toward the old market at the edge of the gravelly beach. "A 'nuff fish we catch. It going to take us a long time fi haul it from di west side back over to di market."

Mr. Wallace frowned. "So, you rather sink di boat and make di fish fall back inna di water?"

Deja looked from the bow to the slip. It was doable. "I agree with Uncle," she said by way of answer.

Mr. Wallace's frown deepened. "No easy fi dock inna this weather, you know, Deja."

Deja glared his way. "I can do it." His lack of faith was typical of most fisher*men*.

"Gwan, Deja!" her uncle encouraged, stepping up on the fly-bridge as well. He was never typical.

Mr. Wallace flung his arms in agitation; he should really cut back on the coffee. "You mad! She can't dock di boat in di slip straight-on. The sea angry, mon, and is only one engine now!" *You'd think this was* his *boat,* Deja thought. "She going go crash it, mon," he went on.

What a crosses! Deja fought back from giving Mr. Wallace the stink-eye. But then again, she shouldn't feel a way about Mr. Wallace. After all, he'd never seen her pilot before, but still . . .

"Rest yourself, Wally. Deja all right," Uncle Glen told him, as if reading her mind. "She have di skill—she going use di wind fi park straight-on. You no know nothing, mon."

Deja smiled, then gripped the wheel and focused in on the slip. It was just like any other parking spot, except that it sat between two other boats—expensive ones. *Imagine the boat has wheels that can turn any way you want,* her uncle had told her again and again when he was first teaching her to dock. She'd just started high school—and Mom was still in Jamaica. Wow, was it really only three years ago?

Uncle Glen pointed at the slip. "Straight-on, Deja!"

Deja counted the weatherworn piles in the slip she was aiming at.

But Mr. Wallace wasn't letting it go. He jutted his chin at Uncle. "Sure you no want take di wheel, mon?"

Uncle made a show of picking at a loose thread on his worn polo shirt. "Rest yourself, Wally."

Mr. Wallace rubbed the back of his head. "Me no want *rest in peace!*"

Uncle shrugged, laughing with his mouth closed. "Is an important skill fi Deja to practice, mon."

Uncle Glen was a master boatsman; he could handle this with his eyes closed. But in truth, Deja had done this maneuver right only one other time. The other attempts had dinged up the green and yellow paint pretty good, not that anyone would notice. *Queen* had been through it all, for sure.

Focus! Deja cut the engine. The boat slowed, heading straight for the dock. If she didn't do this right, she'd smash the nose right into the dock. No, no . . . that was doubt talking. Uncle always warned that it would speak up exactly when she had to concentrate the most.

Basics, Deja. Four letters in port and four letters in left, so the right side must be starboard. Chanting the basics always helped her concentrate. Then she angled the nose of the boat just to the right of the middle of the slip. The wind blasted from the starboard side and gave the boat a shove. Like a judo fighter using the opponent's force, Deja spun the wheel left, put the *Queen* into gear, and gave it a little throttle.

Mr. Wallace tugged the bill of his old Yankees cap. "She doing it to backside!"

Another strong gust swung the boat the wrong way. Mr. Wallace's hat flew off. Deja gasped. The weather had turned enemy. She started working the wheel. A little throttle. A yank of the wheel the other way. The *Queen* closed in on one of the docked boats. Dang it! Uncle didn't have money to fix his own, much less someone else's.

"Deja . . ." Uncle's usual bass approached soprano.

She threw the *Queen* in reverse. Throttled hard. Whipped the wheel. The boat straightened . . . and glided into the slip.

Mr. Wallace picked up his cap, and Uncle threw him a rope. "Wally, you have the honor of tying off after witnessing a most exquisite park by my most exquisite niece."

Deja muted her exhale, tried not to grin. *Never let them see you sweat.* She went back to trying to figure out how many bars of soap Mom had included in the barrel and why she *hadn't* sent the new barrel of stuff yet. And that got her thinking about needing to make some more money. Which was why she was heading right back out to fish herself after dropping Uncle and Mr. Wallace off.

Then, right on cue . . . "Um, Deja, it was a long night." Uncle was rubbing the back of his neck. "You sure you want to go out again?"

Like she had a choice! "Why you don't take some of today's catch fi yourself?" he offered.

"Come on, Uncle, you already paid me to pilot." They'd gone over this before—she didn't take charity. Her mom had drilled that into her head better than a dentist could fill a tooth.

"You piloted half di night—you no want fi get some rest?"

"Not tired." It was true—her adrenaline was still pumping after docking the *Queen*.

"But . . . don't you need fi go see about your siblings?"

"I told you, Straleen is looking after them." Then she got why he was trying so hard to dissuade her. "It's the engine, right? You don't want me to take out the boat with just one engine."

He glared back at the faulty engine. "Well, I should fix it first."

"Uncle, I just docked with one engine. I can go out with one too."

He held up a forefinger for her to wait. "Wally, Deja can borrow the *Gregor*, no?"

Surprisingly, Mr. Wallace agreed. He *must* have been impressed with her docking job.

"Good, good." Uncle Glen clucked his tongue two times. "Free of charge, too. And no worry 'bout unloading; just head on out, mon."

She should be grateful, and she *was*, but her heart sank at the thought of piloting Mr. Wallace's rusty old skiff. Still, she needed the money. So she reached for her fishing rod.

Deja, Thursday, 5:30 a.m.

Three-quarters of a mile away, skies blooming violet over distant mountains shrouded in green, she reached one of her favorite fishing spots, close to a shoreline crowded with sea grape trees, mahoes, and red mangroves. Mr. Wallace's dinged-up boat was only named *Gregor* because there was a dent where the *Mc* in the brand name—McGregor—had been scraped away, probably on a bad parking job. But hey, at least . . . made it this far.

The parrotfish were always biting here, and she could usually get one or two bars on her phone in case something happened with her sibs, and Straleen needed to shout. Deja cast out her line. Yesterday morning she'd caught three parrotfish and a fat snapper, made thirty-five dollars selling them to tourists. For American cash, of course. Her mother always said to get American money; the Jamaican dollars hemorrhaged value.

Her cell phone buzzed. She recognized the 347 area code. It

was from Brooklyn—her mom!—but it wasn't her number. Deja jammed her fishing pole into a rickety holder and answered anyway. "Hello?"

"Hi, Deja." It *was* Mom. What a relief.

"Hold on a second." Deja fished out two SIM cards. Which one was the international one? She needed to have Mom call back so she could switch the cards. No need to pay crazy rates. "Ma? Sorry, I'm on the boat, and—just getting the SIM card—"

"Deja, something happened." The hollowness of her mother's voice resonated from more than fifteen hundred miles away.

One of the SIM cards slipped out of Deja's hand and fell onto the deck. "Mom, are you okay?"

The pause was terrifying. "Mom?" Was she there? Dropped calls were a way of life in Jamaica. But then her mother sniffled.

"Mom, can you hear me? What's wrong?"

"Deja, I . . . I've been robbed."

Wait, what? "What, how? Are you all right?"

"Now, don't feel any way about it. I'm okay." Her mother had a teacher's voice, a tone that made you think you were the only one in the world, but that voice was gone. In its place was the sound of someone else, a frazzled person asking you for directions. "I'm in the hospital, but I'm okay."

"*Hospital?* Oh my God! What happened?"

"Steady yourself, baby. Really, I'll be fine. I was on the street, and some man—"

Some man? Deja's stomach clenched, and the rest of her body followed. Some man . . . "Did what? Did what?"

"Listen, Deja, I am . . . fine."

Whenever anyone told you over and over that they were *fine*, it usually meant that they weren't.

"It's mostly—I lost my partner money," her mother blurted out. "He took everything."

Deja nearly snapped her phone in half. "Everything? You had all the partner money on you?!"

That damn money club! She hated it. Carrying around other people's cash? The dumbest idea she'd ever heard of. Her mom loved it, though—said financially distressed people like them needed to make partnerships where each person contributed a specific amount every two weeks or so. Then you all took turns withdrawing the bulk of the money from the partnership to meet big payments when they came due. *Even millionaires would go bankrupt if they couldn't raise enough cash to meet certain payments at specific times,* her mother had insisted when Deja had scoffed at the old-school ridiculousness. It was all about access to big amounts of cash when you needed it. Deja got that, and yeah, yeah, Jamaicans had been making *partners* forever, but literally carrying around *cash*? It was crazy! ATMs, people! There had to be an app for this.

How much was it, all that money? Then Deja went to a worse thought. A man . . . "Mom, are you *sure* you're okay?"

"Deja, here's why I'm telling you this. There won't be any barrel coming, or any money for school fees, you understand me?"

Damn. Damn! Of course, no money equals no barrel. But still. Damn! "Yes, yes, but, Mom! How are *you*?"

"Don't worry about me," her mother insisted, but her voice, flat, so flat, said the opposite. How could she even suggest that? That was about as impossible as impossible could be.

"Are you *sure* you're okay?" Deja pressed.

"Listen, Donovan's ADHD meds are covered for another six months, so that's okay for now." Her mother was clearly avoiding the question. "But the mortgage is coming up. I'll figure something out soon, and . . ." She sounded like she'd been hiking up a mountain, reaching for breath. "Kaleisha's school fees are due, but you can talk to the administrator. Ask her for an extension."

"I talked to her already—"

"Oh good, so I have some time to work it out. Good. That's some relief."

Crap. Now Deja couldn't tell her the rest. That the administrator had yelled so loudly about the fees that the whole of Springtown Harbour must have heard her. But okay, okay, she'd try to talk to the administrator again . . . or maybe she'd just have to avoid her for another month or so.

Deja refocused on the biggest problem. "I guess the only major thing is the mortgage."

"I know that," her mother snapped. Then her tone shifted. "Sorry, I didn't mean to—"

"No problem, Mom. We'll figure it out." But even as she said it, her whole arm went slack and she could hardly hold up the phone. Mom sounded *scared* . . . and she didn't scare easily.

"*We* will. And . . . Deja, don't tell anybody about this—the mortgage, I mean. I don't want that getting out, okay?"

"Sure, got it," she said with all the calm she could muster given that her brain was screaming that this was *so* bad. "Mom, how did it happen?"

"Don't worry about that, baby. How are you doing for food?"

Deja glanced over at Mr. Wallace's empty cooler. "Not bad. We'll be okay for a few weeks." There was rice and stuff. "I'm fishing right now." Deja waited for a reaction, some acknowledgment that she was taking care of business.

At last her mother said, "Good. I'm . . . I'm calling you from someone else's phone—I don't want to run up their bill."

"Your phone got stolen too?"

"They took that— Yes." Now it sounded like her mom was choking back tears.

"Should I . . . ? Should I come up there, to Brooklyn?"

"Deja, don't be silly. You know you can't do that. I need you there for Kaleisha and Donovan. And not a word to them about any of this!" She exhaled long and hard. "Like I said, this is someone else's phone. . . ."

Deja heard a voice in the background saying it was *no problem*. Someone from her money partner group? A nurse? "Mom. Seriously. Are you okay?"

Deja imagined the thief knocking her down, ripping away her purse with the money she had been carrying. How many times has she told her mother that the partner system was a bad idea? How many? And how much had her mom lost? And how in the world would she ever be able to pay it all back? But Deja didn't get a chance to ask. Her mother was saying goodbye, promising to email.

"Love to the kids. Treat yourself to a packet of coconut drops." And then she hung up.

Deja sat in a daze, the boat rocking. Mom, mugged? Up there with no family? And not a bumboclot thing Deja could do about it. On top of that, no barrel. No money. She tucked away her phone and checked her pole—the bait on the line was gone, but no fish. Of course not! Then she gave a hard laugh. *Get yourself a packet of drops.* With what money? Her mother didn't know she'd stopped eating drops—too sugary. Deja'd rather eat coconut. And how would Mom know? It had been a year and a half since she'd seen her. Mom also didn't know Kaleisha started caring about clothes or that Donovan's crossbite had straightened out. There was so much her mother didn't know about any of them anymore; phone calls and emails only shared so much. And now Mom didn't even have a phone.

With a sigh, Deja picked up the SIM card and stuck it back into her pocket, trying to think of what to do next. Gentle waves headed toward the bow. Some lapped against the boat. Others kept their path toward shore, where they would land and become . . . nothing. Just like her mother's dreams of making a small fortune in Brooklyn, then coming back home. Just like Deja's own dream of going to tourism school, starting up a micro cruise line. Her idea was to take tourists all the way around the country by boat, letting them see the *real* Jamaica and getting them to spend their money outside the resort walls. Spread the wealth among the people who really needed it.

All of it becoming nothing.

Deja reset the line with fresh bait, thoughts skidding in dark directions. Would her mom have to repay the other people too? That would take months, longer!

Bumboclot.

Her mom had started and quit so many jobs over there—each time for a pittance more an hour. Cleaning offices, lugging garbage, scraping away nasty stuff from refrigerators. A part-time cooking job, where shift times changed without notice. And now she was taking care of a doctor's elderly father, a job she considered herself lucky to get even if it meant cleaning the old man himself—though maybe it was the raise that she felt lucky about—five more dollars an hour. She'd filed for a work permit, but until she got that, she was limited to cash-only jobs. Low-paying jobs. But they still paid a lot more than working the same jobs here in Jamdown.

Oh—and her mother probably wouldn't be able to come home for Christmas now! Donovan and Kaleisha were going to be totally crushed—two Christmases in a row. And that was when Deja lowered her head and started to sob.

Birds squawked, and then there was the sound of a distant truck horn. She glanced up, and good thing, because the *Gregor* had drifted close to the shore and its barricade of rocks. She checked her line—still empty. She'd drifted close to a small cove she also sometimes fished at, though it was harder to catch snappers there.

She had just recast when she spotted a boat anchored near algae-splattered rocks guarding the shore like burly soldiers. Weird. It was a sleek go-fast boat. Weirder still, she could swear an arm was dangling along the gunwale. Shit. She stood up, shielded her eyes from the morning glare. It sure seemed like an arm, like someone had fallen in the boat. She motored closer, examining the shore. High grass and chubby ficus plants lay in front of the clusters of sea grape and mahoe trees that dominated the coast. There was no one around. Then she allowed herself to look warily toward the go-fast. Had to be seriously wealthy to own one of those. But criminals also used those boats; they could outrun most anything the police had. No way was she getting involved in that.

Then again, maybe the owner wasn't into anything illegal. Maybe he was sick or slipped or something. Or taking a nap?

Which was as unlikely as it sounded. Whatever was going on, it could only mean trouble.

With thoughts of her mom whirling inside her head, Deja pulled the tiller toward her to swing the *Gregor* back toward Springtown Harbour. No more fishing today. At least she'd have time to spend with the kids before dropping them at school. But the next moment she felt a flush of guilt. What if someone was hurt? She shouldn't look back. She shouldn't look back. She looked back. The arm moved.

Deja, Thursday, 6:30 a.m.

As Deja hurried through the tourist magnet that was Springtown Harbour, her brain was in such a rail. What about the school fees? The mortgage. Was her mother *really* okay? She should go to New York despite what Mom had said. She probably needed help. But what about the kids? Uncle could take them! No, she'd bring them. But—no money!

Then an orchestra of hammering and whirring machines rattled her thoughts away. Two boutique hotels, three restaurants, and a shopping plaza were rising quickly. A big-time makeover of a small town well on its way to medium. Tourism. Opportunity was here—and Deja could make it in that industry; she just knew it. She'd studied every inch of the island, and once she finished school, she'd take the test to do hotel management at the new tourism program in Mobay.

Well, that was true an hour ago. Now all bets were off.

A quarter mile later, she made a left off the cracked two-lane blacktop that sloped out of town and halfway up a mountain, lush with vegetation. From there, she continued along a dirt road that ran parallel to the woods, quiet as always. She passed a neighbor's Toyota Flatty, brown except for the red replacement door—the only car on the block—then two one-bedroom houses that were nearly identical to her mom's. Exhausted, reeking of fish, Deja trudged past the yellow-and-burnt-orange crotons that lined her yard.

Still, she paused to compose herself. She couldn't let anything slip about what had happened to their mom. Then she opened the door, praying that Straleen—her oldest best friend—had her sister and brother ready to go.

Yes! Kaleisha, a hyper-focused look on her face making her appear older than her twelve years, braids draped over her left shoulder, sat fully dressed in her blue-and-white school uniform, doodling in her notebook at the kitchen table.

Donovan, however, was splayed out on the couch, lights-out, school shirt half-buttoned. "Kaleisha," Deja cried out. "Why isn't your brother ready?"

"Me no know. I'm *not* his mother," Kaleisha sassed back, a new attitude she seemed to be trying on lately like a new dress.

"Well, I'm not either, but—ah, forget it. Can you just help him get ready? And where's Straleen?"

"In the bathroom," Kaleisha said just as the toilet flushed.

Straleen cracked open the bathroom door. "Me going put on mi school frock." She started to close it, then opened it again. "Hey, you have a next bottle of the VO5 shampoo?"

"Shampoo? Why?" Deja asked.

Giving her hair a little fluff, Straleen said, "Well, me know you going go want to pay me for the kids since nobody can do you a *favor*, but I'll take a bottle instead of the money."

Straleen came over to watch the kids whenever Deja did early-morning fishing, so this seemed like a pretty great deal, especially given her mom's news. Then again, VO5 was impossible to get on her side of the island. And cost 'nuff money. Like so many other things.

Sensing Deja's hesitation, Straleen put on her best coaxing voice. "C'mon. You won't miss one little bottle. Plus, aren't you getting another barrel soon?"

Barrel. If Straleen knew what a painful button that word pressed, she no doubt wouldn't have said it. Deja had only gotten one barrel since her mother'd left!

And now . . . "Just one," Straleen wheedled, interrupting her thoughts. "I'll include an extra week of babysitting!"

That was way more than what the bottle was worth, impossible to say no to. Straleen pumped her fist as Deja agreed to the swap.

On her way to the cabinet, Deja reminded Kaleisha to get her brother ready for school.

Back in April, when the barrel—a four-foot-tall blue plastic drum—arrived from Brooklyn she had to admit opening it was more exciting than Christmas. It was jammed with so much— cooking oil, Irish Spring (dang, how many bars?), VO5, three shirts and shorts for Donovan, two dresses each for her and Kaleisha, a pair of Nike knockoffs, sandals, Levi's, rice, sugar, corned beef, condensed milk, beans, and so many other things, Deja thought she would never run out of anything.

But now, five months later, as she surveyed the cabinet, there wasn't much left. Three bars of soap, a pound bag of rice, a couple of tins of corned beef, a gallon of cooking oil, and *one* VO5 shampoo. She gripped the smooth plastic bottle. What about Kaleisha's and Donovan's hair, never mind her own? She clacked her teeth, pondering. Stores had shampoo, but who had that kind of money?

"If you don't have one, it's all right?" Straleen called out in a tone that Deja knew from all the way back in primary school. This was her "someone is being uncaring, maybe even selfish" voice. Ugh. Deja thought quickly. She had this memory of her mother sometimes mixing apple cider vinegar with aloe and cloves to make shampoo, but no way was Deja going to ask her about that now.

Still, all that babysitting for one shampoo! Deja wearily closed her eyes for a moment. Nobody expected girls with barrels to have to worry about things like this. In fact, it was an unwritten rule: barrel girls were considered luckier than everybody else in Jamaica and no longer had any right to complain about *anything*. Yet everyone made such a big deal about it—acted like Deja had it made because she got a container of stuff from the States. No one thought about the fact that to get it, her mother had to live fifteen hundred miles away!

With a sigh, she walked over to Straleen, still primping in the bathroom, so tall and shapely, and handed over the VO5.

"Thanks! Sure it's no problem?" Straleen asked, tucking a tress away from her high cheekbones.

"Is no problem."

"Look what I'm making for Mommy!" Kaleisha called out, leaning close to the notebook, carefully curling the long black tail of a Jamaican doctorbird with a marker. "I'm going to give it to her for Christmas!"

Deja froze—she couldn't even look her sister in the eye. "She'll love it," she said at last with forced enthusiasm.

Kaleisha started shading in the flowering hibiscus the bird was drinking from. "Yep! Three more months!"

Deja bit at her lip. "It's good to see you have a grasp of the calendar. Now, for the *last* time, could I see you help get Donovan ready for school, please?"

"No."

Stay calm, stay calm. Yelling never helped. Kaleisha would just yell back. The girl was steeped in some kind of phase. Deja sure didn't remember being like this at twelve years old. She had been too obsessed with playing netball back then—and was too much of a "good girl," scared that her parents' divorce meant that her mother might leave them too if she caused any sort of problem. That was what her father had done six years ago—left the country to work the farms in Costa Rica without even telling them which ones.

At the same time, Deja knew Kaleisha was fronting—she missed her mother and had to take it out on *someone*. That someone being *her*. So Deja took a breath and said, calm, calm, "You want your coconut jelly with brown sugar or without?" She asked it like her mother would have—her tone sweet, in the form of a question, the beginning of the bargaining.

"With."

"Okay. It'll be ready by the time you're done helping your brother." Deja took the machete from under the sink, snatched up two plastic mugs, the Pepsi logos almost worn off, and slipped out the door before Kaleisha could object.

She grabbed a coconut by its stem from a crocus bag full of them from under the porch. Propping it on the ground, she swung the machete into it again and again at a forty-five-degree angle. Several layers sliced away before she cracked the shell. One more whack, and finally, a trickle of juice flowed.

Straleen strode out of the house, backpack in one hand, twirling a scrunchie with the other—her long multicolor nails a kaleidoscope of motion.

"Girl, me could have used those nails to cut this coconut."

"You just jealous." Straleen laughed, hugging her, towering over her. "You haven't lived till you've had fake nails."

"Thanks fi watching the kids."

"No problem." Straleen eyed Deja top to bottom. "When you going get some sleep?"

"I don't have a box to check fi that one."

"Seriously, you been up all night, you know, girl?"

Deja wiped the side of the machete against her pant leg. "Don't worry. I'm finding my bed right after I drop them at school. Now, don't *you* forget to take notes from business class for me."

"No problem, but what about your other classes?"

"Lila is getting some. I'll make up the rest."

"Good. I'll remind her. You know how she is." Then Straleen narrowed her eyes. "Me hear Kaleisha say your mother not coming back fi three months. You can last that long?"

"Longer." But how long, she couldn't say.

Straleen reached out, picked a speck of coconut shell out of Deja's hair. "Aww, girl, you, like, literally have dark circles under your eyes. You want my mascara? Help make your eyes pop."

Now Straleen started brushing down Deja's hair with her palm. "At least, let the hair down today. Less accent on the face."

Now Deja narrowed *her* eyes. "Something wrong with my face?"

"You know you pretty, gal. But if you let the hair down, there'll be less emphasis on the raccoon eyes."

Deja shrugged.

Straleen sucked air through her teeth. "Boys no love when you so fenky fenky, you know?"

"When me have time fi boy?" Deja said evasively.

"Side-man then." Straleen grinned. "And wha' happen with that gangsta boy, anyway?" Dang, Straleen had a way of seeing right through her. Gabriel. Deja had just thought about him yesterday. She barely knew him, but still . . .

"Hold on." Deja aimed her attention at the house; being evasive was one of her talents. "Kaleisha, Donovan, come eat." She flipped the coconut upside down on a mug, letting the juice gurgle out. Then, balancing the empty shell in one hand like her mother had taught her, she sheared off slices—country spoons for the jelly that they'd scrape out of the coconuts.

"Okaaaay!" Straleen said in admiration. "You got skills, girl."

Donovan, shirt now fully buttoned, slumped his way outside. Kaleisha sprinted past him. "I call first."

"You take your pills?" Deja asked her brother.

"Yeah."

Deja pivoted to Kaleisha for confirmation. Kaleisha rolled her eyes but nodded. Okay, then. Donovan didn't like the taste of taking Adderall, but what ten-year-old does? At least he took it.

Watching them eat always calmed Deja, like everything was normal or at least she was doing *one* thing right.

Straleen gave her a nudge, drawing her focus back to their conversation. "Judging by how fast you change up the subject, you must be feeling that guy still."

Deja gave a half laugh so as not to give away her thoughts. "That was over before it started."

"If you say so." Straleen hitched her backpack onto her shoulder, then patted Deja's biceps. "Well, the fishing thing keeping you fit, but don't overdo it. Boys don't like the muscle thing." Straleen was all about finding a boy and settling down, as if love was all you needed. The thought of settling down gave Deja a shiver. She had too much to do before she'd ever consider it. Her micro cruise line idea was her ticket, a big one. She knew it in her bones.

"Swear you'll get some sleep after you take them to school?" Straleen asked, stepping onto the grass.

"Swear!"

"Okay, then. Likkle more."

"Yes, girl, see you later."

And with a quick wave, Straleen trotted off.

Feeling ridiculously glad she hadn't let anything slip about Mom *or* about Gabriel, she ran her fingers along her arm and remembered how her toned shape hadn't bothered Gabriel at all. That was when she let herself wonder how he was doing.

Gabriel, last night, 9:00 p.m.

Sitting at the edge of the lumpy couch that also served as his bed, Gabriel gazed at two unlit candles, half-burned. Ones his aunt used to cover the smell of the garbage she injected into her body. A syringe, traces of brown inside, lay next to the candle on the right. He closed his eyes and imagined what she had done to herself. Unbelievable. Opening them, he rocked the other candle, trying to unstick it from the wobbly-legged coffee table, strawberry scent rising. How was he going to tell her she needed to get help? He'd tried to reason with her about a year ago, but that became a shit show, real quick. She was using *daily* now. So he had to go there again—tell her that if she didn't get treatment, he was out of there. A swirl of irritation like black smoke clogged his chest. The candle broke free just as his aunt flushed the toilet. No sound of running water in the sink, and the bathroom door opened too quickly for her to have even dry-wiped her hands on a towel.

Her eyes, close set and sunken, sandwiching a short button

nose, narrowed. "What deh pon yu mind?"

She could always read him—high or not. Luckily, right now, she was not. So what he had to say had a chance of breaking through—a slight one.

He hesitated at the burden of the fight ahead of him, then blurted out, "Things have to change up."

How much more weight could she lose? Standing there, slightly swaying, she tilted her head. "Oh, is that you a think 'bout?" Her tone was already laced with vexation. "You a tell *me* what fi do now? Mussi think you a big man!"

Big man? Hell no. He felt way too young to be talking about this with his aunt. But he needed to. Just like she needed . . . "You *need* to get treatment." He clenched his jaw, then said again, "That shit's going to kill you."

"Lawd Jesus, you no know what you a say."

"I see junkies all di time, Auntie." Junkies with desperate faces, buying from fellow posse members. "I know."

His aunt leaned forward as if to help her voice travel. "You no know shit." She began hitting at her head with her palm. "Besides, a what me fi do?"

"Get help, that's what you can do! There are places!" His voice went loud—he could count the number of times he had raised his voice in his entire life. It frightened him, raising his voice—made him scared he'd lose control.

Then, exactly like those junkies, desperation filled her face—for the heroin? For help? Which? "Me try that once."

He found a gentler voice, a way to smile. "Second time is a charm, you know?"

She took a seat on a fraying velvet chair and crossed her legs. "Don't think so."

And there went the control. He slammed his fist on the table. "Do you realize that you're killing yourself?!"

"Is my life. And is *my* apartment. If you no like it, you know what you can do." Her crossed leg started bobbing like some out-of-control pendulum. "And rememba, is me bring you out a that orphanage, you know, boy!"

The orphanage card. She pulled it out all the time. As if he were ungrateful. Even though he paid nearly all the bills, rent, groceries, electricity. She'd *lose* this apartment in a heartbeat if he left. Still, he swallowed down the vile words he ached to hurl at her in hopes that they could reach some kind of peaceful agreement. Because even though he knew she was bluffing, he *wasn't* ready to pull the trigger and walk out on her. Not yet.

He pushed at the spent needle on the table. "Jesus. Can you at least not leave these lying around?" Okay, it was a stupid thing to say, but he wanted to get something out of her.

"Okay, Gabriel. Me can do that fi you."

Well, that was *something*.

Gabriel, Thursday morning, 6:30 a.m.

His aunt was passed out on her bed, her dark brown skin flushed, the black Nike Air Maxes he had bought her still laced onto her tiny feet and the vinegar-like smell of heroin haunting her bedroom. She couldn't even go twelve hours without shooting up. He crept close and picked up the needle and foil off the floor, brown residue gooed on where she'd cooked up the H. He balled up the foil and put the syringe in her makeup bag between the skin-bleaching cream and anti-aging moisturizer. Products her thirty-five-years-young face needed to cover up the damage.

As he tossed the foil into the garbage, a thought hit him—where'd she get the money to buy the heroin this time? His stash! Chest suddenly pounding, he made sure she was still out, then used his apartment key to unscrew the panel of the broken electric socket in the living room. He willed his hands not to shake as he reached in, then felt ridiculous relief when his fingers found the paper wad. He drew it out—the stack of bills, nearly all American, was the same size it'd been when he'd hidden it.

He peered over his shoulder once more. Addicts were sneakier than gangsters; his job had shown him that far too many times. His aunt had found one of his hiding places once before. Now he peeled off a few hundred, paused to listen for any movement, then screwed the panel back on.

Money safe in his pocket, he took his pillow off the couch, folded the sheet tightly, then put them away in the closet. Old habit from his orphanage days—discipline first. From under the couch, he slid out a cardboard box filled with clothes. He sifted through the neat stacks for a brown tee that went with his Timberlands. Then he added his chain with the wooden cross.

In the frowsy bathroom, he avoided breathing through his nose to limit the musty odors. The sink was covered in makeup stains—his aunt wore a ton of it. What a mess. He ripped a strip of toilet paper off the roll and began to scrub, so hard the paper shredded. But he kept rubbing—made him crazy to be in here with it all junked up.

In the mirror he could see, dang, that his locs were getting long, to his shoulders. Almost as long as Auntie's. That and their light brown eyes, the color of coffee with cream, were the only family resemblance. He remembered thinking she had the prettiest eyes. Now the whites of hers had crooked red lines through them.

Gabriel's phone buzzed. Hammer.

15

Y?

15

K

Hammer was oak-tree stubborn and didn't believe in casual hangouts, so it had to be important. Plus, Hammer wasn't just his posse partner; he was a day-one from the orphanage days. So "K" it was.

He wanted to meet up downstairs in fifteen. Weird. They didn't have any drops to make. Gabriel hoped nothing unexpected was going on; he'd been looking forward to a day off from doing posse work, just chill, maybe play some video games.

Gabriel peeked between the blinds to see what was up in the courtyard. The trailer part of an 18-wheeler was parked by the side of the driveway. Two pairs of legs poked out from underneath, toes up. Gahh! Gabriel knocked his forehead against the window in frustration. Stupid kids—they still hid under there even though he'd warned them a half-dozen times to find a safer place to crash. He knew from jump that they were homeless, roaming all over the place. Little nomads. Huffing, Gabriel went back to the socket, unscrewed it again, and peeled off another hundred in smaller notes.

Gabriel, Thursday evening,
one week ago, 11:45 p.m.

Speakers the size of refrigerators stacked twelve feet high, twice Gabriel's height, blasted a dance-hall reggae beat all over the parking lot behind the old stone church in Springtown Harbour. Round paper lanterns hung from guano trees. A floodlight on the church wall brightened the night as a dozen guys and girls in a line dance dropped into a squat, bounced three times, sprang up, and made as if pedaling a bicycle. Another thirty or so hung out—some talking, most just swaying, coming across as lonely and out of place. Gabriel's head was on a constant swivel, and every once in a while he tapped the Beretta in his waistband—a nervous tic that had started once he joined the posse. Besides, he didn't know the posse people in this town, and that made him feel like a blind man walking. Ten miles out of Mobay revved up his stress, but being a whole hour away got his whole eye twitching. Were those three guys by the DJ booth all wearing jeans because they were in another posse Gabriel didn't know about? Two other guys were wearing the same chains—for that same reason? And then there was their attitude to watch for, that certain walk or shrug that screamed *posse*.

Gabriel wondered if he should have even accepted Chops's invitation to this party. What did Chops want to talk to him about anyway? He caught sight of Hammer, striding by two girls who watched intently as he passed. There was always a rhythm to Hammer's stride, his pumped-up body swaying to an internal beat that people seemed attracted to. Hammer pulled up when he reached Gabriel, the necks of two sodas wedged between his ringed fingers.

Lifting one, he said, "Di grape fi you." Then he gestured toward a tree by the back door of the church, waved to a cute dark-skinned girl with short hair in a black top and shorts. "Di orange drink fi her."

"Nice." Gabriel nodded and took the soda. "What *you* drinking?"

"Mon, di food free, but you haffi' pay fi drinks. Me going wait till me get home fi have one."

Gabriel reached in his pocket. "Okay—you bought mine, I'm buying yours—"

"No insult me with your money, mon," Hammer scoffed.

Gabriel grinned, left the cash in his pocket. "You seen Chops?"

"Don't you mean 'di priest'?" Hammer mocked. "No, mon. But me a wonder what kinda scam him a run?"

Gabriel didn't reply, as if agreeing. Funny how he did that sometimes, choosing silence over confrontation, like how he'd put off the words he needed to say to his aunt for so long. He squeezed the neck of the soda. "How long you going to stay? Wouldn't mind reaching my bed before the sun comes up."

"What's your rush? How 'bout you relax for once, mon?"

Gabriel shrugged. "You know me no love crowd, star."

"Yeah, well, you need fi work dat out, mon. Enjoy youself. At least until Chops shows."

Gabriel thought about his last conversation with Chops—the way they talked about *living a more meaningful life*, which probably meant leaving the posse. Like Chops had done. Gabriel reasoned that he should say something to Hammer about it. "You know what, mon? Me think him legit. Chops, me mean." He stopped short of mentioning possibly leaving the posse— something he wasn't yet even sure about—something that would probably make Hammer's head explode. No, this wasn't the time.

Hammer smirked. "If him is a priest, I'm di bloody Pope."

Gabriel laughed and glanced over toward the church, where a tall, skinny guy in baggy jeans was now talking to the cute girl in the black top. "Okay, Pope, you better go see about your flock."

"Damn." Hammer walked away without another word. Reaching the girl, he started to chat up the skinny guy as if they were old friends . . . and just like that, they were all laughing.

Hammer had a talent for people—he could talk to anyone about anything. Or maybe it was the joy Hammer took in doing it that Gabriel envied? Because while Gabriel could talk his way out of anything, it always felt like a grind to do so. He manufactured words; Hammer let them flow. At least until he got pissed off. But that wasn't happening now. In fact, the skinny guy was pulling up his baggy jeans and waving goodbye. Damn, Hammer was good.

Above him, the stained glass on the back wall shimmered with purples and reds. The dazzle of color took his thoughts back to Ark Haven, the orphanage in Montego Bay—it was Catholic too. Gabriel, only eleven, his back against the last row of pews, the tangy-sweet scent of incense in the air. The headmaster and two other priests, arms crossed, were wanting to know what he knew about why Hammer had run away.

"Gabriel, are you sure he didn't say anything to you before leaving? A place he might go? Or . . . whether he was in trouble?" The headmaster's voice seemed flush with concern.

He had racked his brain for a clue, but Hammer hadn't said a word about running away, a dis that had made Gabriel wonder if they actually were best friends after all. Not even a note. And as far as Gabriel knew, Hammer had no relatives or friends on the outside.

For the last time, Gabriel told the headmaster he didn't know anything. "And . . . I wouldn't say anything if I did. I wouldn't ever rat him out," he'd added. At that the headmaster had spun away with the other priests, speaking in low tones Gabriel struggled, but couldn't, hear.

"Gabriel."

Gabriel lowered the soda bottle and wheeled around.

"Glad you made it to the bashment." Chops.

"Yeh, mon."

It was still strange to see Chops with his locs shorn off. Hair cropped close. Now, he looked even younger than his thirty years. But the dark under his eyes was still there.

As they shook hands, Gabriel noted that becoming a priest hadn't affected Chops's strength. The collar around his neck could probably pop off with a simple flex. And his palm was sandpaper rough. "Wha' gwan, Chops?"

"Good, man. How are you? Enjoying yourself?"

Gabriel shrugged.

Chops waited, like he genuinely wanted to know what was going on—like he cared. A certain pressure built until Gabriel felt compelled to share. "Party and me don't mix so well, mon."

Chops fastened his eyes on him. "You remember our last conversation?"

Gabriel lifted the soda to his lips and threw back half in a gulp.

"About leaving the posse—think any more about it?"

Gabriel stole a glance at Hammer, now standing inches away from the girl in the shorts. How could he leave his number one? Could he even leave the posse if he tried? Teago didn't "let" his people simply "leave." "It well complicated, mon."

Chops pressed his lips together. "Truly I tell you, if you have faith as small as a mustard seed, you can say to this mountain, 'Move from here to there' and it will move."

Gabriel didn't hesitate. "Matthew 17:20."

Chops's smile spread across his face. "I don't usually drop the gospel on people like that, but I knew you'd know. Ark

Haven wasn't the best of places, but it did do a decent job with Scriptures, eh?"

Chops had lived there too, years before Gabriel and Hammer. Probably why he took so much interest in them. Gabriel gave his soda a shake, listened to it fizz. "Yeh, mon."

"I think there's more for you in this life, G."

Gabriel studied the scar in the middle of Chops's forehead. "That why *you* left?"

"No doubt." Chops seemed shorter than when he was in the posse. Gabriel had him by a few inches. Or maybe *he* had gotten taller?

More people were dancing now, probably because the DJ put on Popcaan—"Elevate." "Nice party, though." Gabriel smirked. "You turn priest and party promoter."

His eyes on the dancers, Chops murmured, "Long way from the posse."

Gabriel thought about how Hammer didn't believe that Chops was legit, so he asked. "How much people know 'bout you? 'Bout di posse and thing?"

Chops's voice stayed steady. "A lot. I haven't been secretive about any of it."

Gabriel raised an eyebrow. "Even what you did in Kingston that night?"

Now Chops grinned. "Oh, that story." He didn't elaborate, just straightened his white collar. Gabriel couldn't help but notice the long, gnarly scar on Chops's forearm. Word was, he got it when a dude from a rival gang slashed him. Then, supposedly, with blood spewing everywhere, Chops beat the guy unconscious. And then carried a wounded posse member across Kingston on his back!

Gabriel wanted to know how true *that* was but decided not to press him and instead asked another question he'd wondered about. "So, uh, thanks for the invite, but—what's up?"

"Nothing much. Just wanted you to come down and relax a little. Talk things over in person that you might not want to say over the phone."

That made sense. If anyone in the posse knew Gabriel wanted out, it would definitely be trouble, if not Gabriel's ass. The only way to leave and live would be to switch over to the relative safety of another posse. Dudes were doing that more and more. But why would he want to go spinning his wheels in a whole new hamster cage? *And* he'd still be in a posse.

Even now Gabriel worried about how much he should say. Leaving was always on his mind, an oppression, like the humidity. Still, he gave a shrug, all noncommittal. "You know . . . me thinking about it, is all."

"No problem, mon." Chops played it cool too—anyone else would be nodding like some salesman, trying to reel Gabriel in. Make him see the light.

Gabriel took another sip of soda. "Me notice you don't come around the posse much anymore."

"My new policy."

"Is wha' that?"

Chops raised a forefinger in the air. "God's plan. At the same time, I don't want to be called away from my calling."

An old woman, eyes wide, forehead furrowed, called out, "Pastor Powell." Chops leaned past Gabriel, waved to her, then cast an intense gaze on Gabriel. "Duty calls. Enjoy the party. Good talking. Let me know if you want to talk more."

Gabriel watched him go greet the woman. Dang. Chops had this way of searching your soul that made you feel like you could have done better. Could be *doing* better.

Restless now, in the grip of a weird irritation over Chops's last words—*duty calls*—Gabriel sifted through the crowd, glanced again at Hammer, still talking to that girl as the selecta mixed in a slow song, then headed for the parking lot.

And that was when he saw her.

Lit by a beam from a security light, brown skin so smooth and toned. Probably a sports girl . . . a sprinter or netballer or something. And, and, and she saw him checking her out and held his gaze. He waited for a smile, but she held her stare. He liked that. He took his time going over to her, already wondering what she was all about.

"Hi," he said, standing into all his height.

"Hi."

"You were looking at me."

"Yes, I was."

"Most girls I know look away or down when they're being noticed," he said.

"Maybe I'm not most girls."

"Seems so," he said. "You look good, too."

"Looks are everything to you?" She bobbed side to side, just a little bit, like she cared about how he might answer.

"Just something I notice. Wanted to see what else is going on with you."

Her eyes, wide set, ginger brown, were bemused, evaluating. She made him feel comfortable, something he definitely was not used to.

He wondered if she didn't feel the party either, so he asked.

She shrugged. "It's okay. I'm not really the party type, I guess."

"Yeah, me neither."

She raised an eyebrow. "So you prefer being alone?"

"Hate being alone."

She immediately laughed.

"I swear." It was true. He did. But it was only when it was out of his mouth that he realized he'd never put it into words before.

"Alone with your thoughts and things?"

Whoa. She zeroed in like a laser. This girl! So he went with it. Nothing to lose, right? "Yeah, being alone with my thoughts makes me feel . . . I don't know . . . even more alone, I think. Sometimes . . . well, I'll even hang out with people I don't particularly like—"

"Just so you're not alone?" she finished.

"Yeah." He shrugged. "But it's crowds I hate most."

She nodded while looking sidelong, gesturing to somebody.

Gabriel instinctively tensed. It was gonna be some dude. But two girls—one tall in a silky red blouse that hung off one shoulder, the other a few inches shorter, hair in Afro puffs, both with their eyes wide—were making their way over.

"Your friends?" he said, low.

She started to fold her arms, stopped, let them drop back by her sides. "Yeah, checking on me."

"What's up with that?"

"Probably think you're cute." She waved them off, and they slid back into the crowd.

Diiddddd . . . that mean *she* thought he was cute? He pushed the thought away, got them back to their conversation. "Um, so, why you come to a party, then hang out alone? Especially if it's not your thing?"

"My girls made me. They think I spend all my time with the kids."

Kids?

"My little brother and sister—I take care of them." She measured their heights out, her hand long, slender. "My uncle is watching them tonight."

"And your parents . . . ?" He trailed off.

She blinked before saying, "Divorced. My mother is working in foreign."

"Which part?"

"New York."

He tilted his head. "Oh, so you getting barrels? Got any extra cooking oil?" His joke clearly fell flat, as her face stiffened. "Hey, wha' wrong?"

Now she folded her arms. "Nothing."

Damn! What had he said? "Come on, tell me."

She toed the gravel. "It's not easy, you know."

"What'd you mean?"

She paused. "I mean, the kids are entirely my responsibility now. Sometimes I feel like a single mom who works *and* goes to school."

"No easy," he agreed, hoping his voice was conveying the sympathy he felt.

"Okay, your turn—what about you?" She leaned against the wall, getting comfortable, like she was expecting a good story.

Gabriel considered deflecting, asking her a question instead. The older guys in the posse, especially Blood Moon and Jamal, had made sure he learned how to avoid giving anything away to the police or possible snitches. And he'd found that those techniques pretty much worked with most people, which was perfect: he was weirdly uncomfortable when people knew too much about his life. Like, unprotected. Yet for some reason, he didn't feel like guarding his story . . . from her.

"Me? My parents skipped out early on—or . . ."

"Or?" she prompted, her face suddenly a frown full of concern.

"Me did grow in an orphanage."

"Oh."

It felt like it suddenly got a lot more humid.

She asked, "When did you leave?"

It so wasn't his thing, spilling like this. But the other part of him that wanted to keep her talking said, "My aunt, my mother's sister, she just showed up one day out of the blue—came and claimed me. I was . . . twelve, twelve and a half, I think."

The girl— He needed to get her name. She rubbed her upper arm like she wasn't sure what to say next. "Well, that was lucky, no?"

"Sort of." When she cocked her head in interest, he made a quick decision. He'd push through his effed-up life and see what this girl was made of. "She's a mess, my aunt. Drunk, high. One night she was really wrecked. I told her"—he paused, then, what the hell, he barreled on—"told her she had to get her shit together. And that's when she told me the only reason she adopted me was because the town paid her for keeping a dependent."

The girl's hand flew up to her mouth. "She *what*?"

Even after all these years, Gabriel could still smell the acrid odor of white rum when he had put his aunt to bed and pulled a blanket up over her, all the while in shock over what she'd just told him. For the money? Then she passed out. Next morning, she didn't remember a thing. Or acted like she didn't. Whatever.

Hand still over her mouth, the girl said, "That had to be awful. Amazing you can even talk about it."

Truth was, he never had. Not even to Hammer. And hearing *her* talk about it made him feel suddenly shaky, like he needed to sit down.

She must have sensed it, because suddenly she was grasping his forearm, her grip strong. "Hey, you all right?"

Gabriel wasn't sure—it was as though talking about his aunt flooded him with everything she'd done—and he felt . . . shame. When it was just *his* awful secret, he had pretty much held it all in check. But now, out in the open, the embarrassment rained down. And yet . . . at the same time he felt . . . well, he wasn't sure, as he'd never quite felt this before, but almost like . . . he was lighter. A sense of . . . relief.

"Hey," she said again. "Seriously, you okay?"

"Yeah. Yeah. I am. Just—it's not something I usually talk about."

"Tough being back there?" Her gaze was soft. Earnest. Like she understood.

He cleared his throat. "That's exactly what it was. I can still smell the alcohol on her breath."

She loosened her grip, but instead of simply letting go, she let her fingers linger. Just an extra second, but the feeling kept going, rippling up his arm into his chest. "How'd you know?" he asked.

She shrugged one of those toned shoulders. "Dunno, guess I could relate."

"How, mon?" He really was interested.

She hesitated.

"Come no? You can't just say you can relate and then *not* relate. You haffi' play fair, mon!" He grinned. "At di same time, me hope you *can't* beat out my story. Strangers tell each other deep things about themselves all the time."

"Is true; why *is* that?"

Gabriel shrugged. "Maybe because they know they'll never see each other again?" he guessed. He thought about that for a moment, how true it actually was. "And chances are we'll never see each other again either. But at least we can have a good time talking." Yet even as he said it, he hoped he was wrong.

"Okay, fine." But she still hesitated. Just as Gabriel was about to coax her further, she blurted out, "My father was in a posse. . . ."

"Oh yeah?" He said it all casual, but it was all he could do to keep his hand from instinctively readying itself on his Beretta.

"He wasn't always—he was a cabdriver, a legit one. But the

company went out of business, and he kept driving as a—"

"A robot," Gabriel finished for her.

"You got it. My mother went on and on about it. 'There's no insurance. What happens when you get in an accident?'"

"Did he?"

"Did he what?"

"Get in an accident?"

"No. And every night when he came home, he said to my mother in this newsman's voice: 'Robot taxis provide a service too.'" She gave a half laugh.

Gabriel detected something under that laugh, something familiar, like buried anger. "I respect that; guy has to take care of his family somehow. Driving a cab without a license isn't any capital offense." *His* father, whoever he was, obviously *wasn't* the kind who took care of the family no matter what.

"He felt that way too. My mother made him quit, though, and I think that was when everything changed. It was like he felt weak or something. Like you said, couldn't provide for the family anymore. Never saw them kiss anymore after that, either. . . ." Her voice trailed off. "Anyway, he ended up leaving, took a job in foreign."

"America?"

"Costa Rica."

"'Nuff people a go there."

"Plenty jobs."

"How's he doing?"

She took a view of the party. "Who knows?"

Now Gabriel frowned. "He checked out?"

"Yeah, he did." She said this so prim and proper, he could instantly tell how hurt she still was.

"He took off without saying anything?" Gabriel wondered what *his* parents had said before leaving *him*. He always wondered that.

"He said this and that, but not much." She rolled her eyes with a *pffft*. "But he left me a gift. . . ." She raised an eyebrow as if to say, *Can you believe that?*

"Gift? What was it?"

She gave a crooked smile, shrugged. "Don't know. I never opened it. I hid it."

"You hid it?"

"Who needs his 'gift'? He ditched us." She waved her hand as if flicking away a gnat.

"I hear you. Don't know if I want to know about my parents either."

"Really, you never asked your aunt?"

Her surprise surprised him. He thought they were on the same page. "Why would I want to know the people that ditched *me*?"

She inhaled, about to say something, but instead turned her attention to the party. Maybe it was time to lighten things up. "But now you have me all curious about that gift. I might have to come and look for it."

"You won't find out where I live," she said. The saucy had come back to her voice. Okay, good. She was back.

"And why not?"

"You'll never see me again, remember?"

Damn—why'd he even say that! Maybe she wasn't serious though? A waft of fried dough with a hint of cornmeal scented the air. He made a show of breathing deeply. "You smell that? The festival is ready."

She nodded enthusiastically. "Festival is my fav."

"Let's go get some!" As he turned for the buffet, she fell into step beside him. How had he missed all this food? The cinnamon of the festival blended with the scent of spicy peppers on the escovitch fish on the next tray over. They glanced at each other, grinning. Gabriel took two plates and put a piece of festival— hot!—on each, then he handed her one plate with a small bow.

She bowed back. "Thank you."

The doughy dumpling was perfect—crispy outside, soft and warm inside. It reminded him of those rare Sunday mornings when his aunt was *not* hungover or high and in the mood to cook. "When did you first have festival?"

Her face lit up as if replaying the moment in her mind. "At the beach. With my parents. My little brother and sister love it like crazy."

"How old are they—your brother and sister?"

"Kaleisha is twelve and Donovan is ten. My sister thinks she's eighteen. Do you—" She stopped herself, blushing, proba- bly about to ask if *he* had brothers and sisters.

"It's cool. It's a normal question." As he thought about his answer, he tilted his plate, rolling the festival side to side. He landed on, "The friends I have are my family. It's funny, though. When I was little, I used to circle the grounds at the orphanage fantasizing, pretending that I had a family out there somewhere.

The priests once asked me if I was haunted because I paced so much."

The girl had raised the festival to her lips, but now she lowered it back to her plate.

"What?" Had he said too much?

"How old are you? Do you mind me asking?"

He didn't. "How old do you think I am?"

"Not as old as you seem—no offense."

"And by that you mean—" He rolled the festival to the other side of his plate.

She squinted, thinking. "Just that—no pun, but you've got a lot to deal with but no one to deal with it with—"

He swallowed; half laughed at how unwittingly right she was. "Like you?"

"My friends say that all the time, that I have to stop trying to handle everything on my own." She gave a lopsided smile. "But if I told them what really bothered me, I'd never hear the end of it. They're not easy, at all."

"So what really bothers you?"

"Let's just say I'm really good at *looking* like I'm in charge."

"A wha' suh?" He dropped into thick patois, to keep things light.

She shrugged. "Well, I'm pretty much an expert at hiding my emotions. I have this trick—"

"Trick?"

"Yeah, see, when I feel scared, and I don't want people to know, I tell myself I'm walking on the bottom of the ocean, and if I open my mouth, I'll die."

He pictured that. Okay, a little strange. But cool, too. "And what does that do?" He was truly curious.

"Nothing. It makes me do nothing." She picked up the festival and let it hover by her mouth. "And when I do nothing, people seem to think I'm cool."

"So, the trick stops you from telling people how you're really feeling?"

She grinned again . . . then popped the rest of the festival into her mouth. He felt so damn close to her. "That's some serious t'ings right there." He put his plate down, shifted closer. "I can use them against you one day."

"Don't think so."

"Why?"

She raised that eyebrow and said for the second time, "You'll never see me again, remember?"

"Well, before I never see you again, I ought to at least know your name—"

She rubbed her fingertips together, wiping sugar from the festival away. "You first."

"Gabriel."

"Nice. Biblical."

He pulled his locs back. "Nothing holy about me. What's yours?"

"Deja."

"I like it."

"Thank you." Her sweet tone called him to come closer.

"I like it a lot." He put a hand on her shoulder, then slid it down her arm. She didn't pull away.

Then she did, in alarm, as shouts and cusses erupted from the courtyard. Gabriel surveyed the grounds behind her, already guessing what was going on. Yep . . . Hammer was standing in front of two of the guys in jeans Gabriel had marked earlier. But where was the third one? Words were flaring back and forth like embers. Only a matter of time before they caught fire. Gabriel scanned the area—where was Chops? Without a word to Deja, he ran through the crowd, hand on his gun. If he pulled it, things would escalate. If he didn't, he might be too late.

He circled behind the two guys, slowed to a stop. "Wait deh, mon!" he commanded.

They spun around. No weapons. Gabriel kept his hand on the handle but was glad he hadn't pulled it out. "We going now!" he told Hammer. "We *going*," he repeated, when Hammer, being Hammer, just stood there.

The two dudes eyed him warily, probably only wanted to save face.

At last Hammer flipped a hand in the air—*done with you*. "No worth it." He stepped away.

As Gabriel backed away as well, Chops strode up . . . no game face. Maybe he *had* changed for real—a legit man of God. Hammer was already halfway across the parking lot. Time to go. Yet . . .

Deja was standing among the crowd that had gathered. She was still holding the empty plate of festival. Things could still pop off. He waved. She didn't.

He left, thinking, *I'll never see you again.*

Gabriel, Thursday, 7:00 a.m.

Their lives had already been far apart when they met that night. Still, the promise of what might be kept tugging at him. What if they'd started something and it stuck?

But it hadn't.

He slid his phone into his back pocket, tucked his gun into his waistband, and took the stairs two at a time out of the housing complex. Past the courtyard were the crumbling, mice-ridden tenements he and his aunt had first lived in. Seeing them always made him think about how Hammer had shown up at his door out of the blue three years ago. It'd been a year after Hammer had left Ark Haven without so much as a "later." Shown up, brandishing an offer to join a posse.

Gabriel had walked Hammer over to an empty playground nearby, the ground dotted with litter and random shards from broken bottles. Hammer had beefed up, neck thicker, chest broad, totally jacked. Only his skinny legs remained of the guy Gabriel had grown up with, the closest thing to a brother Gabriel had ever known. But checking out how big his shoulders and neck had gotten, it was a for sure that wherever Hammer'd been, it wasn't far from some weights and a lot of food. "So . . . how you know where me live?" had been Gabriel's first question.

Hammer had shoved his hands into the pockets of his jeans shorts, yellow, distressed, and camo. The kind Gabriel couldn't afford in his wildest dreams. "Me have connection now."

"The posse thing?"

When Hammer confirmed it with a slight bow, Gabriel thought about the headmaster at Ark Haven, how he'd raged about gangs like he was standing at a pulpit during high Easter mass. *The* Daily Gleaner *says there are more than two hundred and sixty posses in Jamaica. Two hundred and sixty! Yet we are only fourteen parishes. Not even three million people. A shame, I tell you!* He went on a rant about how gangs were growing all the time like weeds, attaching themselves to politicians, businesspeople, even police, strangling the goodness out of Jamaicans, wrapping themselves around the throats of decent people, making them unable to speak out against the criminals and injustice. Selling drugs, committing mayhem and murder.

Sitting there, listening as the headmaster went on, Hammer had leaned over and whispered about how posses weren't "weeds" but "businesses," with a boss and pay that guys like them couldn't find anywhere else.

That had been the clue, the one that Gabriel had overlooked, the sign that Hammer had seen a way out of the orphanage. Looking back, it had to have been his reason for leaving. Had he not thought Gabriel could handle posse life too? Not that

Gabriel'd ever thought about it as an option, but he didn't want to be thought of as weak.

A distant siren trailed off somewhere near the playground.

"How'd you get in?" Gabriel asked.

"Dem always a look out fi people, mon. Surprised nobody recruit you yet."

"They tried." When Gabriel was thirteen, two guys, green bandannas tied around their upper arms, had preached posse life, even threatened him when he'd refused. He was glad to see Hammer had no bandanna at all.

"Which posse?"

Gabriel shrugged.

Hammer suddenly glanced over his shoulder, even though nobody was nearby.

Was somebody after him? Or maybe that was just what you had to do when you did what he did?

Hammer leaned toward Gabriel, spoke lower. "Me and most of the di posse live up in some apartment inna Farwood, about twelve of us, another five scattered all about Mobay—"

"Farwood? Near di airport?"

"Yeh, mon. Di rooms no too big, but dem clean and you have bathroom fi yourself. Di boss run things in di entire district. Pay fi garbage pickup. Make sure all di pickney gwan a school. Everybody can walk pon di street at all hours. Nobody a do nothing to nobody or else dem answer to us. Police all work with we too. We make some drops, mostly ganja, some coke." He glanced across the street, then shifted his voice even lower. "Di big thing is transshipment. Drugs come in from South

America and we send it go foreign . . . England, America." He said this excitedly, like Gabriel should be impressed too. "Tight operation, mon."

Gabrial thought of the headmaster's words and could only wonder if posses grew like *businesses* that gave people jobs or weeds th atchoked the life out of living things.

"So, you want fi join up? Me chat to my don already. Him interested." Hammer kept nodding, backing up what he'd just said. "Me no know if you have job, but you'd probably get a bigger payroll if you join."

As if Gabriel had a payroll now. He had explained how he was in between part-time jobs and his prospects weren't looking good. Even going back to school was impossible, since he needed to make money to help pay rent for him and his aunt.

Hammer had sucked air through his teeth. "Nobody care 'bout we, mon."

A question had gnawed at him almost as persistently as the question about who his parents were and what happened to them. Why had Hammer taken off, taken off and dropped Gabriel like a phone call? When the older boys back at Ark Haven used to give him trouble, who was it who had jumped in to fight alongside him? Hammer. Who was the only one there who hadn't laughed at him when he'd wet his bed because he'd been consumed by night terrors? Hammer.

Guess now was the time to find out why. "Yo, why didn't you tell me you were leaving?"

Hammer visibly flinched. "What?"

Gabriel immediately regretted asking and the weakness it

implied. "Ark Haven." He squatted to retie his sneaker, buying time to swallow his rising anger. Then, standing, he said in a lighter tone, "You didn't tell me you were leaving."

"Oh, that?" Hammer spoke like the answer was obvious. "Out of all of we back inna di orphanage, you was the only one who could someday get a *paycheck* job—"

Gabriel tried to stop him, because compliments made him itchy.

But Hammer hammered on about the top marks Gabriel had gotten in his classes, how he'd even figured out some math the priests couldn't answer. "You had skills, mon. Skills I didn't have. I left Ark Haven to find a posse that would take me. That was *my* road."

Pressure had built behind Gabriel's eyes, and he finally blurted out that *he* wouldn't have left his friend without even a "see you later."

Hammer shook off the comment. Spoke all cool about how he hated goodbyes. And how it was better to just leave. "G, you wasn't ready for no posse thing back then, even if you wanted to."

"And you're asking me to join your posse now. Why?" Gabriel asked.

Hammer looked back in the direction of Gabriel's run-down apartment building. "It no look like things are happening fi you."

Gabriel sighed at the truth in Hammer's words while he surveyed the broken glass scattered all over the ground.

Hammer's face brightened. "Gang life no easy, but di posse will have your back." He looked over his shoulder again. "And you need that round here. Nobody else is going to look out fi you. But me need fi know now. Teago, my boss, him moody. Me talk you up, and him interested now, but that interest nah go last, mon."

Hammer was asking him to choose. A life in a mouse-ridden apartment with his drug-addled aunt? Or be part of the "weeds," the only "business" around here that would pay real money?

The memory left with the rumble of a military jeep coming down the street, a soldier in full combat gear at the wheel; two others sitting in the back, weapons pointing down. The one closest to Gabriel shouted, "Hey, youth!" Gabriel hated how grown-ups used that word. Flexing superiority. But worse than that, what if they decided to search him? Found the Beretta? Shit.

The soldier's eyes were slits. "Is what you doing here?"

Gabriel knew he had a right to say nothing, but that would be stupid. Ever since the prime minister called a state of emergency three months ago, soldiers had been crawling around check-ing for teenagers in gangs with *guns*—as in, Gabriel. "So, I live here," he answered quickly.

"Where?"

He pointed up to his apartment and launched into a full chat in hopes he could deflect their well-armed interest. "Up so. Three-L with my auntie, Paulette Williams. She works at the old-people home Prestige Wellness in Port Shore Heights, just over—"

The soldier waved him off, slapped the side of the jeep, twirled his forefinger in the air in a helicopter motion. They drove away without another word.

Gabriel swallowed hard. He forced himself to walk naturally toward the parked trailer of that 18-wheeler, his legs rubbery. All the while, he fingered the safety of his gun to make sure it wouldn't go off if the soldiers circled back and he had to throw it away quickly.

No sooner had the rumble of the jeep faded when it was replaced with the roar of a motorcycle engine. Hammer. The sight of his shaved head catching glints of morning sunlight was a relief. But Gabriel still had something to take care of. He squatted in front of the trailer and tapped a boy's leg.

"Hey, mon, wake up!" he called out—jeezum, they couldn't be older than eight!

One boy popped up, hitting his head. His dingy khaki shorts and marina top were so worn they probably couldn't survive even a gentle washing. The smaller boy woke slowly, rubbing his eyes.

"You still here in spite of what me tell you!" Game face on because this kid was hard.

The boy yawned. "Where else me fi go?"

"How much time me tell you the man that own this truck don't play. No telling what him might do if him catch you sleeping here."

"Me can take care of myself."

How many times had Gabriel said *that* to somebody?

"G—" Hammer was loud even when he whispered.

Gabriel held up a hand—wait. Then he reached into his pocket and peeled off twenty US. He held it out.

The smaller boy frowned. "What me have to do?"

"Find somewhere else fi sleep, and don't come back."

With a slight shove of the smaller boy, the bigger one took back the lead in the conversation. "That's it?"

Gabriel sharpened his tone. "Just no come back."

The boy tilted his head toward his smaller friend. "What about him?"

Gabriel knew the boy was trying to play him. "Take it or leave it, but either way, me going to make sure you both leave this place. It no safe."

The boy snatched the money. Gabriel gave him a hard stare, then joined up with Hammer, who straddled the souped-up motorcycle he was rocking back and forth. "More charity work?"

"Moving expenses."

Hammer eyed the kids, evaluating. "The one you was talking to look strong. Could make it inna di posse life, maybe."

"No, mon," Gabriel said.

"Why not?" Hammer hiked his shoulders. "You prefer him live on di street?" The boys were now crawling out from under the trailer, taking their strips of cardboard with them. "The little one look useless. But for real, the tall one could make it in the posse, mon."

And Gabriel got that. Probably why Hammer would rather see the kid in the posse than on the streets. "No, mon, the posse isn't for him."

"Why you say that? You no want fi help him?"

"Maybe I don't want to be the one that gives him a gun," Gabriel said. "I feel he would use it."

"Wait deh! Is *me* bring you into this posse. So, what you

saying about *me*?" Hammer tapped his own chest with his palm. If he wasn't touchy about *everything*, he wouldn't be Hammer.

"I don't mean anything." Gabriel sort of did, though. He didn't want some kid involved in the same mess he wanted to get out of. But Hammer didn't know *that*. "So, wha' gwan?"

Hammer cut his eyes left and right, then low-voiced, "Listen, mon, me hear something."

"What?"

"You no go like it."

Gabriel didn't already. "Gwan, mon."

Hammer stared at Gabriel for a seemingly endless moment. "So, what you know 'bout di state of emergency t'ing?" Other thing about Hammer—he really liked to ask questions he already knew the answer to.

"Come on, already. Just tell me."

"I heard that last time, a bunch of soldiers got in big trouble with them high command because them didn't find enough guns and, get this . . . didn't arrest enough *gang members*."

Gabriel thought about the jeep that had just left. "So . . . you're saying *we're* in trouble?"

"Me saying they're searching for more people to arrest this time."

"You're saying we're in *a lot* of trouble?"

Hammer rubbed a hand over his head. "Me hear the boss was talking about giving up someone to the soldiers to get them off his back."

Hammer was always hearing things—some of them true, some of them about a flat earth. "Who said this?" Gabriel pressed.

"You no trust me?" Man, everything riled Hammer up.

"*Who?*"

"Don't worry about who. Worry about . . . *you.*"

"You're talking crazy, mon."

"You hear me, though?" Hammer kept rubbing his head, clearly irritated. "The someone is you, G."

Gabriel paused, trying to put things in place. "Wait, you saying the boss wants to set *me* up . . . to get *arrested*?"

Hammer didn't hesitate. "Arrested. Killed. No matter to him."

A woozy feeling came over Gabriel. "Me?" It couldn't be, not after three years in the posse. Only one drop had gone bad, and that was when he'd just joined. But he'd been perfect since. The boss liked him; he'd said so. This was *family.* "No way, mon."

"Yes, mon." Shit. Hammer's lips made a thin, angry line. He was serious. Gabriel felt like puking.

"But . . . but . . . *why?* I do a shitload of the dirty work around here! I mean, who does the hard collections? Who makes the drops when police dem sniffing around?"

"Hey, mon, you don't have to convince me of nothing. Me know who you are." Hammer shifted the bike left, right, left, right. "Word is, it's because di boss hear you want fi leave. Bonefide left di posse, and di boss can't afford fi have s'mody else leave. It look too bad on him."

Gabriel racked his brain to figure out who could have told Teago *that.* The only person he'd talked to about leaving the posse was Chops. And Chops wouldn't talk . . . would he? He shook off the entire thought. "I don't think so, mon. Can't be."

Hammer hesitated a moment, genuine concern in his eyes, then said in a rush, "Listen . . . me hear a setup coming fi you.

And you'll know when it's going down if di boss ask you to switch up the stash house."

"Switch up the stash house?"

"Yeh, mon."

"What kind of foolishness you talking, Hammer? No way would the boss want to risk losing the stash just to set somebody up."

"Rest yourself, mon. And hear me good," Hammer said in a harsh whisper even though the closest people around were the two kids, now a block away, still dragging their cardboards. "You'll get asked to move the stash house, but when you get there, there won't be any stash to move, just soldiers to take you away."

Gabriel swallowed. He never should have talked to Chops! He must have slipped up, said something. But then again, would Chops rat on Gabriel? Would Teago actually set him up? "I don't believe it, mon."

"Damn, G. Blood Moon tell me. And Jamal backed him up."

Shit. SHIT. *They* would know. They were the most senior guys in the posse, after Teago. Shit! Gabriel yanked his phone out of his back pocket.

Hammer waved it away, as in *don't try*. "Me been trying fi reach them, but them nah pick up."

Gabriel called anyway. Straight to voice mail. He tried Whatsapp . . . waited . . . grinding his teeth . . . nothing.

"Me tell you. Them nah answer dem phone."

"Wait . . . they're doing a drop at the cove." Gabriel's breathing sped past his control. "But—why didn't *they* tell *me* about this stash house thing?" He wanted to chuck his damn unanswered phone. Damn it!

Hammer had a funny expression on his face, his thick brows almost touching. There was something he wasn't saying.

"Why? What is it?" Gabriel crossed his arms, hard.

Hammer started, then stopped, then said it. "I don't mean no offense, but you're not the one people tell things to."

"*What?*"

"You don't really . . . talk to anyone."

"I talk to you all the time!"

"Yeah, me, but you no really talk to anyone else—"

Okay, true, but . . . "Man, you can't go tell everybody your business." Needing other people was necessary . . . but dangerous.

"G, calm down. Me never say that. Me just saying that when you *don't* tell people things, they make up the things they *think* you're doing."

"People have 'nuff things fi say, mon." Friggin' gossip was what it was. No way was he being set up. No way!

"G, focus. If it's true, you need fi get out di posse. . . ." He clamped a hand on Gabriel's forearm, hard. "I talked to Webber. Actually, a *him* reach out to me. . . . Him have a way out."

"Webber? The shipping agent?"

"You know him know things."

He did. Webber was into everything, legal and illegal. Webber had warned them about a setup once, pretty much saved their lives. Because he knew things.

Webber.

So this was *real*. At last Gabriel went into laser focus.

In the silence he heard cardboard scraping the pavement. The boys were coming back, makeshift beds under their arms. Gabriel hoped against hope that they weren't headed for that truck. If they were, he'd have to give them a beatdown. He jammed his hands into his pockets. "Fine, I'll call Webber."

"The meeting set, mon."

And *this* was why he was Gabriel's day-one. "Okay . . . where?"

"Freeport, by his office. Six inna di morrows."

eja dug out the white meat from the shell of a second coconut, laid it on a plate. Fully expecting her siblings to fight over it, she studied Donovan's face. Wait, what was that? A split lip? She gripped his chin, angling his face up to the sunlight.

He snapped his head away. "Cut it out."

There was also a bruise on his cheek. "What happened?" she demanded.

Kaleisha drank down the last of her coconut water, then said, "He got in a fight."

"Shut up." Wow, Donovan was cranky.

Deja grabbed his chin again. "Were you fighting?"

"See what you did?" Donovan snarled at Kaleisha, who shrugged carelessly. To Deja, he insisted, "It wasn't my fault."

"So, then, what happened, Donovan?" Deja let go of his chin, the whole time madly trying to figure out how she had not noticed this until now. Oh! Straleen had picked them up from school yesterday. And by the time Deja got home from her hotel management study group, he was in bed. Okay, she wasn't a *total* failure as a fill-in mom.

"One of the guys, Kelvin, said something stupid."

"So, what did he say?" Deja's mind was still racing—had she forgotten to tell him to take his second pill yesterday? Gosh, she couldn't even remember what she'd had for breakfast yesterday.

Donovan scowled. "He called me a crybaby."

"Well, you are," Kaleisha snarked.

"Shut UP!"

"Kaleisha, behave yourself," Deja interrupted. "Why did he call you that, D?"

"Mi no know. I just said Mommy was in Brooklyn. And . . ."

"And what?"

Donovan touched his lip. "He said I was a crybaby and that I should stop crying because we got barrels." He pulled away and stomped back into the house.

Deja guessed the rest. One time, when an adviser at school had asked Deja if *she* was having a hard time being a barrel child, she had been shocked. Deja quickly said she was fine, but the adviser went on and on about the psychological danger, how Deja wasn't the only one in this predicament. Apparently, kids all over the Caribbean had to deal with it—the jealousy from other kids who *didn't* get a barrel and the expectation to be grateful and never complain about your parents being away from home. Great. Now Donovan was dealing with it too. This wasn't because he didn't take his meds—anybody would have gotten mad.

Kaleisha sighed. "I guess you want me to go talk to him."

"Thanks, but I got it."

Inside, Deja squatted beside her brother, who sat, arms crossed on the couch. "Is who start it?"

He shrugged. "I did."

She told herself not to stack troubles on top of his troubles. "How come?" she pressed, gentler.

"It's just . . . I miss Mommy." He began digging through the backpack.

Oh, Donovan. "I miss Mommy too," she told him.

He looked up, eyes widened. "You do?"

"Yeah, you don't think I want to wash your underwear all my life, do you?"

He fake gagged. "That's nasty."

"Tell me about it." She palmed his head. He ducked, and she palmed it again.

"You miss her bad, huh?"

He pressed his lips together.

"You go ahead and keep missing her, okay? There's nothing wrong with that." She imagined her mother's face, how soft her eyes grew at moments like this. "I mean, imagine if you *didn't* miss her."

"Why would I *not* miss her?"

"Well, you wouldn't miss her if she was a bad mom."

Donovan gave her the squint-eye. "She's not!"

"Exactly! So, you go ahead and keep missing her." She didn't know if he got it, but he didn't appear *so* sad anymore. That was something. "Come on, better get some coconut before Kaleisha piggies it all up." She reached for his hand. He pulled it behind his back but followed her outside. And that was something too.

She headed over to the blue plastic barrel with a mug to get milk. The big-deal barrel from Brooklyn, the instant Christmas, gifts galore. She felt like kicking the damn thing. And yet who knew when there'd even be another one? Oh, Mom!

She remembered the cab ride all the way to Mobay to pick it up and how it took forever. The customs agents had been so rude, checking and double-checking her paperwork, even making her pry open the lid for an overly long inspection. Well, at least she wouldn't have to deal with any of that for a while . . . if ever.

Then she had a funny thought—imagine opening a barrel and her mother actually popping out! *That* would be the best barrel ever.

Now the barrel, which came up past her waist, was empty of surprise and half-full with rainwater. She gazed up at the patches of blue sky, the parts clouds hadn't yet found, hoping for rain, hoping she could keep using the rainwater instead of the tap—that'd help on the water bill.

She dipped the mug, took a long swig, then rallied her siblings for the twenty-minute trek to school.

By the time they reached the main street, the one that curved around the horseshoe-shaped harbor, Deja's forearms were glistening—it had to be ten degrees warmer than when they'd left. At least it was early. Later, when the stores opened, Jamaicans and tourists packed the sidewalks, voices and reggae music would crisscross the air, and all the cars—half going east toward Montego Bay and the other going west toward Negril, to or from the gated resorts—would only make it hotter.

Donovan, the little weirdo, was squinting. He always did this when he got downtown—he liked how the reds, greens, beiges, and oranges of the two-story buildings blended together when he partially closed his eyes. Ten-year-olds were a trip. Kaleisha, ogling her fingernails, each one painted a different color, nearly banged her head into a lamppost. Deja would have to keep her away from Straleen or she'd want *acrylic* nails too. That definitely wasn't in the budget.

She glanced toward the clock tower down the street. School started in five minutes. Then, *Shit! Shit! Shit! Kaleisha's school fees!*

No way was the school administrator *not* going to hit her up, palm open for the cash. Deja couldn't take it, not today.

She glanced around for somewhere to duck into. It would be just her luck for the administrator to happen by. The old church? No, too far. She guided the kids across the street to the shade of a bus stop.

"Where are we going?" Kaleisha demanded.

Deja landed both hands on her sister's shoulders. "Kaley, can you take Donovan to school from here?"

Kaleisha cocked her head. "Oh, you trust me today?"

"Can you do it?"

"Of course I can do it."

Deja could tell she was trying not to roll her eyes. "Good. Thanks, Kaley. I'll pick you two up after school."

Kaleisha stood taller, lifted her head imperiously. "I can get us home, too."

Now was not the time to bruise her confidence, so Deja

quickly said, "I know you can, but I miss you guys when you're gone all day, so I'll come meet you at school."

Donovan stuck out his lower lip. "You no miss us! You 'fraid we ah go get inna trouble."

He was speaking so much patois lately! Ugh—she was thinking exactly what her *mother* would think. And so what if he was? Little kids spoke the Queen's English *and* patois all the time. *Don't be your mother,* she told herself. She ran her hand over Donovan's tight curls. "Okay, smart man. Be good at school."

"Oh, a remember me remember! Me make something fi you." Donovan reached into his backpack, took out a pin. Deja's name was written in red marker on a piece of balsa wood that was pasted onto a plastic pin, dried white glue spilling out from the edges. He must have made it at school.

Deja smiled. She started to pin it onto her tee, then paused. She'd made a pin exactly like this for their mother when she was about his age, something just as rickety. It said *Evangeline*.

This pin should say Evangeline. Mom should be here now, pinning it on her blouse. Deja cleared her throat. "Mommy would love to have one of these." She waited, hoping she had said the right thing.

"But I made this for *you.*"

"And I love it!" She finished attaching it to her T-shirt. "See? Hey, but maybe Mommy would like one too, though? You know how to spell Evangeline?"

"To send to Brooklyn? How much is that?" Kaleisha said nonchalantly as she ogled her nails. "I don't know if we should be spending like that with school money due, you know?"

Deja glanced at her sister. How did *she* know *that*? She'd have to be more careful talking to Straleen and Lila.

"No problem, Kaley, we can afford it," she said easily, then shifted back to Donovan. "So we'll make one for Mommy, okay?"

"I'll use a different marker, though."

"It'll make her so happy!" Deja patted the pin, and the balsa wood broke loose and fell onto the pavement.

By the look on Donovan's face, you'd have thought he'd dropped a slice of his favorite lemon-iced cake. "I should have used more glue," he moaned.

"*More* glue?" Kaleisha pointed at the pin. "Looks like you slapped a whole bottle all over it."

"Shut up!"

"It's okay." Deja picked up the balsa wood and squeezed it back onto the plastic base. "There. How's it look?"

Donovan smiled. "Criss."

Deja pulled him into a hug.

"Let's go. We'll be late." Kaleisha hooked her thumbs under her backpack straps.

"What are *you* doing?" Donovan asked, not yet moving to leave.

"Me? Maybe go fishing on the *Gregor*."

Kaleisha rolled her eyes. "That lousy boat. When's Mr. Wallace going to get a new one?"

Donovan cut in. "It's yellow, though. I like yellow."

"Yellow and sucky," Kaleisha scoffed.

Deja placed a palm on each of their backs. "Okay, enough; you're going to be late."

"'Kay." Kaleisha took off, and Donovan broke into a jog to catch up.

Occasionally glancing back at her siblings, Deja passed the courthouse but then couldn't see them. Pivoting, she jogged back and still didn't see them.

Panic rose until she finally spotted them, much farther along than she'd anticipated, almost across the schoolyard.

She felt like a balloon deflating. At least she'd avoided a conversation about school fees for one more day. Okay, then, back to the boat.

Money. Money. Money. She could ask Uncle Glen to see if Mr. Wallace would let her take the *Gregor* out again. If by Friday she caught a half-dozen parrotfish at about eight hundred J a pound and maybe a few snappers for three times that, she could make a few thousand. But there was Kaleisha's twenty thousand J school fee, not to mention auxiliary fees for science lab, math, and PE. Shit. It'd take months to make that! And that was if she were lucky. And she usually wasn't.

At the harbor, a go-fast, bright green, was gunning out to sea, its wake massive. She stopped with a jolt—suddenly remembering the one she'd seen earlier.

"Deja, wha' gwan?" her uncle called out from the open-air bar by the floating wharf.

She shoved the thought away and joined Uncle Glen and Mr. Wallace, who were drinking Guinness mixed with milk. Breakfast of champions. "Uncle, I want to go back out, but—I'm guessing you haven't had time to fix the *Queen* yet?"

"No, but Wally won't mind you taking the *Gregor* out one

more time." When Mr. Wallace hesitated, Uncle Glen smiled sweetly while ramming his elbow into his friend's arm.

"No problem," Mr. Wallace said, rubbing his arm.

"And no charge. Isn't that right, Wally?" Uncle's eyes bulged as he waited for the answer.

Mr. Wallace shot him a stare, then gave up and took a sip of his "breakfast." "Yeah, yeah, no problem."

"What a *gracious* human being. You should get one of dem peace prizes, mon." Uncle Glen grinned wide. "Free of charge. And me no want no argument, neither."

For once, she wasn't going to argue. "Thanks, Uncle, Mr. Wallace. See you soon."

Stepping onto the dock, she weighed the pros and cons of her two favorite fishing spots. If she went to the same one as earlier, she could check on that go-fast boat. But when she thought about her other favorite, she remembered the beach *it* was near.

Deja, last Sunday, 10:30 a.m.

White sand so fine it was almost powder. A boundless canopy of blue sky. Jamaicans by the dozen. One or two tourists. A rare beach where the people born here were allowed to swim. Not reserved for tourists alone. Deja would work on integrating the turquoise waters when she made it into the tourist industry. A hope for a coming day.

She slathered sunscreen on Donovan's forehead, keeping an eye on Kaleisha, already ankle-deep in the water. All too eager, Donovan started bouncing on his toes. "Hurry up!"

"Stay still. Almost done."

She dabbed finishing touches on the bridge of his nose. "Okay." Donovan pivoted, kicking up sand onto her, and raced to the water. "Don't go in too deep. And stay with your sister," Deja yelled after him. Of course, he didn't acknowledge her, and that only meant she'd have to watch him like a hawk. Going to the beach used to be so easy—the biggest concern had been how cold the water would feel when she first got in. Now she had to worry about the sunscreen, the lunch, the depth of the water, whether there were jellyfish or prickly sea eggs.

"You're not going in?"

She swung around.

Gabriel?

What?

Her first thought was her hair, which she'd shoved under the old red baseball cap she used for fishing. Her second, the ratty old oxford shirt she'd thrown over her swimsuit. Couldn't do anything about it now. Then—*Gabriel?!*

Here?

"Uh . . . hi? I didn't expect—um—what are you doing here?"

"Heard you were down here. Thought I'd stop by. Also, thought *I'd* 'never see you again.'" A perfect smile. His eyes, narrowed against the sun, were warm, thoughtful, teasing. The rips in his jeans were patched with black that matched, and he wore a pair of Jordans. She hadn't noticed at the party how long his legs were. She did notice that he looked genuinely happy to see her. And man, he was cute. Then she reminded herself about how he'd *ditched* her at the party. "How did you know I was here?"

He grinned. "People love to talk, especially if you ask them the right way."

"And you went around asking about me *why*, exactly?"

He took a step closer. "I didn't say a proper goodbye the other night."

That she had not expected. "You came here to say goodbye?"

"I hope not." Sunlight edged his locs.

Deja tried not to show how flustered she was that he was here and quickly followed up with "So, what was that all about, when you left, I mean? You were in a big hurry. . . ." Was he the type to get into fights? Naw, his face was too . . . perfect.

"Some guys got into it with my friend Hammer."

"Your friend's name is Hammer?"

"Trust me, it well suit him."

She glanced at the water, checking on the kids. They were running toward her. "A longtime beef, or did it just happen?"

Donovan, reaching Deja's side before Gabriel could answer, asked, "Who's he?"

Gabriel gave him a chin up. "A friend of your sister's. I'm Gabriel; what's your name?"

Donovan didn't answer, but he did give Gabriel a once-over.

"He's Donovan, and she's Kaleisha." Kaleisha at least gave *him* a chin up, while Deja wiped water off Donovan's face. "You two go play. I see some good waves coming. Not too deep, though." They ran back into the surf.

Gabriel shaded his eyes to study them. "They're watching out for you."

She laughed. "I wish."

"What do you mean? That was good, them coming back to check on you."

"Yeah, it's not that." She sent herself to the ocean bottom before she started to complain. She got barrels from her mother. She had no right to complain. That was the rule.

"What is it, then?" He tilted his head. "Are you on the ocean bottom?"

Now he'd surprised her a second time—he remembered that. "My mother—"

He finished her sentence. "Working in foreign . . . New York, right?"

She tried not to show how impressed she was, flattered even.

"Not easy," he went on. "And you don't have anybody to help you?"

Just as with the other night, Deja couldn't get over how well he understood her . . . situation. It gave her a degree of relief. "I do, but I try not to ask much, if you know what I mean?" she let herself say.

"Yeah, you said something about that the other night." He looked back at the kids splashing each other, Donovan stumbling, losing his balance, landing face-first in the water, them both shrieking with laughter as he got up and shook his head at Kaleisha like a wet dog. "Does it bother you, taking care of them?"

She thought about that, pulled the brim of her cap down lower, didn't answer.

"I like your cap."

He was changing the subject—he must have sensed she didn't really want to talk about it. Huh. Most guys, Deja thought, wouldn't have picked up on that.

She tugged on the brim again. "It's my lucky fishing cap."

"You fish?" He sounded surprised.

"Yeah, I sell some, make a little money, you know."

"Huh. Fishing good around here?"

"*My* spot is." She looked westward. "About a quarter mile out that way."

"You go out with the fishing boats?"

"I do, but I take a boat out myself."

He arched an eyebrow. "Fish and sail, too?"

"It's a *motor*boat, so it's not sailing—" She caught herself, no need to overexplain, get show-offy.

"Still, respect due." He looked at her raptly, as if he'd discovered something he didn't expect to find.

Deja felt a glow—a surge of happiness. Other guys—they always said something stupid about fishing not being a thing girls did. Always.

She focused on Donovan and Kaleisha and finally looked back and answered his initial question. "And . . . I don't mind taking care of them. Not all the time, anyway." She paused.

"But . . ." he encouraged, sifting sand from hand to hand—in no hurry. She dared to think he actually wanted to know.

"But . . . well, sometimes—it's sort of like I lose myself a little. Taking care of them all the time makes me feel like I don't have a grip on my *own* life." She folded the paper bag she'd packed for their lunch. "I tell you what, I really feel for single mothers."

"I think you're lucky. Family is everything," he said, letting the sand spill from his hand.

Lucky? Her face went instantly hot. "I don't think you get it."

His brow instantly furrowed. "Get what?"

"You're just saying that because guys never have to take care of the kids."

He held up a hand. "Hold on—"

"No, for real. It's not easy."

"Deja, I'm sorry—I guess it didn't come out right. What I meant was that I think it's great that you have a family. I wish I had a little brother or sister." He cleared his throat. "But I get what you're saying. . . . Women do mostly have to take care of the kids and all."

And now Deja wanted to smack herself in the head. Idiot! She was the one who hadn't understood. It also occurred to her that a barrel wouldn't mean much to *him*, either, not when weighed against having parents. But the sorry that she wanted to say was caught in her throat, entwined with a lump of embarrassment.

For once, though, the kids had perfect timing. They were scrambling back toward her and Gabriel. "Look! Look! I think we found gold," Donovan was shouting, opening his hands to reveal scallop-shaped seashells and several small stones.

Kaleisha snatched out a gleaming pebble. "This one! Here!"

"Hey, that's mine!" He grabbed it back.

"Chill! I'm just showing it to her."

Deja looked at the wet stone. She knew it couldn't be gold, but it *did* look like it. "It's really pretty, D, but I don't think it's gold."

Gabriel peered close, pointing at the yellow part. "That part there is probably a mineral called pyrite. It fools so many people into thinking that it's gold that it's called . . . ?" He put out his hand, giving them a chance to answer.

"Fool's stone," Kaleisha said at last.

"So close—good answer. It's called 'fool's gold.' Know how you can tell?"

She swung her head side to side, sending water droplets spraying from her braids.

"Gold has unusual shapes, but fool's gold comes in cubes or crystals. What shape is the yellow part?"

Kaleisha held it up to her eye. "It's cubes," she said, dropping it back into Donovan's hand.

"Aww, shoot." With a scowl, Donovan lifted his hand as if to throw the stone into the sand.

"Hey, you should keep it. It's not gold, but it's still pretty hard to find!" Gabriel sprang to his feet in one swift move. "Plus, these other stones? See how flat they are? They are the *best* for skipping. Me know me can skip farther than either of you."

The kids stared up at him eagerly as he went on.

"Hey! Let's have a contest! You two get to add your skips together versus my skips. You first!" And there he was, jogging off to the water's edge, the kids following, already arguing, "No, *you* first!"

Deja sat there stunned. This was weirder than weird. She had to admit, she'd been kinda annoyed and, yeah, pretty bummed when Gabriel took off at the party. But here he was, not only apologizing but now having her siblings, who were skeptical of everyone, practically eating out of his hand—bending down to be at their height, flicking his wrist to show them his *secret* rock-skipping technique, and even showering them with encouragement. And . . . he had deliberately come and found her. But—what was up with his friend? And the way they had hustled out? Clearly something was going on.

A few minutes later, Gabriel jogged back as the kids continued skipping stones. "They're pretty good. *Somehow* they beat me by one." His face was bright, happy.

"Yeah, they're pretty coordinated," she agreed. Dang. She was feeling him too much, too soon. "So, what's going on with you?"

He plunked himself down into the sand. "Me? What'd you want to know?"

"The other night at the party . . . it was nice."

He adjusted his shirt. "Yeah, me feel so too."

"But what happened at the end was crazy." Her directness, coming at him, so quickly without notice, made him bite his lip. "I mean, do I need to worry about you?"

He lowered his head, took his time shaking the sand off the wet edges of his jeans. "I'm not gonna lie." He looked over at her. "I'm in a posse . . . but no, you don't need to worry about me."

Shit. She *knew* he was too good to be true. "Why? I mean, why *not* worry?" She thought of her father. Look how *that* turned out. *Shit.*

Gabriel glanced at Donovan and Kaleisha, then back to her. "Maybe because I'm . . . feeling you."

She put her hand flat on the sand, the rough grains warm against her palm. "I don't know what to say to that."

"Fair. Maybe I shouldn't have said it—but it's the truth."

She couldn't let the posse thing go, so once she brushed the sand off her hands, she asked, "So, why are you in it? A posse, I mean."

He shrugged. "Not much for sufferers, you know? Things are

hard right now. Even a loaf of hardo bread is expensive."

That was all true. Straleen and her other day-one, Lila, had been searching for part-time jobs for forever. Still . . . a *posse*?

He ducked his head to peek under her cap. "So, your turn— truth. How you feeling about us? Can we hang out?" There were flecks of sand on his left cheekbone. She wanted to reach out, brush it off, but didn't.

"The thing is, I never have any free time—" She *wanted* to tell him that the posse thing was a turnoff, a complete turnoff. She wasn't a girl who hung with guys in a posse, but using the kids was a better excuse.

He nodded. But the smile didn't reach his eyes. And suddenly there wasn't much to talk about. A man selling sodas chanted his sales pitch as he walked by. A Jet Ski whirred as it cut through the ocean. A baby being rocked in a mother's arms cried out. Then the kids sprinted from the water, racing each other back yet again.

"We're hungry," Kaleisha shouted.

"Me belly a touch me back," Donovan one-upped her, bouncing around, all fidgety.

Had he taken his meds . . . ? Yes, but it had been more than five hours since. "Think it's time for your medicine," Deja said.

"Nooo." He danced a weird half circle. "I don't need any."

Kaleisha put on her sass face. "Yes, you do."

Donovan dropped to the sand, legs crossed, both fists to his cheeks. Deja was searching for something new to say, new words to motivate him.

Gabriel stuck a finger in the sand. He was drawing something she couldn't make out. "Somebody once told me that I should take some medicine too. I didn't listen . . . but maybe I should have."

Donovan lifted his head.

"For what?" Deja asked for Donovan's sake and, truth, for her own curiosity.

"Stress, anxiety, you know." Then he gave her a wry grin. "I don't so love being in crowds and things."

Like at the party.

"You know, meds might have helped me, Donovan." Gabriel patted Donovan's shoulder. "Maybe yours help you. And who knows, maybe later on you won't need them." He stood. "I'll let you guys have your lunch."

Donovan whirled to Deja. "Can he stay?"

Just as she was saying, "Sure," Gabriel was saying, "I'd like to, but I've got to go. You two are good at skipping. I'll get you next time, though."

"No way," Donovan fronted.

In spite of what Gabriel had just told her—the posse thing—Deja felt something pull at her, like she was throwing away a stone that had a sliver of real gold in it. So she blurted out, "We've got extra sandwiches. It's bully beef and hardo bread."

He met her eyes with his own. "Thanks, but I really do have to go. But why don't you give me your number?"

She hesitated. He was in a posse. And yet. That pull. And . . . she didn't want to be mean.

The kids got all giggly as she told him; she made eyes at them to stop.

"I'll hit you up sometime," he said, giving the kids a wave.

As he headed up the beach, Deja unfolded the paper bag and took out the wrapped sandwiches, thinking of the joke they'd shared when they'd met. *I'll never see you again.*

Deja, Thursday, 10:00 a.m.

Deja'd been so busy thinking about Gabriel's beach visit that it had barely registered that she'd chosen her fishing spot near the cove. Maybe she wanted to distance herself from the memory of him, even though he was still on her mind. Weird. But now, a hundred yards away, she could see that nothing about the go-fast boat had changed. Except there was no arm hanging over the gunwale. What had happened to him? What should she do?

The smart choice would be to go to the other spot, memory of Gabriel or not, and catch some snapper and parrot. The harder choice would be boarding the go-fast, where someone could be lying on that deck, sick, hurt, maybe dying—definitely in need of help. Ugh. But later on, if she heard that somebody found on a go-fast boat had died in the hospital, she would be haunted forever—if only she had checked, maybe she could have saved that person. Gahhh! Then an image of her mother struggling to get to her knees on some Brooklyn street after being mugged flashed through her mind. Had a passerby stopped to help *her*? She had to have gotten to a hospital somehow. Probably someone did. Someone stopped and helped.

She steered closer. Then gasped. Two holes pierced the stern of the boat. Bullet holes!

This was a mistake!

Still. She was here now. She had to find out. Cutting the engine, eyes on the go-fast, she reached under the rotted seat and felt around until her fingers found the anchor. It was heavy, sharp—a decent enough weapon if she had to use one. Hefting it, she eked out a tremorous, "Hello?" Nothing. "Hello?" Louder.

She let the slow drift take her over, then grabbed hold of the boat's gunwale. Waves lapping rocks was the only sound. Tightening her grip on the anchor, ready to swing it if necessary, she leaned forward and eyed the deck. A long brown smear stretched from one side to the other—blood? And it led to a body, a man! His back was against the gunwale, his head bowed, his right leg straight out, a pool of blood underneath. Deja fought not to recoil. She didn't see any other wounds—maybe he'd only been shot in the leg? And was he alive? Deja swallowed hard. "Hello. Can I help?"

Nothing.

Just as she decided he must be dead, his arm twitched. Deja jerked back, losing her balance, nearly impaling her leg with the anchor. Hands shaking, she took a deep breath. *Pull yourself together, Deja!* She called out "Hello" again. Nothing. She put down the anchor and pulled out her phone—maybe by some miracle there was service? No. Damn it.

Okay. Okay. She had to get over there. She wrapped the *Gregor*'s line around the go-fast boat's cleat and sprang onto the other boat's stern. Hulking twin outboard motors sat there. . . . Man, they could probably go ninety miles per hour. Two three-foot-tall steel containers were roped onto the back of the deck. This was definitely a drug dealer's boat. *What the hell am I doing here?* Deja knocked on them. The thuds let her know they were still full, probably with gasoline for the return trip from wherever. She glanced at the man—he for sure wasn't making any return trip anywhere.

Then she noticed that his thigh was wrapped with gaffer tape, the roll still attached, as if he'd passed out while he was doing the wrapping.

A chain hung around his neck, a small black wallet dangling from it. Deja bent down, again whispering, "Hello," to be sure he was still out, then reached for it. It held a shiny badge that read SPECIAL AGENT, DEA. The American Drug Enforcement Administration? What? She fumbled the wallet, caught it again. Steady. Steady. The card on the opposite side said his name was GONZALEZ G. She dropped it fast, looking everywhere at once. The fact that he was some sort of police didn't do anything to make her calmer. There were lots of corrupt police in Jamaica. But he was American, she reminded herself. Not that they didn't have their own issues.

She was wasting time; she needed to *do* something. Fishing out her phone once more, she dialed 112 for help. Still no service. Of course. Of course, there had been some a hundred yards back. Shit. She crept forward as if to a dog she didn't trust, then gave the man's shoulder a gentle shake. He didn't respond. The smell of sweat was oppressive. Could it just be sweat? The stench seemed to be coming from the shore. Weird. She eyed the gaffer tape around his leg and thought for a moment. In health class, the teacher had said the first thing to do with a bad wound was to stop the bleeding. Clearly that was what this guy had been attempting.

She surveyed the rest of the boat. A handgun barrel was wedged behind the steering wheel mount. Below that was a box-shaped leather briefcase, like an airplane pilot's. Two holes in the side of the console. More bullets? Then she took in the wide, messy path of blood across the gunwale. The guy had probably been trying to get to the radio to call for help. The radio! Maybe *she* could call for help?

Then came a groan. The man's eyes fluttered open! Deja reached for the gunwale of the *Gregor*, ready to jump back in. His eyes searched hers, almost as if he wasn't sure he could believe what he was seeing. He groaned again, then lifted a trembling hand toward either the briefcase or the gun, she wasn't sure. He had to be delirious to think she was stupid enough to bring him a gun! His eyes closed once more. But his chest was still rising and falling—still breathing. The relief that he was alive made her near light-headed.

Deja willed herself to move, creeping closer, closer, until she could reach for the roll of gaffer tape. He was alive. She'd radio for help or go get some. But first—first . . . he wasn't going to stay alive if he bled out. So, drawing a deep breath, she gently lifted the man's leg. He moaned, louder. The stink made her want to gag. As quickly and as tightly as she could, she wound the tape around his leg until the tape ran out. It wasn't the best tourniquet in the world, but it might do. His face looked gray beneath his tan. He had to get to the hospital! But no way she could carry him to the *Gregor*; he was big, more than six feet at least, maybe 180 pounds, muscular. She could radio for help! But that would take time he might not have left. Damn. She thought again about her mother. What if no one had tried to help her? Bracing her legs, Deja put her arms under the guy's armpits, around his chest, and, gritting her teeth, heaved him up about a foot.

He groaned out a "No." His eyes opened again, begging her to stop.

She lowered him back down. "I have to get you to town." Her tone was like the one she used with her siblings to get them to do something they needed to do.

"No time." He raised his arm a few inches, as if trying to show her something, then dropped it down, wincing. He pointed again. "The case. The case."

The briefcase. She went to it. Clicked open its two silver latches. Eased the sides apart. Bumboclot! It was filled with American hundred-dollar bills! Filled! She looked to the man, slack-jawed. What did he want her to do with *this*? His eyes were drifting closed again. What he needed was a doctor. Her heart started hammering—was he even breathing? His forehead felt cold, and purple blotches were blooming on his skin.

But now he was pointing again? "Water," he said, his voice

cracking. Deja studied the deck—a thermos. He had to be parched—why hadn't she thought of this? She snatched up the thermos, spun the cap so fast it fell and rolled along the deck, then held the bottle to his lips.

The man got down a few small sips, then, with trembling fingers, reached into his shirt pocket and pulled out a card. "Take it," he breathed.

She set down the thermos, took the card. DEMARCO WEBBER. There was an address in Mobay and a phone number. Was he an agent too? "Bring him the briefcase. Don't let them get it." His eyes closed once more. His voice was so garbled, she wasn't sure she'd heard him correctly.

"The briefcase? Bring this—this Webber man the briefcase?" she stammered.

"He'll reward you." He swallowed, grimacing. "Just bring it to Webber." He lay his head back in apparent exhaustion.

This was insane. "*You* need a hospital!"

He motioned again for the water, grimaced as he took a bigger sip. After a moment he added, each phrase a gasp, "There's five hundred K in there. Don't take it. We marked it. Webber, he'll see you're paid. Please."

"Who's them?" She waited for an answer that didn't come. And in her mind—she couldn't help it!—she was thinking, *Reward? How much?* Enough to help her mother? Pay Kaleisha's school fees? Her mind raced. Maybe even the mortgage! She snapped the case shut, picked it up by the handle. Then—fool! What was she even thinking? This man could be dying!

"No. I'll get you to a hospital first." She set the case down, made for the wheel—how had she not thought of *this* before? She could use his boat! She'd have him in Springtown Harbour in fifteen minutes, and she could radio for help on the way. She eyed the controls. She couldn't resist running her fingers across the sleek black acrylic dash—definitely custom. But why did they put the autopilot way off to the side? Whatever. Weird, but whatever. At least they hadn't messed with the gauges—those she recognized. She made to turn the key for one of the engines, then remembered about the blower. She glanced back at the man. She didn't want to waste the three minutes to blow out any lingering fumes. So, saying a quick prayer, she made sure the shifter was in neutral and turned a key. One of the engines growled to life, but then . . . died. Deja groaned out loud. She could try the other engine but decided to turn the same one again. It started . . . and died again. Her third try didn't even turn over the engine. So she tried the other key. Nothing. What had she done wrong? Was it the blower? Then the smell of gas wafted into the air. Damn! She'd flooded the engine. Damn it! It would take half an hour for the gas to subside. A half hour neither of them had. Okay, the radio. She jabbed the button. Again. It was dead. A fuse? How to even start fixing it? She spun around to tell the man she'd have to go back to the harbor alone to get help.

But he had fallen, face flat on the deck.

A rank odor polluted her nose and mouth. She lurched for the gunwale and retched. Holding vigil as her grandmother had passed, her hand on the beloved old woman's wrinkled cheek, the same thing had happened. The same smell of feces. The whiff of death.

She put her hand under Gonzalez's nose, accidentally touching his cold lips. She snatched her hand away, watched his chest—no up and down. Deja didn't even know him, but to her surprise, tears pricked her eyes. He wasn't breathing.

A seagull screeched as it flew overhead. Waves broke against barnacled rocks by the shore.

The least she could do was cover the guy. She yanked open the storage compartment, sifted past a stern anchor, a coffee thermos, a battery, and found a blanket.

As gently as she'd cover a baby, Deja laid the blanket over him and made the sign of the cross. It wasn't much, but at least she'd done something.

Now she had to think . . . *think*. He wanted her to bring Webber the briefcase. *Don't let them get it. He will reward you. Don't let them get it*, he'd said.

She eyed the circling seagull, debating. Five hundred K in marked money! *Could* she get it to Montego Bay? To this Webber guy? Then she could at least tell this Webber guy to get his . . . friend? What might the reward be for this much money? Even a hundred US would be a huge help. And it *was* this man's last request. She looked to the east. Montego Bay was an hour away by car. Maybe the guy could meet her at the harbor? No— she didn't want him to know anything about her. If she did this, she would have to go to him.

And who was "them"? *Don't let them get it.* At that very moment a low whistle cut the silence. She crouched, eyes following its sound to the shore. Was someone there, in those grasses past the boulders? A surge of panic—was it "them," the people who shouldn't get the money?

Briefcase in hand, Deja crawled to the edge of the go-fast, peeked over the side. She saw no one, but still she stayed low. She had to leave—now.

Deja, Thursday, noon

With the *Gregor* at full throttle, Deja swung into the mouth of Springtown Harbour. Wind whipping at her face, she could feel her pulse all the way to her fingertips, every molecule prickly. She hadn't felt this hyper-focused since playing netball.

Who was this Webber guy anyway? And who else was looking for the money? Well, whoever put a bullet into that guy's leg was. And—*backside*, what if this Webber dude had something to do with *that*? But she had to do something with the briefcase. No way was she keeping the money. The guy said it was marked. Plus, it wasn't hers. *Okay. Okay. Think.* If she handed it over to the police—yeah, right; that would be a joke. No one would ever see it again. And no reward.

The reward.

Her thoughts circled around that poor Gonzalez guy, gaffer tape wrapped around his leg. He didn't even get last rites. And now he was lying there in the boat—that wasn't right!

Deja yanked out her phone, about to dial 112. Then she froze. What was she thinking? As soon as she called, police would be dispatched to check the go-fast. They'd see a gunshot wound and immediately suspect that drugs and cash were involved. They'd track this very call, and that would bring them straight to her. And the briefcase.

Think. *Think.* The SIM cards! She fished them out of her pocket. Each one was attached to a different phone number; hundreds of people bought random cards every day, right? And so they probably wouldn't be able to track it back to her. She popped the card in her phone out and put a new one in. Placing a hand over the speaker to mask her voice, she made the call.

"Hello. Where is your emergency?"

"Near . . ." Her voice squeaked. She took a breath, started again. "Near Green Island, there's a . . . a man on a boat, just outside a cove. He's dead."

"What is your name?"

Deja pressed her phone hard against her ear. "It's the cove near Green Island. He's dead."

The person on the other end of the phone kept saying "Hello, hello." Deja had done what she could. She couldn't risk any trouble with the local police—so she hung up.

But what to do now?

Don't trouble trouble until trouble trouble you. That was what her grandmother would be saying right now, bobbing her head, *uh-huh, uh-huh.* But Deja had taken the briefcase and invited trouble into her life.

And maybe it was a *solution* to trouble, this briefcase. Go for it, girl! She pulled the briefcase closer. It was quality material. Too bad she'd have to throw it away the first chance she got. They would be looking for a briefcase, whoever they were. She'd have to transfer the cash into some other bag.

She was about to slide the *Gregor* into its slip, and—oh damn! Of *course*. There was Uncle Glen leaving the beach bar, a clutch of buddies calling after him. If he saw her, he'd come over, see the briefcase, and ask too many questions, because that was what Uncle Glen did.

At the far end of the beach, she saw a crew of fisherwomen. They'd be done scaling the morning catch and were probably frying by now.

Deja steered toward them, careful not to look in the direction of her uncle. The smell of sizzling fish, Scotch bonnet peppers, garlic, and some thyme reminded her she hadn't even eaten breakfast yet.

"Anybody have bags to sell?" she called out, springing from the boat, pulling it to shore.

"You no have fish fi sell?" asked Mrs. Waul.

Deja had totally forgotten about fishing! "No luck."

"Then what you need di bags for?"

Be calm, Deja. "Um, for tomorrow. Going out early-early. Should be good fishing."

Mrs. Waul pinched her chin. "Give me nine US, nuh, dear?"

Deja knew the price should be three or four dollars.

"I can give you two."

"Baby, make it five dollars and yu have a deal."

"Four," Deja said.

Mrs. Waul reached down and picked up three burlap bags. "Is a long time me have these, yu know?"

"Never mind, no trouble. I can go over to the bar." Deja was all polite.

"Oh, it's okay. I don't want you fi use up your gas."

A good haggling session meant Mrs. Waul would respect her now, all without an ounce of suspicion. Deja held up four dollar bills, and the two made their exchange—smiles abounded. She gave a nod of small honor to Mrs. Waul, and the sand around her sandals glimmering with fish scales, like a sea of jewels.

"Maybe you work for me someday, dearie," Mrs. Waul said, a hopeful lilt in her voice.

"Maybe," Deja conceded, hoping she'd never see that day.

A minute later, she was heading out of the bay, as if to try her luck fishing again. As soon as she was far enough out, she checked for other boats, and, all clear, killed the engine. Hands shaking, she unlatched the briefcase. Shit. She'd never even dreamed she'd see so much money. Drug money. Marked, he'd said. Still, it was dizzying to think what she could do with that much money.

She opened the briefcase wider and took out the first stack of notes. She couldn't stop searching the horizon, then searching again. *Act natural,* she told herself. *Calm down.*

Her heart was racing, but the rest of her seemed to be in slower motion. *Slowest* motion. Each stack—almost three inches tall—felt like a thick hardo bread sandwich, and there were probably twenty of them. She filled one burlap bag, then the next. Neatly. She made believe she was packing the kids' lunches. Everyday stuff. No big deal. When the briefcase was empty, she grabbed its handle, leaped into the water, wading to shore. There she stashed the case behind the only mangrove tree on the beach. A minute later, she was hoisting herself back onto Mr. Wallace's skiff.

This time she motored slowly and casually into the harbor, just a girl coming back after a great fishing day. And damn, her uncle was *still* hanging around.

Deja edged the *Gregor* between its ragtag siblings of old and tired skiffs. Tying off near the *Queen*, she emptied the cooler of its ice, slung the burlap bags over her shoulder, and hoped against hope that the bags' bulk wouldn't stand out.

Uncle Glen was waving. Of *course* he was. She thought about just walking on as if she didn't see him, but no way would he not be suspicious. Deja and her siblings were the kids he'd never had; he was interested in everything about them.

"You come back quick-quick. Must have been lucky today." Uncle Glen nodded at the bags over her shoulder. "You catch all the parrot in di sea." Then he tilted his head. "Why the bags?" He knew too well she didn't make it a habit of wasting money on bags.

"I have to go, Uncle. Have some things I have to do back home." She took a step, hoping to divert him.

"If you have a problem, you can talk to me, you know?"

She almost stumbled. How—

"Deja, I spoke to your mother," he went on.

She nearly stumbled again, this time in relief. "What did she say? How is she?"

His eyes smiled. "No worry, mon. Your mother is as smart as my Lisa was. She'll figure something out."

Uncle's eyes always got like that when he talked about his wife. She'd passed ten years ago, but she was no doubt alive and kicking in his memories. "But you sure Mummy's okay?"

"No worry, mon. New broom sweep clean, but old broom know every corner. She can handle herself."

If she knew every corner, she wouldn't have been carrying all that partner money on her, Deja thought bitterly. "What did she *say*?"

"Well, we chat 'bout 'nuff things, but . . ." He slurped like he was drinking soup, something he did when he was thinking, a habit Deja liked as much as she did teaspoons of castor oil. "Me thinking of a way fi maybe sell the *Queen*, so me can get a little money fi help out your mother."

Sell the *Queen*? He loved his boat! It was his life. His livelihood. "What? How? No!"

He rubbed his ample belly. "No problem, mon. Me can figure something out."

"Uncle, you can't live without the *Queen*."

"It's amazing what you can get used to, Deja."

"But, Uncle, the way things are, do you think you could even get a fair price?"

"Oh, you turn economist now? You sound like your mother!" His laugh boomed. "But you know, you right at that. . . . I probably couldn't bring myself fi sell her."

Mr. Wallace called out from the bar, "How's my boat?"

Uncle Glen cupped his hands around his mouth

megaphone-style. "Your dingy is fine. And it had never had a better pilot, neither." He smirked, but when he pivoted back to Deja, his brow was furrowed. "You don't look so good, mon. Maybe you should make me drive you home?"

So, *that* couldn't happen. "Thanks, Uncle. But I'm good—just worrying about Mom."

"You sure you sure?"

"I'll be fine." Her tone sounded way perkier than she felt. "Likkle more, Uncle."

Crunching her way over the sand toward the sidewalk, she was unable to shake that moving-in-slow-motion feel. Did anyone notice?

Well, Uncle Glen did. Right on cue, he yelled, "Shout me if you need me!"

The second she got home, she dropped the bags. Her stomach was growling, and her throat felt parched, but first, where to hide the bags? The passports, important documents, and a few paltry dollars were stashed in the broken drainpipe out back, but this was way too much to fit in there. Too thirsty to keep thinking, she drank straight from the jug of water in the fridge—if Donovan or Kaleisha were there, they'd lay into her like she did to them for doing the same thing.

Now that she was no longer thirsty, a wave of fatigue hit hard. She sank slowly to the floor, jug still in her hand.

From the window, a shaft of light blanketed the bags in a golden glow.

She needed time to think. Was she safe from them? No one

had seen her except the DEA agent. So no worries there. But what about the emergency services she'd called? What *if* they could trace her number—and suspected *she* was involved in the agent's death? She felt instantly sick. They could arrest her, and what about the kids? She shook that thought away and tried to focus on the money. *Come on, Deja. What to do? What to do?*

Her old backpack. It was somewhere in the closet. That would be perfect for getting the cash to that Webber guy. But what if someone came and searched the house? She looked frantically around the room for a hiding place, then spied it. Couch pillows! She would hide the cash in them, in plain sight. That always worked with her siblings. They'd never once found their birthday gifts.

After another swig of water, Deja stood and peeked out the window. The street was empty. Relieved, she closed the curtains, scooped the pillows off the couch, and started yanking out the stuffing.

Gabriel, Friday, 6:10 a.m.

Gabriel paced in the shadows of a thirty-foot stack of shipping containers in the cruise ship port. The sickly sweet smell of oil permeated the air. Man, he was wiped. He'd slept like crap—*Switch up the stash house* had looped in his mind till dawn. He'd texted and Snapped Jamal and Blood Moon a bunch of times, but nada.

And where the hell was Webber? He should have been here ten minutes ago. The priests at school had drilled into Gabriel that punctuality was one of the truest signs of trustworthiness, so could he really trust Webber?

Gabriel circled over to Hammer, who was shining a handlebar on his bike with his shirtsleeve. "So, what's this deal, anyway?"

"Relax. Webber will tell you, mon."

Gabriel pulled out his phone. "What's up with Jamal and Blood Moon, anyway? Haven't heard back. You?"

"After drops, them go hang out sometimes, you know?" Hammer tweaked his nose, indicating that they dipped into the coke supply for their own use. In fact, everybody in the posse except Gabriel and Hammer got high, especially the boss. Bumboclot, Teago could party.

Gabriel knocked on a metal container, the echo sounding hollow. "Hey, doesn't the boss hate Webber?"

"Sure does. Webber screwed him out of a mega deal, mon. Never seen him so mad."

"So why should *we* trust him?"

Hammer shrugged. "Because the boss tried to screw Webber first."

Gabriel jammed his hands into his pockets and looked up: cirrus clouds, moving fast like his thoughts.

"Wha' gwan, G?"

"What?"

"Chuh, mon, me know you, you know? You up to something."

He *was* up to something. He had a plan, actually *plans*. He just wasn't sure which one to try. "I'm going to test him."

Hammer *pfffft*ed. "Test him, what test him? All you need fi do is listen, G. Di man going tell you how you can get off the island. What more you need to know?"

"Everything. Maybe it's my life we talking about."

"Backside!" Still, Hammer studied Gabriel for a minute. "Okay, look, it no complicated. . . . Webber can get us in with a posse in foreign. America at that."

Gabriel did a double take, not sure he'd heard right. "Us?"

Hammer's mouth fell open. "What? You no want me fi go?"

Gabriel hadn't intended to insult him. So he said quickly,

"Didn't say that. Just didn't know you wanted to go." Plus, why shouldn't Hammer want to leave? Guys were switching posses so much lately, it was hard to keep up. "Where in America?"

"Miami."

Gabriel gave a slow whistle. "Like Bonefide?" Nobody disrespected Bonefide—dude had good sense.

"Yeh, mon, like Bonefide."

"Wait, *Webber* got Bonefide to the States?"

"No that me a tell you, mon!"

That was something, at least. Last he heard, Bonefide was doing pretty well for himself. Gabriel whistled again. "Okay, okay, I get that. I get that. But still, something feels weird." He trusted Hammer, but could he trust who Hammer trusted? "Don't know, man. I just feel we still need to test Webber. Who knows, *he* might be setting us up."

Hammer waved Gabriel off. "Me believe him, mon."

"You believe the earth is flat, too."

"Prove it isn't." Hammer poked a finger in the air as if putting a period at the end of a sentence. Then Hammer was suddenly motioning toward the grimy two-story office building that bordered the lot. A man walked outside.

Gabriel exhaled. "Here we go."

"Yeh, mon."

Webber came striding toward them, rimless sunglasses up on his head, Afro cropped short, T-shirt gleaming white, carrying an energy drink. He was old, probably around forty-five, but when Webber got closer, Gabriel noticed a neck tattoo. A barcode. Odd. Desk-job people weren't usually into tattoos, much less ones that could be easily seen.

When he reached them, Webber took a big swig of his drink, and Gabriel saw his opening to take charge. "Webber, check it. I want to know—"

But Webber just launched straight into a rant. "Time's ticking. Feel me? You're what, seventeen, eighteen—that's a grown-up. And if you didn't know, a teenager wasn't even a thing until about sixty years ago. Before that you were either child or grown-ass man. So, you better listen good to what I'm about to say and think like you're grown."

Webber eyed Gabriel from head to toe before going on. "Opportunity doesn't knock. It fucking booms in your bloody ear. Children have the luxury of not listening because they have time on their side. Grown-ups don't. They must take bumboclot action before the bumboclot opportunity is even fully explained. Why? Because somebody else is going to pull every dirty trick in the book, and the addendum, to beat you to it. So, listen up. . . . I have a connection to the Third Phase posse in Miami."

"You never tell me it was Third Phase!" Very little impressed Hammer; clearly this did.

"That's right, the Third effing Phase, boys." Webber raised his can at Hammer as if to cheer. "They are vertically integrated, and if you don't know what that means—"

Gabriel cut him off. "Means a company has taken over control of different phases of its supply chain."

Webber leaned back in mock amazement. "Okay, Wikipedia . . . nice entry."

"Him well smart, mon," Hammer said.

"*Smart* people shut up and listen." Webber gestured with his can of energy drink. "As *I* was saying, the Third Phase has the economic clout to produce goods on a wholesale and retail level, and it's all legal thanks to their political allies. That's the kind of power that can one day fill your pockets, boys."

"But why do they—" Gabriel started.

Webber kept talking as if Gabriel hadn't even opened his mouth. "So, here's the offer. Take it or fuck off."

Who the hell did this guy think he was? Still, Gabriel held his tongue. Smart people listen.

"The Third Phase is happy with the quality of soldiers I've been sending them, and they want more. Now, hear me, and hear me good. They take my word for new recruits, but they still require a task."

Gabriel had been waiting for the catch. Here it was. "What task?"

Webber shot Gabriel an arch look. "More listening. Less talk. I'm about to tell you." He took another chug of his drink. "Now, to be crystal clear, the price is a package. I'd say ten kilos of cocaine or fifteen keys of good ganja should do it. Why? It's a bumboclot test is why."

And Gabriel wanted to test *him*.

"Some posses jump you in; some make you beat up a guy to get in, right? But we're talking Third Phase here. This is the big time, boys."

"Where we supposed to get that much drugs from?" Hammer asked.

"Crazy, right?" Webber cut loose a maniacal smile. "I'm guessing you'll have to steal it. Seriously pissing off whichever don you rip off, placing a bull's-eye square in the middle of your heads. This way they'll know you're effin' serious, cuz you put your asses in the fire—"

Gabriel jumped in when Webber paused. "So what's in it for you?"

"So nice, you care so much about me," Webber mocked.

Gabriel really wanted to hit him. But then Webber said, "Okay, I'll tell you. Once you get the drugs, you bring them to me. I take my minor cut and use my access here to put you and the package on a South Florida–bound vessel, where a contact from the Third Phase will be waiting to welcome you to the land of milk and honey." He drained his drink, crushed it, shot toward a trash can. It clanked right in. "Let me know when you get a package." He flashed them a peace sign and strode off.

Gabriel and Hammer gaped at each other. The second Webber was out of earshot, Gabriel exclaimed, "Bumboclot! Where are we going to get ten kilos of *anything*?"

"Hell if I know!" Hammer shrugged, then started to grin. "But you sure you don't want fi bring him back and test him?"

"Okay, you have jokes." Gabriel watched Webber stroll back into the building.

"You believe him now?"

Gabriel shrugged. "Not sure. But I think he doesn't care if we do. . . . Maybe that's why I kind of believe him."

Hammer swung a leg over his bike. "So, you ready?"

"For what? To rip the drugs off Teago and gamble that the

Third Phase doesn't just dead us off once they get what *they* want?" He didn't add that if it worked out, he'd still be stuck in a posse. Damn. Even if he ended up a winner, he'd be a loser.

Gabriel's phone buzzed. Had to be Jamal or Blood Moon. They would clear all this up. But when he looked at the phone number, it was Teago's.

Deja, Friday, 5:30 a.m.

Deja woke drenched in sweat, her tee clinging like a second skin. For a nanosecond, nothing made sense, not the machete she was gripping in one hand, nor why she'd been sleeping with three pillows propping her up. Maybe that was why her back was so stiff. She'd been having a dream, one where she hadn't taken the money from the agent and had driven the *Gregor* back to town but suddenly found herself walking *with* the bag of cash next to a skinny cow in the middle of the street. What did that mean? Then a panic of images played out in her mind. The man. The boat. The money. Then she recalled putting the kids to bed and staying vigilant for a while, intending to keep an eye out for "them" all night. But sleep must have overtaken her.

She sprang up from the couch and hurried to her mother's bedroom. Pushed the door open. The kids were asleep. Okay. Okay.

Closing the door gently, she made a beeline for the closet. That old backpack was in there somewhere. Yes! She pulled it out, and eeww, it smelled like fish. When she zipped it open, a few shimmering scales spilled out. She tipped the backpack, gave it a good shake until she was sure it was empty. She reached under the couch for the down and feathers she'd removed yesterday. She immediately began gutting the pillows of their stacks of American hundreds and stuffing them into the backpack.

A knock at the door.

Them?

Deja froze.

Another knock.

Deja grabbed the machete, backed away from the door. Kaley. Donovan. How could she get them out?

"Deyyyyja—" Straleen.

Deja almost dropped the machete in relief as she remembered they were coming over early to cram for the big statistics test next week.

"Deyyyja," Straleen singsonged again.

The relief was momentary—she'd want to come in! What the hell should she do now?

"Dejaaaaa," Lila echoed.

Oh great. Both of them! With an exhale, she swung open the door but didn't move to let them in.

Straleen gave her a dubious stare. "Girl, what is up with you—you look so crazy!"

Deja tried a fake smile. "What are you talking about?"

"The way you look." Straleen didn't play, and the fake smile didn't work.

Lila adjusted her glasses and said in the gotcha-gotcha way, "Um . . . the machete?"

Shit. Shit. Deja should shoo them away. "Just, kind of busy right now—"

"Doing what?" Straleen insisted.

With blank in her mind, Deja started to close the door. "Hey, see you later, okay—"

Straleen put a hand on the door. "Hold on, hold on. Seriously, what is up with you?"

Deja couldn't force the door closed. What to say? What to say?

Lila leaned past her. "And what's that on the floor?"

Deja tapped the flat of the machete against her leg. She couldn't keep standing there with the door open, arguing with her friends. This might invite other eyes. Wake the kids. Make her lose her freaking mind.

"Deja?" Straleen demanded.

Bumboclot—this was all too much to keep to herself, anyway. "Fine, come in. But keep your voices down. The kids are asleep."

Sitting at the kitchen table, explaining everything to her friends while dealing with their wide-eyed expressions and gasps of disbelief left Deja feeling more exhausted than if she hadn't slept at all. Her friends had a zillion questions and were unable to resist touching the blocks of bills. Lila even began stacking them like toy bricks until Straleen smacked her arm. It was surreal. Deja loopily answered Lila's repeated questions, careful not to tell them about her mom.

It was all so, so strange, as if she were telling a story about someone else. Except it wasn't someone else, and the disbelief on her friends' faces confirmed it. This was a disaster, one that was all her fault.

Lila, who'd been firing questions at her like she was police, paused long enough to pour a glass of water. She thrust it at Deja, then poured one for herself.

Straleen tapped her nails on the table to get Deja's attention. "Girl, me nah say this to scare you or anything, but serious thing. . . . I pray nobody is out there looking fi dead you off."

And those words were what cut through the fog. *Dead you off.* Deja picked up a brick of bills. "I've been wondering the same thing." But oddly, at this moment, she wasn't as scared. Now that she'd said it out loud and talked it through with the girls, it wasn't too big for her. It was like when she'd docked the *Queen* despite the bad conditions yesterday. It wasn't a good situation, but she could handle it—because she *had* to handle it. There literally was no choice.

Double-teaming, Lila leaned forward, head leaned to the right—her *I've got something serious to say* gesture. "I would have calmly looked around to see who else saw me, reversed that boat, and then kindly taken my backside back to my yard."

"It's funny—last night I dreamed about doing exactly that." Deja gave half a shrug. "Then again, I dreamed about a cow in the middle of town, too."

Straleen's eyes went wide. "Cow?! Cow dream is a warning, mon. You need fi heed that."

Deja shook her head. "Stray, you need to stop being so superstitious."

"And you need to stop being so stupid," Straleen shot back.

Easy to say, Deja thought, annoyance starting to burn. They weren't dealing with what she was dealing with. They weren't feeling what she was feeling, seeing what she was seeing—her mother lying on some hospital bed in Brooklyn. Alone. No money.

Lila fixed her a look. "You should have never taken this money in the first place."

"That's not *remotely* helpful, Lila! I *took* it. It was hell out there, you know? The guy was a DEA agent!"

"He could have been 007 himself! I wouldn't have taken the damn case." Lila rubbed at her temples as if she were the one in trouble. "Chuh, mon, this is a bumboclot mess!"

"You think I don't know?!" Deja struggled to keep her voice down—she couldn't wake the kids. Then a new thought occurred to her.

Not for nothing, but for both her friends, gossip was their currency. They would trade it with other friends. And *that* couldn't happen. She reached for their hands. "Listen, for real—you two can't tell *anybody* about this."

Straleen slammed back in her chair. "Tell anybody? Think we want to die too?" She pitched herself forward just as quickly. "Oh no, I see you. You going fi deal with this whole money thing by yourself." She slapped the table. "You won't let us watch Kaley or Donovan for free. You even pay your uncle fi use him boat when you know he'd let you use it for free; you won't let nobody do *anything* fi you."

"You *know* that's right, Deja," Lila added. "But listen, baby, you can't handle anything from your grave, not even the worms."

Straleen piled onto the admonishment. "I mean, me could understand maybe if you did need a money, but you have barrels—"

Okay, enough. Enough of the fear they were whipping up in her. Enough of the finger-wagging. Enough. Enough. Enough. Deja landed her elbows on the table. "Here's the deal." She cleared her throat. "My mother was mugged. She lost every damn cent she had over there, plus her freakin' partner money. There *are no more* barrels coming! I'm freaking out. Me no want fi live pon street with Kaleisha and Donovan. So, what di hell unu talking!"

In the following shocked silence, Deja could hear one of the kids rolling over in bed.

Straleen looked stricken. Lila looked away, blinking hard.

Deja was so mad, she couldn't even swallow. Here she was with a major situation, and they were going on about barrels. "And you two have to stop it with the barrels. Don't act like I have more than you because I get one. I would gladly exchange it fi my mother, you hear me?"

More silence. At last Lila, tears in *her* eyes, reached over and rubbed Deja's shoulder. "Sorry, baby. Me never know about your mother. Hope she's okay?" Then she pulled Deja into a hug. Deja let her, then squeezed back, hard.

"Okay, don't break me back," Lila groaned. When Straleen joined in, Deja's troubles ceased to exist, at least for that moment. Then the moment was over when Straleen, ever practical, asked, "So, say again who you supposed to bring this all to?"

Deja dug the business card out of her pocket. Straleen read it aloud.

"Demarco Webber. Number 10 ac Barnett Street, Montego Bay."

"So . . . think I could just mail the cash to him?"

Straleen nudged a stack of bills. "You put that in the mail and I bet you're breaking at least ten laws. Not that you're not already breaking some by having it in the first place—sorry! I'll stop." She squinted in thought, then put the card on the table. "Maybe take it to a police station?"

Lila instantly disagreed. "No, mon. They might arrest her on the spot. Or worse, they might take the money for themselves and *then* arrest her on the spot. You gwan like Jamaica no have plenty corrupt police." They were expressing out loud the conversation Deja'd already had in her own head.

Deja coughed into her elbow, thinking about the phone call she'd made to emergency services. Then decided not to say anything about it. This was messy enough.

Lila was madly scrolling on her phone. "Webber . . . Webber . . . Look! He's a shipping agent. Here's a picture."

Straleen grabbed the phone. "Handsome!"

"Really?" Lila said, grabbing her phone back and handing it to Deja.

Straleen shrugged. "Wha' wrong with that? Besides, a man that looks like dat isn't any killer. And no act like you no notice when a man well handsome."

Deja took a long look. Webber's page said he was an expert in shipments and cargo and the client always came first. "You think this is his cover?" she mused.

"Cover?" Lila pursed her lips. "What, you a detective now?"

Deja gave her the stink-eye. "Hello, I was on a damn go-fast boat with a dying man with a DEA badge and five hundred K in marked money! I think I'm allowed to say 'cover.'"

"Okay, okay." Straleen held up her palms for peace in the valley. "Deja, you are officially allowed to say 'cover.' But let's say you take the money to him, and something goes wrong and . . . you *DIE*? What's going to happen to those kids in there?" She pointed to the closed bedroom door.

"Yes, that's it. That-is-it." Lila took Deja's hand and squeezed. "Girl, you need to get rid of the cash right now. Just disappear it."

Deja pulled a few inches of the curtain aside and searched the street. "Okay. I'll get rid of it."

"Good." Straleen let out a long exhale. "You want help?"

"No. I got it."

"Where you thinking?" Straleen asked.

"The big garbage dump downtown." Deja loaded the remaining stacks of cash into the backpack. "And actually, you *can* help. Can you take the kids to school?"

"I got you." Straleen grasped Deja's forearm. "And please don't tell me you want to pay me. I heard you about the barrel thing, okay?"

Deja grinned for the first time in twenty-four hours. "Okay."

Lila, however, who was big-time frowning, pointed toward

the end of the street. "There's a big forest out there. You could just dump it. That'd be quicker."

Then Straleen practically jumped out of her chair to add, "Or maybe you could burn it with some leaves?"

"You know the neighbors around here, bloody nosy, all of them. And I don't want to throw it out anywhere close to the house. I'll toss it in a dump downtown." And with that, she zipped her backpack shut.

Gabriel, Friday, 7:30 a.m.

Heading up Brandon Hill, Gabriel kept replaying Teago's words in his head. The boss had only said for him and Hammer to come to his house before abruptly hanging up, but had anything hinted that this was a setup? It couldn't be, not at Teago's fancy house. His mansion—and most of the others up here on the hill—had gigantic columns out front, one percenters for sure. And the perfectly manicured gardens looked like they belonged in those rich tourist hotels down below in Montego Bay.

Hammer veered the motorcycle onto a side street, then stopped at an ornate gate; the metal grilling favored a spider-web. The wall around the yard—pink concrete—was lined with life-size sculptures of skulls. It was freaky, but a mansion worthy of the name.

Hammer cut the engine.

Gabriel whispered, "Suppose him dead us off, right now?"

"Right now pass and we no dead yet."

"True. Besides, you said he wants to set *me* up, not you."

"Me with you, mon."

They fist-bumped. "Respect, brethren." Gabriel glanced around. The neighborhood was quiet, nobody on the streets. "Nothing bad ever happens here. We'll be all right."

"Want to try Jamal or Blood Moon again?"

Gabriel called. Straight to voice mail. Those two were really partying it up this time.

"You going to ask Teago 'bout the thing?"

"No, mon." Gabriel started for the gate, then paused. Maybe he *should* find out what was going on, once and for all. Then again, Teago was like a box of fireworks. No need to toss a match at him.

Hammer trailing, Gabriel pressed the buzzer on the gate. It was one of those electric jobs that would open all by itself. He waited, then pressed it again. The gate didn't budge, but then the massive front door flew open. The boss came striding out, phone in hand, wearing only black boxers, probably silk, that blended with his skin, and gold slippers dotted with rhinestones. His face, a slightly lighter color than the rest of him, told Gabriel that he'd been using bleaching cream again, like some of the dons of rival posses who also weren't pleased with their darker skin.

Teago kept the gate closed, nostrils flaring. "Me call this long time. Where the hell you two been?"

"Teago, we came as soon as you called." Gabriel casually lay a hand on a skull, took in Teago's pinpoint pupils. Dude was high.

"Me want you fi tell me what unu was out here doing just standing in front of me house?" He was well paranoid, too. He must have been watching through a window.

"We were calling Jamal."

"Him answer?" Now the boss gripped the gate, a ring on eight of his ten fingers, eager.

"No."

"Damn it!" He gave the gate a shake. "Look, Jamal and Blood Moon were doing a drop for the transshipment yesterday morning, and me no hear nothing from them since!"

Gabriel held his hand out for caution. "Boss, maybe you shouldn't talk so loud."

"Loud! What you think this place is? Everybody round here is a damn thief. You know how much lawyer and politician live round here?"

The boss must have been doing coke—he was usually crazy discreet. The transshipment deal between the Bolivians and that big Louisiana posse was the most important part of his business.

"The last time them didn't call me, me hold back some pay. But this time me going to show them that me is no joke!" He slapped the gate, then finally lowered his voice. "Now listen, me want you two to go search fi them."

"No doubt, but where?"

"Me send Brickyard to go check where them live in Farwood. And Blocks and Stinger a check downtown. Now, you two go check di cove near Springtown Harbour."

That was where the transshipment was supposed to go down yesterday. "But . . . the deal is done already," Gabriel said.

"You no know that. Maybe them didn't even go to the damn drop spot. Maybe them was high and now them too embarrassed fi call me. Maybe them kidnapped by aliens. Me no know what . . ." Spittle gathered at the side of Teago's mouth.

"But why didn't you send somebody else there first?" Gabriel asked. After all, there were sixteen other guys in the posse. "That's the first place I'd look—"

"Boy, why you love question me so much?" Teago's eyes were slits.

"I was just thinking it through, and—"

"*Thinking?*" Teago couldn't be more sarcastic. "If you was really thinking, you woulda realize that is only Blood Moon, Jamal, and you two that have di damn code to di gate. Me no want *everybody* inna di posse fi know *that*." He waved both hands in the air, as if he was pleading. "Now, go . . . and call me when you find them." He spun around and stalked back toward his gleaming front door, then paused and glared back at Gabriel. "And listen, me no want no backside trouble. If is a problem, fix it." Then he went inside.

Gabriel caught a glimpse of the chandelier in the hallway— were actual jewels hanging off it?

Hammer pinched his nose, signaling what Gabriel already knew.

"Yeh, mon, him well high."

Hammer got back on the motorcycle. "He was probably partying so much, he forgot about Jamal and Blood Moon until this morning."

"No doubt." Gabriel got on behind him. "One good thing, though."

"What?"

"He didn't say, 'Switch up the stash house.'"

Deja, Friday, 7:15 a.m.

Deja couldn't stop scanning the area. She was nearly down-town, the courthouse just ahead on the main drag. She moved quickly but not so fast as to cause suspicion. A car was turning a corner; two women were standing and talking on the sidewalk, holding plastic bags. Were they looking at her, at her backpack? No. Why would they be? Deja's heart was trampolining in her chest. She couldn't get rid of this thing quickly enough. She told herself to stay chill—just blend in but be ready to drop the bag and run if it came to that. A woman strutted past her with a large knockoff Fendi purse. Her mother had one exactly like it, probably where the partner money had been the night she got mugged. Damn.

The reek of a sun-ripened collection of rot and waste told her she was almost at the garbage collection area. If she closed her eyes, she could have followed the odor. Around the bend she saw a rusted garbage truck, the driver's eyes closed, probably stealing a nap. A middle-aged woman in a sun visor was coming toward the garbage bins—at least a half dozen of them standing side by side. Passing the truck, Deja eased the backpack off her shoulders and pretended to check her phone, waiting for the woman to go by.

As soon as she had, Deja eagerly approached the very first bin. Pee-yoo! It was overflowing—they all were. The stink—whoa, she struggled not to gag as she hoisted the backpack up onto the pile. It hit a jumbo-size trash bag and tumbled back down. Great. She heaved it again, arms out, ready to catch it if it fell again. But this time it stayed put. Dizzy with relief, she glided away as nonchalantly as she could.

A door creaked open. Though Deja kept on walking, she couldn't resist peeking over her shoulder. Oh no! The garbage truck driver was about to pick up the backpack. It must have fallen off the pile!

Just make a run for it was her first thought. It would feel so good, such a relief. But, damn it, the man was about to open the zipper.

She sprinted back. "Mister!"

"This your backpack?" He held it out.

"Yes, um, I must have forgotten it . . . when I was checking a text."

"You young people would forget your heads if they weren't attached to your necks." He shook his own head. "Just like me son."

Deja reached for the backpack. "Thank you." She took it by the strap, managed a fake smile, and turned on her heel. Where to go with this bumboclot backpack now? It was like a damn boomerang.

Deja turned onto the next street, lined with stores. Waved to the heavyset owner of the souvenir shop, a friend of her mother's. Where to ditch this bag?

Across the street, a row of tourists was approaching a minivan driver. Deja slowed down. . . . They all had backpacks. An idea jelled.

And sure enough, the tourists began taking off *their* backpacks, laying them by the back of the van. An older couple put down what looked like ski poles. They were probably going hiking. Deja looked left and right. No one was paying a speck of attention to her.

She crossed to their side of the street, just a girl out for a casual stroll with a backpack that wasn't full of cash. *Just be cool. Just be cool.* She'd stick her bag with the tourists'. It would then be a problem *they* could handle. No one would accuse tourists of anything. They'd just wonder how it got there; turn it over to the police or something. And that would be the end of it.

The minivan driver was deep in conversation with a lady wearing an enormous yellow sun hat, hopefully too preoccupied to notice anything. Deja quickly went up to another woman who was standing alone. "Hello," she said, smiling huge. "Are you going hiking today?"

The woman's bespectacled face brightened. "Yes. Are you one of our guides?"

"No, but I'm training to be one, though." Deja grinned. "You going to Negril?"

"Yes! Have you been?"

"I have. It's beautiful! Barely a half hour that way." As Deja pointed in its direction and as the woman's eyes followed, Deja set her backpack beside the others.

"Oh good. I hear the sunset is one of the best on the island," the woman said enthusiastically.

"It definitely *is*. And there's a great bar called Rick's Café. They do cliff diving there."

"No kidding?"

"It's a lot of fun to watch, so if your guide doesn't tell you about it, be sure to bring it up. It's great out there, twenty-one miles of perfect white-sand beach, water so clear you can see little guppies swim by. And be sure to take a trip up into the mountains if you can. More plants and trees per foot than almost anywhere in the world."

"You're so sweet—thank you. I just love this island. Everybody is so nice."

"No problem," Deja said. "Like I said, I'm getting into the tourist industry—I love to tell people about my country!"

"Well, again, thank you so much. Have a great day!"

"You too!" Deja moved on, feeling a thousand pounds lighter. Oh, it felt good. Wow, she'd never make it as a special agent! Which caused a thought to jolt through her. Her fingerprints. They were all over the bag. Would the police be able to detect them? Find her? Could you even get fingerprints off a backpack?

Someone calling interrupted her surge of panic. "Miss! Miss!" No. Noooo. But yes. She spun around to see the minivan driver jogging toward her, waving the backpack in the air like he was a hero.

In the background, the tourist lady was waving too. "You forgot your backpack, sweetie!"

Deja managed to wave back at her.

"You so rich, you can just give your things away?" The van driver raised one eyebrow, held the bag just out of reach.

Had he seen inside? But no, no, he was flirting. Okay. Deal, Deja.

"Oh, thank you," she forced herself to say, hand out for the bag.

"I'll trade you the backpack for your information?"

There it was. "Sorry, I can't do that. But thanks again!" She took the bag.

"Oh, you have a man?"

Why did guys automatically assume that if she wasn't interested in *him*, it had to be because she had a man already? She forced a smile.

"So, nothing for me?" he asked, now giving what he must have imagined was a smoldering look.

"My sincerest gratitude." She swung away, trying to think what to do next. People on the sidewalk didn't bother to hide their nosiness. *Imagine if they knew what was* really *going on,* she thought wryly.

Strange how she couldn't get rid of this money! And then she noticed, up ahead—almost unbelievably, a cross, from the same church where she'd met Gabriel.

A new thought jolted her. Maybe something divine kept interceding—maybe she was *meant* to have the cash? It kept returning to her, so maybe it *was* destiny. Her mother used to say in her deepest patois, *what a fi yu cannot be un-fi yu.* Huh. So, maybe this was the universe saying this task was meant to be Deja's. Jeez. She was getting as superstitious as Straleen.

And the minister there—Pastor Powell—several times after mass had asked about her future. He was so easy to talk to—calm, open. He'd had a hard past, something about drug dealing—at least that was what she'd heard. And about how he found God and how that had saved his life. And now he wanted to save others. He gave you the sense that he could make things work out, no matter what. He didn't just play the game; he *was* the game.

She should take the bag to him. Get his advice. Yes. And just like that, a sense of calm washed over her. Which meant she should do it. She passed the bakery, smelling meat frying and dough baking for beef patties, making her stomach growl. Outside a souvenir store, she went by a rack of T-shirts sporting sayings like JAMAICAN ME CRAZY and STRAIGHT OUTTA JAMAICA.

Then she laughed out loud. Straleen and Lila should see this—she was going to someone for *help.* Just as quickly, her thoughts twisted. What if Pastor Powell *wasn't* who he seemed to be? What if . . . he still worked with the gangs? This was Jamaica. Everybody needed money—everybody knew somebody scuffling in the drug business.

Deja shook her head to rattle the doubt loose. She was at the rectory and needed to knock before she lost her nerve.

When the door swung open, Pastor Powell's welcoming smile greeted her. Whoa, he had great teeth. Did posse members *have* great teeth? Then again, that Gabriel guy she'd met did—that gap in the middle was really cute.

"Deja, hello! Come in."

She was glad Lila and Straleen weren't with her—they always joked about how they would date him in a hot minute if he weren't a minister. And even that was something they might overlook! Was it sacrilegious to even be thinking this? Deja blinked the thought away.

"Good to see you. It's been a slow day." He had the sweet, gravelly voice of a radio DJ.

She forced a short smile. "Do—do you have a few minutes?"

"Of course. Let's go to my office." He gestured to the pine door in the corner.

The room's high ceilings and stone walls gave it the airy feel of a castle, one that smelled like old books. Deja's sandals slapped against the tile floor as she followed the pastor to an old-fashioned desk cluttered with papers. As she slid the backpack off her shoulders, he motioned for her to take a seat. That was when she noticed the tattoo on his wrist. *Chops.* A gang name?

He must have noticed her noticing, because he said easily, "It's a name from another life. Sometimes I think about having it covered up, but I keep it to remind me of when I was lost. Helps me remember that people can change."

She gave him an uncomfortable smile.

"How's the family keeping?" he asked smoothly, sitting beside her.

"Good."

"Your mother?"

She rubbed her arm. "Good. Fine. She's fine."

He seemed to be looking through her, maybe already reading her first lies. "A non-Sunday visit. Must be important." He cracked his knuckles by just making a fist. "Sorry, old habit. Go ahead."

"I just—want to ask you something." Well, that was stupid. Of course she did. She rubbed her arm harder. How to say it? By just saying it. "What do you do if you're about to do something that might not stand good with God?" She didn't fully believe in God. There was no evidence, not in her life, but she wasn't entirely sure.

He ran a finger along the hook-shaped scar by his left cheekbone. "Well, in my life I've had moments—no, long periods—where I did not listen to God. You may have heard about that."

She considered her words carefully. "You've mentioned things in some of your sermons. . . ."

"Good. That saves me from going through that whole sorry saga again." Now he grinned. "So, I can give you a verse from the Bible or something like that, and we can call it a day, or you can tell me a little more about what's on your mind. Maybe then I could be more helpful."

Helpful. Help. That word again. And yes, she needed help. It was time to fess up. "I found this." She nudged the backpack with her foot.

"And it belongs to someone else?" he prompted.

"Probably—actually, I think it's some criminal's." Her face went hot—had she offended him?

"It's okay. I *was* one once. Go on."

Okay, time to go for broke. "A man wants me to deliver this to someone else. . . ." She watched him carefully; his face barely registered surprise.

"Someone wants you to be a mule?" he asked, his voice gentle, as if she were a horse he was trying not to spook.

The mineral-like smell of the agent's blood flooded her memory. A whiff of leaking gasoline. "I'm not sure?"

Pastor Powell waited patiently for her to go on.

"Okay. Ah, let me start from the beginning. I was out fishing yesterday morning and I saw a boat drifting, with blood on the gunwale. I . . . I wasn't sure what to do, but I was worried someone was hurt, so I motored over. And there was a man on board, badly wounded—gunshot. I think he was some kind of American agent. He had a badge around his neck." She remembered the blood-covered gaffer tape, his light brown eyes. They were so clear, even though he had to have been in so much pain—how?

Pastor Powell could have been a statue. At last he gave a near-imperceptible nod for her to continue.

"So, first I tried to help him with his wound—there was blood everywhere. That's when he told me to take the . . ." She couldn't find the words. Her tongue felt heavy, stuck in her mouth. So she unzipped the backpack and tilted it toward him, revealing the stacks of American cash.

He looked it over like a clerk tallying the goods in front of him. Then he sat back and waited. He had the patience of Job.

"And, well, the last thing he said was for me not to let them get it."

"Who?" Calm, so calm.

"I don't know. He didn't say." She wondered if she was forgetting something. "But . . . he gave me a business card of a man in Mobay—said to deliver the case to him. And then . . . and then he died."

He leaned back at last. "Well, that's not your everyday confession."

"I don't think it *is* a confession." This was a choice, she thought.

"The cash, it's probably safe to say it's marked?"

Pastor Powell was badass. "Yes, that's what the guy—the agent—told me."

"And tell me, are you thinking of doing this? Delivering the . . . backpack? Rather than, say, bringing it to the police?"

"My mother . . . I wasn't quite truthful before." And now her voice nearly broke. "She got mugged. She's still in New York, and they took all her money and the partner money of a bunch of other people."

Now his eyes went wide. "I see. Is she okay?"

"I think so?" She didn't really. "There's been no barrel for months. My sister's fees are due for school, and the house has a mortgage. And I go out and fish every morning before my own classes, but it doesn't cover much. . . ."

"Deja, I am truly sorry to hear this." He squeezed her hand, his own as rough as tree bark. "Thank you for trusting me." As he cleared his throat, Deja knew she'd been right to come to him. He really did care. "Now, you said the man is dead?" he asked.

"Yes." Gah, that stink. "I would have called the police, but . . ." She lost her focus, the images of all the blood taking over.

"I understand," the pastor said gently. "Since he's dead, there's no need to incriminate yourself. But once you figure things out, we should notify the police. His relatives should know."

"I called emergency services, told them where he was," she said.

"Smart. What did they say?"

She shrugged. "Don't know. I hung up after I told them where he was. . . ."

"That's okay." Now he leaned forward. "So, what do *you* want to do?"

She had expected a sermon or some keen posse insight. But his question, and the way he asked it, was so casual, like he was asking what she wanted for lunch. It left her with a clear thought. She *did* want to deliver the cash. She wanted to keep her word to the dead man. And more than anything, help her mother. "He said I would get a reward if I got the money to this man."

"You up for that, Deja?"

"I need to be." When she first stepped onto a netball court, people'd said she was so short she'd have to play with a ladder. Fishermen like Mr. Wallace scoffed at her as if only men could pilot boats. Screw all that. "If I'm not up for it, I'm just another barrel girl." She paused, then added, "Without a barrel." She looked from the backpack to him. "So, what do *you* think?"

"I see . . . problems. Many. But if you're asking me about the morals of this decision, well . . ." He exhaled. "You've told me that an agent of the law asked you to do a job for pay. I don't see the moral problem there." He rubbed that little fishhook scar again. "But the world you'd be dealing with is one I know and one I had to leave before it destroyed me morally and mortally." He paused, stretched his neck like his collar was too tight. "I won't read you any Scripture, but I will say simply that entering this world creates a destiny. What a fi yu cannot be un-fi yu."

That couldn't be a coincidence! He said what her mother had said. Deja smiled and immediately saw he wasn't expecting that kind of reaction.

"Are you sure you're okay, Deja?"

The backpack—her way to help her family. *What is for you cannot be un-for you.* "Pastor Powell, thanks for your help." She stood to leave.

He held up a hand. "Deja, I'm not sure what just happened here. I don't know if you want me to get more involved. . . ." He seemed more than ready. And more than a little concerned.

She felt a sudden strong need to leave. She'd involved enough people in this mess already. This was something she had to work out herself. She wished Straleen and Lila weren't involved either. That they'd never shown up when they had. "It's okay. Honest," she assured him. "I know what I have to do."

Frown lines appeared, deep and many: he thought he'd made a mistake—or that she was about to. "Are you sure you don't want to think this through a little more?" A sudden knock on the door nearly caused Deja to jump out of her skin.

"Can you hold on?" he asked.

Deja bowed her head ever so slightly so as not to be rude, but she'd made up her mind. She watched as Pastor Powell opened the door and talked to someone, all the while tapping the door-frame. Impatiently? Nervously? It wasn't clear. He held up a finger. It might have been a gesture for the person to wait. Pushing the door shut, he strode quickly back to Deja. His eyes were guarded, the frown lines deeper.

Was it *them*? "Is anything wrong?" she dared to ask.

"No, just a couple of guys I need to see. I'm so sorry, but could you come back in an hour? This can't wait, I'm afraid."

Deja, Friday, 9 a.m.

A cloying clutch of humidity enveloped Deja as she stepped from the rectory. Two guys who'd graduated from the high school last year stood outside the door, ill-fitting ties around their polo shirts and grim looks on their faces. But they shot her chin-up expressions of acknowledgment. She recognized them—the Fleming twins. She wondered what mess they'd gotten themselves into this time. They were always in trouble with the police. Pastor Powell was probably going to try to straighten them out. Good luck with that. Still, she returned their greetings.

"Deja, I'll be free in an hour," Pastor Powell reminded her.

Deja nodded, but she was good. The minister had ministered right to her answer.

She could use *67 to keep her phone number from appearing on someone's caller ID.

That was what she needed. Swapping out the SIM cards again might be pressing her luck—who knows, maybe somebody was onto her. But her mom, before she'd left for the States, had rattled off a bunch of things Deja should do to keep herself safe, and one was to punch in *67. Of course, Mom would lose her mind if she knew Deja was going to use her advice for what she was about to use it for. Then she thought—dang—if Webber was an agent too, he might have a workaround for *67. Still, what were her options?

Deja veered into an open lot filled with ficus trees and ducked behind one. Under the shade, business card in hand, she thought about what she might say. Should *she* tell *him* how much she wanted? Or did he have a set sum for these situations? She had no clue. How much had been stolen from her mother? Not like she could call her and ask. She thought about the mortgage and school fees for Kaleisha; at least she had a vague sense of what that came to.

Fifteen thousand American dollars—that should cover everything, maybe with a little left over, she finally calculated. But what if she was wrong? What if she was demanding too much? No, it would have to be 15K.

After all, she was risking a lot by toting this cash around, a walking bull's-eye.

She punched in the number from the card.

"Yes?" A voice, smooth, youngish, answered. She'd expected someone much older, for some reason.

"Is this . . . Mr. Webber?"

"It is. Who's calling?"

"Um—a man on the boat"—bumboclot—"he said to get something to you." That hadn't come out right at all.

There was silence. "Who am I speaking with?"

She wanted to tell him. She wanted to explain this all so it could just go away. But that wasn't the smart move. "I . . . I just want to get this . . . bag . . . to you. He said, 'Don't let them get it.'" Her voice quavered; she sounded like a six-year-old.

Emotionless, as if he got calls like this every day, he asked, "What did he look like? Did he give you his name?"

She had to be just as matter-of-fact. Not give too much away too soon.

"Well, do you know?" he pressed, more forcefully.

"Gonzalez. . . ," She remembered the man's eyes, struggling to stay open. "Brown eyes. Brownish hair. Tallish."

"Describe the briefcase."

How did he know there was a briefcase? Webber *had* to be an agent—and now *he* was testing *her*. She almost started describing her backpack, she was so nervous, but she caught herself in time. "Square. A lawyer's briefcase kind of thing. Or like the ones pilots carry."

"Where did you find him? What did the boat look like?"

"Outside Springtown Harbour, near Green Island." She fought off the image of the man's leg and all the blood. "It was a go-fast boat."

"Is he dead?"

"I think so. I'm pretty sure." The phone went silent.

"What's your name?"

She shook her head as if he were in front of her. Dummy—he couldn't see that. "I don't want to say," she said aloud.

"Fair enough." He paused. "Where are you?"

Her hand was trembling. *He* was asking all the questions, and she didn't really know anything about him. "Are you an agent?"

"So *where* did you say you were located?"

"I'm at—" She paused. He was avoiding her question and trying to get info from her. Fine. She could play this game, and so instead of answering, she asked another question. "You're DEA?"

"You read that on his badge, did you?"

"Yes. So, are you?"

"We can't talk about that right now, but I'm not one of the people you're probably worrying about, *if* that's what you're worried about."

She had to bargain. No, she had to let him know without a doubt what she wanted. "He told me you'd give me a reward."

"Reward?"

"Yes, money." She hated how weak she was sounding. She had to be more forceful!

"Why didn't you keep the money?"

"It's not mine. Besides . . . it's marked. That's what he said." She swallowed. "I just want what's fair." She watched a couple pass by, laughing at something, looking so relaxed, the flip side of how she felt.

"How much are we talking about?"

She hesitated yet again, then told herself that there was a *fortune* in that bag. "Fifteen thousand American."

"Fifteen thousand *American*?"

"Yes."

"You moving to America or something?"

He was playing with her. Fine, let him. It was something to push against. "Look, mister, the man was dying, okay? He was bleeding out. I was going to take him to shore, okay? It's why I went to the boat—there was blood on the side. But I couldn't lift him. *He* asked me to bring this money to you. *I* just wanted him to freakin' live. *He* said you would give me a reward, all right? So, will you or won't you?" As she waited for him to answer, she wiped away tears that had sprung to her eyes.

"Okay. I'll have your money." He cleared his throat. "But I hope you're not thinking of raising the price, because that's not going to fly."

He didn't bargain. Everybody in Jamaica bargained! But he was an agent. Did they bargain? Could he be trusted? And should she ask for more anyway, just to see what he would say? She sneezed.

"Bless you."

"Thank you."

"So, do we have an understanding?" He sounded like he was good with the price. Maybe she shouldn't ask for more after all. It was nothing like bargaining over the price of fresh parrotfish. Maybe too easy. Was it a trap?

"This offer won't last." Now he sounded like a TV ad. He was so comfortable with this, he could even joke. Crazy people were like this. Like some boys in school who could talk about killing a cat, then make a joke, then ask to borrow money to buy a beef patty.

And yeah, what *she* was doing was crazy. But she was glad she'd used *67, at least. "Okay."

"Now, where are you?"

No way was she telling him. No way was he coming anywhere near her family. "He gave me your card. I have your address. I'll bring it to you."

"Sure you don't want me to come to you? It's not a problem."

"No. I'll come to you."

"The address you have won't work." He paused. "But I know a place. Do you know Anchovy? The train station?"

It was a stop on the old train route, the last one before Montego Bay. A bird sanctuary was nearby—her mother had taken them there once. But that train station was abandoned now. Lila's words practically smacked her upside the head. *Dead you off.* "Why there?"

"Miss, I'm making accommodations for you. And you have to understand that as much as you don't know me, I don't know you."

Okayyy. He was right. There was his side to all this. She must have sounded crazy to him. Even though he was an agent, even though he was silky smooth, he probably *didn't* get calls like this every day. Still. "I don't want to be in some lonely place with somebody me no know."

"I understand," he said. "Okay, there's a restaurant down the street from the station. Miss Jane's Food Place. Seats outside. Broad daylight, so you don't have to worry. Can you meet me there at four thirty?"

She shouldn't bring the backpack to meet him. She'd have to stash it somewhere. Where? Well, there had to be plenty of places.

"That okay with you?" he pressed. "Miss?"

She refocused. "Yes."

"Call me on this number if you're going to be late."

"Okay. But how will I know it's you?"

"I'll be wearing a white shirt and black jeans, but don't worry, I'll probably know it's you." He chuckled.

She didn't know why, but he'd changed, lightened up. "Okay."

"What was your name again?"

She started to answer, then caught herself, sidestepped the trap. "You asked me that before. Why do you keep asking?"

"I like to know as much as possible about the people I'm meeting."

She had to be firm. "I'll see you there."

"All right. Good luck. Call me if there's trouble . . . but you should be okay. The trip from Springtown isn't too bad."

The air was sucked right out of her lungs—how did he know she was calling from Springtown? She pushed out one word. "Okay."

"And don't worry. You deliver the cash, and I'll do my part, okay?"

Finding another breath, she repeated, "Okay."

He hung up. She stood moored to the ground like a ship to a pier. Bumboclot! *How did he know where I was calling from?* Wait—she'd said where she'd found the boat. So he was just guessing; it was the closest harbor. But still. What if—somehow—he was watching her now? She scanned the area. Just ahead, a cat ran off the sidewalk and into the street, an

SUV approaching. Halfway across, the cat stopped. The SUV kept coming. Deja gasped. At the last moment, the cat ran back to the sidewalk.

That was what she should be doing—scampering back to safety. Instead of going to meet some random guy with all this cash. *Think, Deja.* Webber had figured out where she was calling from. So maybe he was police? Criminals didn't have that kind of tech. Or did they? No, he had to be some sort of police.

Even if it had been a guess—he now knew. Shit! What if he found out her name, or worse, that she had a family? *What if.* She'd never forgive herself if anything happened. . . .

Then she knew what to do.

Uncle Glen.

He'd take the kids. She'd just tell him some BS like she had to go on a class trip somewhere. Yes. Uncle could take them on a boat ride, maybe to Montego Bay or wherever—it didn't matter where as long as they were out of town. Deja broke into a jog.

At the school gate, the security guard in his little guardhouse barely noticed her as she breezed by. Full of nerves, she walked across the dirt yard, suddenly desperate to see her siblings.

Inside the office, she waited for the school secretary to get off the phone, each moment dreading the footsteps of the administrator with her hand out for school fees. At last the secretary finished her call, and Deja checked the kids out for the rest of the day, explaining that they had a doctor's visit. As the woman left to get them, Deja hesitated under the crushing weight of uncertainty, until she heard the secretary call after Donovan, warning him not to run in the hallway. But he came sprinting into the office, his little backpack bouncing. "We don't have no doctor's appointment!" he announced.

Deja shushed him, thanked the secretary, and led him and Kaleisha, who trailed behind him, into the schoolyard. Halfway across, Deja took Donovan by the arm. Her other hand went around Kaleisha, who shrugged it off, eyeing her older sister suspiciously.

"Listen, it's a secret, but we're going on a little trip with Uncle Glen!"

"Where?" Donovan asked. "And what happened to the pin I made you?"

Deja froze, wondering if it had been on her shirt when she got home yesterday. Bumboclot! It wasn't! It was gone. "It's . . . it's at home," she bluffed. "But listen, we're going on an adventure!"

His eyes widened. "For real?"

"Why?" Kaleisha said, her voice suddenly coated with worry. "Is Mommy sick?"

"No, Kaley, she's not sick."

"We in trouble?" Kaleisha pressed, eyes stormy.

"Of course not. Now, let's get going."

Donovan grinned, psyched, but Kaleisha wasn't buying it.

They were just blocks from the wharves when Donovan announced he was hungry. The smell of fresh bread was overpowering, but Deja couldn't risk stopping.

"We'll get something to eat at the dock."

"Pleeease," Donovan pleaded.

Deja was hungry too. Still, "Soon," she promised.

"Why are we going this way?" Donovan asked as Deja led them down an alley between the back of the stores and the seawall.

Deja ignored him but caught Kaleisha watching her, reading her unspoken lies. She hurried on, clutching their hands. The sun poked through a cloud and lit the seawall with a blinding brightness. She prayed it was a good sign, a shining ray of hope. And at last, her knees going weak, they were at the wharves.

And, oh, thank God, there was her uncle, in his favorite spot at the beach bar, his hand conducting as he serenaded two other fishermen with some tale or another.

"Uncle Glen!" Donovan broke into a run.

Deja grabbed his hand, corralled him, her grip slick with sweat. "Hold up! Wait here with your sister until I come back."

"Why?"

"Just wait. You'll ruin the surprise!" she snapped. Both he and Kaleisha froze in unison. Dang. She must be making them nervous.

As she approached her uncle, she considered telling him everything. But no. If it all blew up, she didn't want him involved in any way. If this became a shit show, who would take care of the kids?

Uncle Glen smiled wide upon first seeing her, but then he squinted, arms folded. He could read her like a poker player.

Willing her face to betray nothing, she said, "Uncle, I need you to do something."

"Soon come," he said in patois to the other fishermen, and made his way across the gravel. "Wha' gwan, Deja?" He glanced the kids' way and waved. "Them should be in school, no?"

She reached into her pocket and pulled out two American twenty-dollar bills. It was a big splurge, but she could at least make it up with the reward money. She hoped. "Uncle, I need you to take Kaley and Donovan to Mobay."

He eyed the bills but didn't reach for them. "Okay . . . but you want fi tell me what's going on?"

"One is for food or whatever they need. The other is for you, for gas . . . some of the gas . . . a little of it. Maybe you can show them around like last time? I can meet you there by six . . . at that restaurant, um, the Hot Time Grill near Doctor's Cave Beach. I need to do an errand. I'll come find you."

He rubbed his belly like a Buddha. "And how *you* getting there?"

"The bus."

"This about your mother?"

"Yes."

"This about what was in those burlap bags?"

Her breath caught. Her uncle missed *nothing*. And this was no time to lie. "Yes."

"And you don't want to tell me about that?"

"No."

"And you want me fi keep di money, and you won't take no fi

an answer, even if I say that I'm your uncle, and it's my solemn duty to take care of you when there's trouble?"

He could always make her smile. "That's right, Uncle."

Uncle Glen raised his chin, as if considering, making her sweat, for sure, but then he reached for the cash.

She threw her arms around his burly shoulders. "Thanks."

"Okay. I'll start working on the *Queen*."

Deja gaped at him. "You haven't fixed the engine yet?"

He aimed his arm back toward the bar. "We had important things to talk 'bout." Searched her eyes. "No worry, Deja. The *Queen* will be up and running in an hour, tops. And I will take the little ones to Mobay."

"You sure?"

"Yeh, mon."

"Okay, so Donovan is starving, or so he claims." She started to dig in her pocket again. "Here, let me give you more—"

"No problem, mon. I'm rich today." With both hands, he snapped the two American notes she'd just given him. "Oh, and what kind of danger we in, sister Deja?"

She held his gaze. "Enough."

"No problem. Me going take good care of them."

This was the best way. She didn't want them out of her sight, but she also knew Uncle Glen would die for them. At last, she waved them over.

"Okay, the adventure starts in just a little bit," she began as they reached her. "Uncle Glen is making sure the *Queen* is super ready. Then he's going to take you on a boat ride to Mobay!"

Donovan fist-pumped. "Yes! Remember that restaurant we

went to with Mommy? They had the best burgers. Can I get one?"

"Yes, you can," Deja said, eyeing Kaleisha, whose face was unreadable. "And what will you get, Kaley?"

"Where are *you* going?" Kaleisha countered.

"I'm taking the bus to a place near Mobay. I have to do something there, but I'll meet up with you later."

Uncle Glen placed a hand on each of their heads. "My goodness, you two just might be big enough now to steer the *Queen*."

Donovan broke into a happy dance, and even Kaleisha let loose a grin, saying, "Can I go first?"

"No, me," Donovan said, hopping on his toes.

Before they could get into a good brouhaha, Deja pulled them both into a bear hug. "Listen to Uncle!" she told them. "And I'll meet you in time for dinner."

Which prompted Donovan to moan about how hungry he was.

"You no think Uncle Glen have sandwich?" Uncle boomed.

Donovan pointed to his uncle's prodigious gut. "You like you nyam plenty sandwich, Uncle."

Uncle Glen patted his stomach. "That's not fat, you know."

"What is it then?" Kaleisha asked, one side of her mouth raised in a smirk.

"That's muscle at rest, my dear." Hands on their backs, he guided the two toward the outdoor bar and grill. "Now, tell me wha' happen at school. And don't tell me *stuff*, or else me will eat your sandwiches for you."

Donovan laughed. "No, you won't."

"I want bully beef," Kaleisha said earnestly.

"Bully beef? You know how much bully beef cost? How about a cheese sandwich?"

"I hate cheese."

Uncle Glen let his mouth drop open like he was flummoxed. "No, really?"

"You know I hate cheese."

"Oh, me did forget." He winked at Deja.

Deja's heart was falling, even as she was saying a silent prayer for safe travel to Saint Mary, the patron saint of the sea. It was what Uncle Glen had told her to do when he'd first taught her how to navigate a boat. She wasn't leaving anything to chance.

Gabriel, Friday, 9:45 a.m.

Gabriel and Hammer bounced along the cracked asphalt of the old road heading toward the cove. The trees here were shorter, thinner, at a more sideways bent than the ones back in Montego Bay because of the ocean wind. Gabriel licked his lips and tasted salt. They were close.

But he wished they could just ride around the island for a week. The thought of what lay ahead made his shoulders clench—finding Jamal and Blood Moon, doing more drops, collections, maybe getting set up by his own boss. It all sent Gabriel spiraling back to the years at the orphanage, back to the long sleepless nights, the loneliness and disappointment gnawing at his insides, thinking that better must come.

But this wasn't it.

He was nowhere close to better. He needed to do something. More. He had to get out of this. But how?

Hammer pulled up at a chain-link fence, thick bush behind it. They were about to go into a drop zone. *Wake up, idiot!* Gabriel told himself. *Focus on the task at hand.*

Hammer cut the engine twenty yards from the entrance. He had a rule: never park at the place you're actually going to when you're on a job. Don't make it easy for whoever might be watching.

As they walked toward the gate, Gabriel thought about how Jamal and Blood Moon still hadn't called. Yesterday they were supposed to get a package from a plane coming in from Bolivia, then proceed to the cove, where they would trade the drugs for cash that a courier was bringing in by boat. A simple transshipment. How the backside could it go wrong? But it must have.

"It's a routine thing. They've done it a million times." Hammer, mind-reading again. "Still, Teago say check, so we check."

They passed the NO TRESPASSING signs that the posse itself posted. It'd been Gabriel's idea to put them up. He'd convinced the boss it would make the area seem less suspicious. Make it like all the other beachfront property that had been bought up by rich people and fenced off from regular Jamaicans.

Hammer reached the gate first. He grabbed the lock, then stared at Gabriel, his eyes wide. The lock had been left open. Either someone had intruded, or Jamal and Blood Moon had gotten lazy, or . . . Hammer squatted, pointed to the tire tracks in the sand. There was only a single set. There should have been two. If Jamal and Blood Moon had driven in like they were supposed to, they should have driven back out the same way.

Now both Gabriel and Hammer had their hands on their weapons. Bumboclot. Two vehicles approached on the road behind them. Gabriel went on high alert until he recognized them as tourist vans. As soon as they were out of sight, he began calculating. Going straight to the cove would be too dangerous if somebody had set a trap.

"Let's tek di trail in case there's police or somebody," Hammer, again on the same wavelength, said as he eased open the gate.

Slices of sunlight cut through the canopy as they crept down a path in the bush that paralleled the sandy road. A sudden loud flapping sent Gabriel's heart pounding. In a flash, his Beretta was out. It was a John Crow, a bird old people always took as a sign of evil. It was also times like this when he wished Hammer carried a gun instead of a knife.

The path hadn't been used in forever—Hammer had to use his knife to hack past overgrowth. The musky scent of moss and dead leaves weighed like a fog. Stepping over a fallen guango tree, Gabriel caught sight of an opening. He crouched and pointed. A black RAV4 was parked up ahead, its front tires sitting on the very start of the rocky beach, the passenger-side door ajar. Shit. Jamal's car. This was bad. No way was this not bad. He raised his Beretta; Hammer let him edge past out from under the trees and into broad daylight.

Attention focused everywhere at once, tamping down a wave of panic, Gabriel approached the RAV4, Hammer right behind him. Someone might just pop out of the back seat and start blasting! But there was no other way—he had to check. See if Jamal and Blood Moon were in there.

He pushed the door all the way open. Nothing in the front seat, the back, or the trunk, not even a soda can. It was like Jamal just had the freaking interior vacuumed.

Hammer put a finger to his lips, pointed to the beach. Gabriel again led, stepping flat so as not to rattle the stones. He steadied the Beretta with both hands, took two more steps, then two more, until Hammer dropped to one knee like he was reading the sand. There were boot prints. Jamal and Blood Moon always wore sneakers. And then . . . two small prints . . . maybe a bare foot . . . Had to be children. What the . . . ?

"Backside," Hammer muttered, looking to Gabriel, confused.

Gabriel scanned the cove. "Bloodclot! Hammer!" he hissed, motioning toward a jumble of boulders at the far side of the cove that just barely hid . . . the tip of a speedboat. Blood pulsed at Gabriel's temples.

Hammer's nod came quick—he saw it too.

They were there in moments. Creeping from boulder to boulder, Gabriel was eyeing the boat for signs of life when he picked up a wicked smell, a metallic smell, the worst smell.

And there, at the water's edge, just past the next boulder, were two motionless bodies, incoming waves lapping at their legs. Jamal and Blood Moon.

"Bloodclot!" Hammer cussed in two intense syllables, then broke into a run, his boots splashing the low tide. Gabriel dropped to a knee, covering him, scoping out the brush. His breath went staccato. Bumboclot! He wanted to shoot whether anyone was in the bush or not. But nothing moved. Even the breeze had died down. He eased himself up and, eyes still on the brush, walked backward to where Hammer stood swearing. This was beyond messed up.

"What a fuckery!" Hammer squatted beside Jamal and Blood

Moon—their friends!—bandanna over his mouth, head swaying side to side, the way mothers who'd already cried themselves dry did. Gabriel spat, spat again, trying to lessen the impact of the stench.

Jamal could have been just chilling at the beach if his arm weren't bent behind his back in a way arms weren't supposed to bend. Blood Moon—shit—Blood Moon was a damn mess, as if some alien had exploded through the side of his neck. Gabriel held down a gag, knelt beside them.

He'd seen dead bodies, sure, but only in ceremonies. Folks crying, wailing. This . . . this . . . was all wrong.

"This is so fucked up," Gabriel said at last, furiously waving away horseflies that had gathered.

"Yeh, mon." Hammer, shock plastered on his face, went on, "It could have been us, you know?"

The horror was hard to capture, taking crooked circles in his mind. Gabriel tried and tried to get a grip, but it was like snatching one of these flies between his fingers.

"Is who coulda do this?" Hammer's voice was thick with rage.

Gabriel focused on the question, a light to follow. He couldn't get his brain to work—it just kept pulsing. *They're dead, they're dead.* Then the state of emergency joined his thoughts. "Soldiers took the package? Killed them?"

"No, mon. Soldiers wouldn't have left them here. Soldiers already in trouble fi not capturing enough posse people. No, mon, them woulda take di bodies."

Gabriel's left eye twitched. "So not soldiers. Not police."

Hammer leaned in, patted the men's pockets quick, quick,

as if he was afraid the death would spread to him. "Huh. Nothing in them pockets. No guns around. No shells, either." Jamal usually packed a Colt, long-barreled and silver. He used to brag about the recoil when he fired, kicking back like some cowboys' pistols did in old movies. Blood Moon carried a sawed-off shotgun that he nicknamed Mr. Enthusiasm because every time somebody saw it, they got jumpy.

Hammer stood. "Di boat?"

"Yeh, mon," Gabriel said.

They warily made their way from boulder to boulder, until they were just feet away. The boat's side was smeared with brownish red. Blood. How did this make sense? Had Jamal and Blood Moon been on the boat?

Gabriel glanced back at Hammer, gave a quick nod, then sprang forward onto the long, flat deck at the boat's front.

The boat was empty. More streaks of dried blood.

Hammer jumped right after him, crept toward a set of hatches, bobbed his head as if counting three . . . two . . . one, then yanked the doors open as Gabriel positioned himself behind him, ready to fire.

Life vests, a rope, and other equipment. Hammer poked around inside, pulled back, and checked again. No one.

Gabriel lowered his gun, suddenly exhausted. "This *has* to be the drop boat—"

"Yeh, mon." Hammer rubbed hard at his forehead. "Must have been a nasty little shootout."

Gabriel ran a hand over the Beretta, thinking. "Who tried to rip off who?"

"No know. But no cash and no package."

"And no nobody." Gabriel glanced back to the rocky shore. Whoever had taken the package could only have gone that way, then escaped through the bush.

Had Jamal and Blood Moon suspected something and over-reacted? Gotten spooked? Maybe the boat driver tried to rip them off? Or . . . "You don't think . . . Hammer, you don't think—Jamal and Blood Moon—that they tried to rip off the drop, right?"

"Ah, so it go sometimes, mon." Hammer gave a hard nod. "Me hear 'bout how Gaza posse people in Portmore ripped off di cash from a plane drop a few weeks back."

"Heard that too. Maybe Jamal and Blood Moon did too, and figured—"

"Yeh, mon. A copycat thing."

Back at Ark Haven, one of the priests always talked about considering the contrary when doing critical theory. So Gabriel flipped his thinking. "If it was the pilot of the boat, he would have used it fi getaway. So this blood has to be the pilot's—"

Hammer narrowed his eyes, so focused Gabriel could practically see the wheels turning inside his head. "It make sense that it was Jamal and Blood Moon who started it. Zeen?"

Gabriel followed his thread. "But where's the pilot? Where's the cash? Where's the drugs?" Hammer sprang off the boat to the closest boulder, headed for the tall grass that lined the shore, eyes down, searching.

Gabriel kept watch, brain churning. *What the hell happened?* Jamal and Blood Moon were so experienced. The *most* besides Teago. What a waste! And Gabriel felt a stab of guilt for even thinking this, but now he couldn't ask them about Teago setting *him* up—

"Don't see nothing," Hammer called, hopping back onto the deck.

But wait. What was that? From the corner of his eye, Gabriel saw . . . movement.

Somebody ducking behind one of the boulders. He was sure of it. His chest went tight. Hammer must have seen it too, because suddenly they were both off the boat, running. Gabriel's foot slid on a mossy patch, his balance gone, but Hammer caught his arm. Gabriel peered down, finger on the trigger.

And damn, it was a boy, a little boy. Eight? Ten? No shirt, tattered khaki shorts that were probably once school pants. Just another homeless kid, most likely. He thought about the boys under the trailer. Orphans were plentiful, like fucking seashells. Still, "Don't move," Gabriel ordered.

"What the backside you doing here, youth?" Hammer added.

The boy didn't seem to be even remotely afraid of them.

"How'd you even get in here?" Gabriel demanded.

"The hole in the fence." The boy's voice was high but not nervous. He was unarmed. His skin was ashy, and though skinny, he had a potbelly. Probably some sickness.

"Boy, you're lucky I didn't shoot you!" Gabriel said, beyond thankful he hadn't.

"I *would* have shot you." Hammer made a point of flashing his knife at the boy. "This ain't no puppet show. Get di hell out of here."

But Gabriel motioned for the boy to stay put. "Hold on! Did you see what happened here?"

The boy said a quick "No."

Hammer waved his hand to shoo the boy. "Well, get di hell out of here—"

"But mi friend see it," that young, high voice said next.

Gabriel leaned farther over the rock. "What?"

"Mi friend, him hear di shooting and is him tell me 'bout it."

"When? When was the shooting?"

"Yesterday. Di morning."

"What did he see—your friend?" Gabriel stuffed his gun back in his waistband.

Looking up, the boy shaded his eyes with his ashy hand. "You going fi pay me?"

Hammer lurched forward. "What di backside!"

Gabriel held him off, focused on the boy. "What did your friend see?"

The boy scratched the back of his head. "Mi want a money."

Gabriel gauged the kid's steely sunken eyes. Why would he risk coming over here? Why make up something that could get him killed? "Okay . . . okay, you'll get your money. But you gotta talk first."

Hammer gaped at him, incredulous. "G, him probably going fi make up some stupidness."

Gabriel ignored him. "I'll pay. Now, what exactly did your friend see? Did he see the shooting?"

The boy shaded his eyes from the sun. "Mi friend did leave after the shot dem, but when him come back him see di boat."

Gabriel narrowed his eyes, trying to focus. "A yellow one?"

After nodding, the boy pointed in the direction of the go-fast. "Him say a man take di bag and then drive away."

Gabriel squinted. "What man?"

"Him no know him. But him was short and did have on a cap."

"What did it look like? The bag?"

"Him say it was some businessman bag, about so. Black." The boy extended his arms about two feet wide.

That was a close enough description of the briefcase the transporter usually used to carry the cash. Kid was telling the truth. His friend couldn't have known that without actually seeing it.

Hammer pointed in the direction of Jamal's and Blood Moon's bodies. "Di man, him go over to dem?"

"Mi friend never say nothing 'bout that."

Gabriel visualized the sight line from the boat to where his friends lay. "The boulders, they're in the way. The man couldn't see them unless him check the area."

Still suspicious, Hammer got in the boy's face. "If this 'friend' was here when this happened, him mussi thief something?"

For the first time, the boy looked uneasy.

"What him take?" Hammer boomed.

"Gun . . ."

"What?"

"A gun."

"Describe it?"

"It big."

"How big?"

"So . . ." The boy measured it out with his hands. The length of Blood Moon's shotty.

"What about the other gun?" Gabriel demanded.

The boy dropped his eyes.

"Talk up, mon."

"Yes."

Gabriel raised his voice. "Yes *what*?"

"Yes, him take that one too."

Hammer stuck a forefinger inches from the boy's face. "What kinda gun?"

"Regular one." Now the boy spread his hands about six inches apart. "Di barrel long, so."

That was accurate too. "So you came here to see what you could get—that why you here? Why didn't you come yesterday?"

"Him only tell me today."

"Why *him* no come back?" Hammer didn't seem convinced.

"No know."

Hammer persisted. "And you, you no fraid fi dead?"

The boy shrugged.

Gabriel understood. The boy had nothing. So, nothing to lose. Gabriel knew it well. "Did he happen to say which way the yellow boat went?"

The boy thought, then pointed east.

"Springtown Harbour?"

Another nod.

Gabriel gave Hammer's arm a swat. "You know any wharves between here and Springtown?"

"Some coves, but the closest dock is in Springtown Harbour, far as I know."

Gabriel focused on Jamal's SUV. So what the hell happened to the drugs? "Your friend didn't see another bag?"

The boy cocked his head. "What other bag?"

"Travel bag. Hard shell. The kind that rolls?"

"No, mon." He scuffed a bare foot back and forth in the sand. "So, you going fi give me a money?" he asked at last, a hand on his belly.

Gabriel reached into his pocket and peeled off a US twenty.

"So much!" Hammer protested. "You give him all that and I—"

Damn, Hammer was cheap. "Look at the boy! Besides, it's not your money. Chill." Gabriel held out the note, but as the boy reached for it. Gabriel pulled the money back. "You going to tell anybody about this?"

"No, mon."

"If you do . . ."

"Me know, me know." The kid was matter-of-fact. He knew how things went down—Respect!

Gabriel grinned. "You tougher than you look." That was what people always said about *him*. Money in hand, the boy scampered over the boulders, then paused to ask, "Wha' happen to di man on the go-fast?"

Gabriel swallowed hard. "What man?"

"Mi friend say a man was on di boat." He said it like Gabriel was dumb.

"Wait deh," Hammer exclaimed. "Your friend see di man

who was driving di boat?"

"What did he look like?" Gabriel asked.

"Him never say."

Gabriel crossed his arms in frustration.

Hammer pointed at the boy. "Sure your friend don't know where di man gone?"

When the boy shrugged, Hammer flicked his hand. "Get di hell out of here then."

The boy made a beeline into the high grass.

Gabriel had so much to say about Hammer's attitude, but he dialed it back. "Why you do that?"

"You no see di boy was fucking with us?"

Gabriel thumped his forehead, gesturing to Hammer to think. "He knew about the briefcase and about Blood Moon's shotty and Jamal's Colt."

"Lucky guesses?"

"No, mon. Me no think so."

Hammer heaved a sigh. "Then what di backside a gwan then?"

"Maybe I should call Teago?"

"More foolishness. Let's check out di harbor first. Then we can call di boss." Hammer ran his hand over his head. "If the boy *was* telling the truth, it worth checking out. All now, it might be too late."

"Hammer, we need to call Teago. At least tell him about—"

"Damn it, he's not your daddy." Frustration laced Hammer's voice. "Look, all him care 'bout is finding di package. If it's like the boy said, somebody took it. They could be anywhere. So we need fi go Springtown Harbour. Now."

That was a shit thing to say! Of course the boss wasn't his father. But Gabriel had to do the right thing. He punched Teago's number into his phone. It rang and rang. "What's wrong with him, mon? He's all panicked, sends us out here and can't even answer?"

"High on his own supply," Hammer said matter-of-factly.

Gabriel considered the go-fast. "What about that boat?"

"Fuck that, mon. We haffi' get di package or the cash, if there ever was any cash."

"But . . . the boy identified the briefcase, so the contact *brought* the money, and . . . since we can't find di drugs . . . Like I said, maybe Jamal and Blood Moon never brought them and had planned to rip off the cash from di start."

"Me no know." He turned to leave.

Gabriel grabbed his arm before he could. "Wait, mon. The usual package is worth what, half a million US? That's what, twenty kilo? No way that much cocaine coulda fit in the brief-case. . . ."

Hammer circled a finger, telling Gabriel to get on with it.

"So, since di boy saw the briefcase, I think whoever *took* the briefcase has *the cash*."

"How me fi know? All *me* know is cash *no* here. Drugs *no* here. And me two friend dead." Hammer pushed past Gabriel. "Is a bloody mystery."

True that—at this point everything was a guess. But when they reached Jamal and Blood Moon, Hammer stopped. Dropped to one knee, made the sign of the cross.

Gabriel had never seen Hammer do that before—had thought he didn't believe in God despite all his time at Ark Haven. And maybe—just maybe—he didn't want the posse life either but just didn't know what to do about it? Still, this was no time to ask him about that.

But then those thoughts triggered the strangest sensation—it was like Gabriel was floating. He had no sense of contact with anything on the earth. He should feel . . . something. But he didn't even feel grief. How could that be? Would the mourning come later? Or had he used up all his grief on posse members who'd been killed in the past? Maybe he wouldn't feel that kind of sadness ever again. The very thought scared him. He knew too well that people who felt nothing could do *anything.* "What about their . . . bodies? Maybe we should put them in the car?"

Hammer huffed. "Fi what? Them nah drive nowhere."

"Just . . . just maybe we shouldn't leave them out here."

"Them not getting no sunburn, either. Let's go, mon. We need fi check the wharves. Two of them in Springtown."

Still, Gabriel hesitated. "You know what, maybe we should see Chops."

"What now, you want fi give them eulogy? Me never hear 'bout Blood Moon and Jamal ever going to no damn church."

Gabriel thought maybe they should have. Maybe *he* should start going to church again. Hammer, too. "I think Chops might know something. Just do."

Hammer's tone went sarcastic. "But him a priest now, or so him say."

"He knows the posses around town, mon. So, him must

know the runnings, and who knows, he might have a lead on the yellow boat."

Hammer raised an eyebrow. "Aha! So him still in the posse life?"

"No, mon, him trying to help them find God."

"Hmm . . . then him might know something after all. Okay, then."

Gabriel hoped that "something" also included whether Chops had told Teago about their discussions about leaving the posse.

Or anything about "switching up the stash house."

Gabriel, Friday, noon

Hammer parked a building away from the rectory, keeping to his rule of never parking at his destination. The whole ride there, Gabriel wondered why the hell he had told Chops about wanting to leave the posse in the first place. An idiot thing to do.

"Hey, mon, we haffi' move fast," Hammer said, backing up the motorcycle the moment Gabriel had swung his leg over to get off. "Me going go check the wharves."

"Me not going to be here that long, mon!"

"Chops could chat a whole heap even before him turn minister. Now me 'fraid him going go kill yu with chat." One corner of Hammer's mouth edged up. "Just make sure in all that chat you ask him 'bout di yellow boat."

Gabriel rapped on the rectory door, taking note of the security light on the side. Funny, the beam from that very same light had held Deja in a glow only a week before. It was what had led him to her. Chops probably would have called it a guiding light, one that had gone out for Gabriel and her.

He shook the thought away and was about to knock again when the door swung open.

"Gabriel!" Chops seemed pleased to see him, hand already extended.

Gabriel glanced at the scars on the minister's knuckles as they shook.

Chops noticed. "Doesn't go away so easy. But in time, everything changes, doesn't it?"

"You still trying to tell me something, Chops?" Gabriel asked as the pastor ushered him inside.

Chops answered silky smooth. "Don't know. What are you hearing?" He answered silky smooth.

Gabriel could sense the preacher's preachiness coming on. "The boss would always tell me no to listen to the noise, listen fi di sale."

Chops grinned. "Him no change. But I heard something else, mon. Something better."

"I've been through the religious thing, if that's what you're hinting at, mon."

"Yeah, I know, Ark Haven . . ." He met Gabriel's eyes. "Didn't seem like you hated it. Maybe you should give it another try—the religious thing."

"You don't think I can make it in the runnings?"

Chops frowned. "No, no, no. Just think you might be something better than that, Gabriel."

"What? A priest like you?"

"With your talents, I think you could be whatever you want."

Now Gabriel laughed out loud. "My talents?" Did he even *have* talents? That weren't posse related? He wasn't sure.

"You have many, Gabriel. Smart. Empathetic. Resourceful—"

Gabriel held up a hand, practically begging Chops to stop, embarrassed by the praise. But . . . he did have visions of doing other things: sitting in an office, having a proper lunch inside a restaurant, and . . . maybe . . . who knew—a family one day—all things that had nothing to do with posse life. And, yeah, way up there on the list, even the thought of not being *dead*.

Chops adjusted his white collar. "Okay, so I'm guessing you didn't come to pray. . . ."

Gabriel suddenly felt uneasy. Like the stained-glass windows might just start shattering despite Chops's invitation in. And how many kinds of wrong was it to come into a church or rectory packing? "I need to talk to you about a transshipment," he blurted before he chickened out.

Chops widened his stance. "You know I'm not associated with the posse in any way anymore, right?"

"Yeah, but you work with posse people, no true? Showing them the 'right' way?"

"Fair enough." But Gabriel saw a flash of disappointment in Chops's eyes. "So . . . you're looking for information?"

"Yeh, mon. You remember Jamal and Blood Moon?"

Chops didn't say yes. But he didn't say no.

"They were supposed to sell a package yesterday, and it went bad."

Chops's gaze passed straight through Gabriel, all the way back to Montego Bay. "Them dead?"

Even as Gabriel started to nod, Chops was already making the sign of the cross.

"There was some little kid by the cove," Gabriel explained hurriedly. "He said his friend saw a man take a briefcase from a go-fast and drive off on another boat."

"His *friend* said?"

Gabriel shrugged, knowing Chops wanted a verification he couldn't give him. "Only clue we have, mon."

"Okay . . . so he came here, to Springtown Harbour? The one who took the case?"

"That's what I'm trying to find out. So, I was wondering—maybe you know something?"

Chops frowned. "No, but if you want, I can ask around."

"Yeh, mon."

"You have the same cell?"

"Yeh, mon." Okay. With that taken care of, he had to ask about Teago—had Chops said anything to him? It would be totally messed up if he had. Still, Gabriel had a hunch that Chops hadn't. And a priest from Ark Haven once said, a hunch might be truth that we know in our hearts, but doomed to our subconscious. Stop wondering and just ask!

So he did.

Chops tipped his head back, but his eyes were glued to Gabriel's. "You in trouble?"

Gabriel tried not to move a muscle, give anything away. "Everything's cool. Cool, cool. Just wondering."

"No need to wonder. The answer is I've had my share of head knocks, but I don't think I'm slipping, not like that. I wouldn't do you like that."

"Yeh, mon. Respect." Now Gabriel felt like total crap. He should have known. Chops must think *he* was crap for even asking. Damn. Okay. Time to go. "Um . . . let me know if you hear anything. Likkle more."

"Gabriel—I hope things no salt."

"No, mon, no troubles."

This time as they shook, Gabriel took in the simple Timex with a leather band on Chop's wrist. He used to be iced out— gold chains for days. A Rolex or something, at least a fake Gucci.

"Listen," Chops said as he led Gabriel to the door. "No lectures, mon, but the good news is that God has a plan for your life, so you can hope and prosper. He says, 'I am making a way through wilderness and streams in the wasteland.'"

Gabriel knew the passage. Knew why Chops was saying it. "We'll see about that." He closed off the thought before it could take any hold on him.

Chops gripped the side of the door, ready to close it. "Well, I hope to see you inside this door again. Anything else you're wondering about?"

There was so much. But there was one thing that Chops had opened the door to—the thing he'd always wondered about Chops. Gabriel grinned. "Speaking of 'making a way through wilderness,' and if you mean it, about wondering about anything—what about that story? You really beat a guy to death? And you still became a priest?"

Chops put a fist to his mouth, seeming suddenly far, far away. Then Gabriel heard, almost as if from a dream—

"There were two; they'd seriously wounded one of the men in the posse by the time I got there. Cut him pretty badly. And something just clicked in my head and I went at them . . . just fists." He seemed like he was listening to his own tale. "I beat one down . . . didn't kill him. The other guy freaked out, ran away. Then I carried my man a few blocks and called for help."

Huh. Stories always grew when people passed them on. "But who was the guy, your 'man'?" Gabriel couldn't resist asking.

Chops gave a quick neck crack. "Teago."

Gabriel took a step back. "Bumboclot!"

"Yes, so you see, we can *all* change, even you." His voice was singsong.

Gabriel paced the sidewalk, mind buzzing, connecting the dots. *That* was why Teago let Chops out of the posse. He owed him! He owed him! Just as he was thinking he had to tell Hammer, his phone buzzed. He glanced at the number. Not Hammer. Teago. Shit.

Gabriel put a smile into his voice. "Yeh, mon. I was just about to call you."

"Why di backside you no call me before this?" Gabriel could imagine the spit flying as he shouted.

"I *did* call you. You have my number on caller ID, so you *could* call me back."

"Oh, so me work fi you now? Is you pay *my* salary? That it? Me must call you back?"

Damn, Teago must still be high. "No, I meant, I figured you'd call."

"Me know what you mean! Youth, you keep calling me till you get me, you hear? Me is a busy man."

The boss and he always talked like this, but there was something . . . different . . . about the tone. "Boss, I'm just saying I did call you."

"No more foolishness. You find di package?"

Gabriel swallowed. "Jamal and Blood Moon are dead."

The silence was short. "Okay. Yu find di package?"

Gabriel pressed his head against the phone. Shit. They'd put seven years apiece into the posse. And Teago only cared about the freakin' package?

"What did Chops say?"

Hold on. What? Gabriel felt instantly nauseous. Did Chops—Hammer! Teago must have already talked to Hammer.

"Well?"

"Nothing . . . Chops didn't know anything, but he's going to ask around."

"Bloodclot! What about di boat?"

"Um . . . Hammer's at the dock, looking."

Then silence. Had Gabriel said something wrong?

"Mi calling Melville," Teago said at last.

"Melville?" No way! *That* kind of police was always double trouble. What the hell was *that* about? Hammer and Gabriel had come through so many times. Nothing had ever gone wrong when they did transshipments, collections, or even street sales. There was just that one little mess up back when Gabriel started. But, for sure, nothing would have gone wrong this time. Nothing would have gone wrong this time if Teago had chosen them, not . . . Anyway they'd be able to figure this out. Melville didn't need to be involved. "Boss, we don't need police."

"We? There is no *we*, just me. Is me make the decisions, not *we*, you understand?"

"Hammer and me can handle it," Gabriel assured him, striving for calm, striving not to get caught up in Teago's fury.

"Damn it. Me want that package, boy. Me call who me want fi call."

Gabriel heard the hum of a motorcycle. Hammer pulled up, gestured with his chin to ask who was on the phone.

Gabriel mouthed *Teago* just as the phone clicked off. Okay, not good. Gabriel called him back. He didn't answer. The mailbox was full. Gabriel called again. Still no answer. Asshole.

Hammer rocked the bike from side to side. "Wha' gwan?"

Gabriel's mind was now flushed with fury. He didn't know where to start. "Damn it, he didn't say one word when I told him about Jamal and Blood Moon. Nothing!"

Hammer blew out a stream of air. "Yeh, mon, me just talk to him, and all him saying was that him want the package."

Jamal and Blood Moon were completely expendable. So were they. None of them meant shit to Teago. Just package this, package that—

Hammer licked his thumb and rubbed something off his handlebar. "We just sufferers, mon," he said as if reading Gabriel's mind. "The whole country is sufferers. I mean we no have di juice fi produce no cocaine."

"What?" Gabriel had no idea what Hammer was getting at.

"We're just movers, mon," Hammer explained.

Huh? "What the hell are you talking?"

"In the transshipment game. Me mean, when you check it

out, you see di cocaine grow down a Bolivia and dem only need us fi move it from one drop to a next one. We no have no lab pon di island. We no control. Nothing. We just move it. Could be moving mango or orange. No matter."

Yep. Gabriel got it. They weren't very different from people who moved furniture. Replaceable. Expendable. Movers.

"Chops say anything?" Hammer asked now.

Gabriel waited for two older women to pass by, both wearing V-neck sweaters even though it had to be eighty-five degrees out. Must have gotten them from relatives in foreign. "Nope. Said he'd ask around, but now I'm beginning to doubt that he will."

Hammer brushed sweat off his brow with the back of his forearm. "Why dat?"

"Don't know." Gabriel remembered Chops's last words to him. "Maybe because he's a minister now."

"Like me say before, if he's a real minister, I'm di bloody Pope."

Gabriel tugged on his shirt, venting in some cool air. "Well, if you are, we need your prayers. Teago's pissed and he's calling Melville."

Hammer slapped the handlebars. "What a fuckery! We can handle this!"

It *was* a fuckery. Something else was a fuckery too. "Why do you think he didn't give a shit about Blood Moon and Jamal? He didn't even seem . . ." And something struck Gabriel—a terrible thought, a terrible, terrible thought.

Hammer went stiff. "Noooo. You don't mean . . . ? *Do* you mean Teago set them up?"

A chill iced down to Gabriel's back. "No, you're right, couldn't, no real motive." He pushed away the thought.

Hammer bobbed his head. "But I tell you, mon, Teago not who you think him is." He grunted, loud. "He didn't say anything about switching up any stash house, though?"

"No." Gabriel went back to pacing. "No joke, we *have* to find that package. It will definitely make the boss chill out."

"To hell with the boss." Hammer's words were heavy with innuendo.

"Whaaat—" But Gabriel was already sensing what Hammer was getting at.

"If we find di package, we should keep it, mon. Then call Webber." Hammer's eyes went suddenly wild. "G, it's our way out of the posse and off the island."

"You mean, get us into another posse."

"It's our ticket out of *here*, mon. American life sound good to me." Hammer rubbed harder at the spot on his motorcycle. "You still no ready fi open your ears, even though yu see how Teago no care?" He exhaled hard, the fire in his eyes gone. "Me check di wharf on the west side of town. Nothing. But make we go check di one on the other side."

Gabriel hopped on the back of the bike. Hammer was probably right about taking Webber up on his offer. Still, what could he have done to make Teago want to set him up?

Gabriel, Friday, 12:45 p.m.

S hit, it was hot. Gabriel visored one hand over his forehead to cut the glare as he searched the streets for any kind of clue. A minivan packed with tourists whooshed past them a good twenty miles over the speed limit. Even though Springtown Harbour was too small-time for the state of emergency to have installed soldiers here, he made sure to check the police station and the old courthouse as they drove by but saw nothing out of the ordinary. Tourists spilled in and out of small shops—and the line at the bakery went out the door. Its doughy smell reminded him of eating festival with that girl again. Deja. As they neared the wharf, Hammer parked between two trucks in front of a MoneyGram store, and they walked the rest of the way.

A half-dozen guys were drinking at a bar near the shore— probably fishermen. Hammer motioned over toward a narrow dock where the boats were anchored. The wooden boards had spring to them as Gabriel and Hammer stepped out onto the pier, the sea breeze sweet and cooling, but the stink of fish soured it. They saw the small yellow boat at the same time. Next to it, gently swaying, was a bigger motorboat with two kids sitting by the steering wheel, eating sandwiches.

Gabriel stared and stared some more. Two kids—no. No. No. It couldn't be!

Donovan and Kaleisha.

Deja might be here. Gabriel smoothed out his tee, then put a hand to his locs, wishing he'd had time to have the ends cut. But it was going to be awkward no matter what. At least he could ask her about the yellow boat. Since she sailed, she might know something.

"Hey, it's Gabriel," Donovan, his mouth full of food, exclaimed, nudging his sister. "What you doing here?"

Kaleisha edged closer to her brother. "He's here for Deja." They knocked their shoulders into each other's, giggling.

"How you two keeping?"

"We're okay," Kaleisha said in her cute voice.

Gabriel played it nonchalant. "Is your sister around?"

"No," she said, then swallowed.

He didn't have any time to talk to Deja anyway. "Hey . . . tell me, you know whose boat that is?" He pointed to the small yellow one.

Kaleisha narrowed her eyes. "Why?"

He lied. "Um, I might want to rent it. Go do some fishing."

Kaleisha frowned. "Oh, Mr. Wallace's old boat! Every time Deja goes out on it, she's scared it won't even start."

His breath caught. "Oh . . . ? When does she go out on it?"

"She went just the other morning," Donovan said.

Gabriel tilted his head. "Like two days, three days ago?"

Kaleisha turned to Donovan. "No. It was yesterday, right? Remember, your dumb pin broke?"

"It's not dumb!" Donovan's voice went high. "Just needed more glue."

Gabriel pulled the conversation back on track. "Yesterday? You sure?"

"Yeah," Kaleisha said, then pulled the cheese out of her sandwich and handed it to her brother, who finished it in two bites.

Gabriel cut a quick glance toward Hammer. Then he smiled at the kids, despite the fact that his heart was drumming. Deja couldn't be involved in this. She just couldn't. "Hey, any idea where your sister is?"

"She went to Montego Bay," Donovan said offhandedly, eye on his sandwich.

"No, somewhere near Mobay," Kaleisha corrected him.

"You sure?"

"That's what she said."

"Okay, thanks, Kaleisha." Then Gabriel pointed at the yellow boat. "Um, you said that's, ah, Mr. Wallace's boat, right? Know where *he* is?"

Kaleisha shrugged. "Haven't seen him today." Then she eyeballed Hammer. "Who's he?"

"He's . . . Ivanhoe."

Both kids cracked up. "Ivanhoe!"

Hammer hated his real name even more than getting a nick on his motorcycle, still, he forced a smile, bowing as if his name were a magic trick.

Gulls squawked. A gust brought whiffs of fish and salt as Gabriel scoured the wharf with his eyes. No other yellow boats. No Mr. Wallace. No Deja. No leads. So Gabriel asked as nonchalantly as he could, "Your sister—she's been gone a while, eh?"

"No. She just went to the bus park a little while ago," Kaleisha said.

He played it cool. "Shoot, so I just missed her. Okay, thanks. Nice to see you two." He gave them a double thumbs-up. "Enjoy those sandwiches."

"Want us to tell her you were looking for her?" Kaleisha asked.

"Nah. I'll just give her a call." He started to turn when Donovan jumped up. He pulled a shiny stone from his pocket. "I feel it's pyrite, but check it, no?"

That day at the beach rushed in. Surf, light blue, bright. Skipping rocks. Deja in her baseball cap. Her *baseball cap*. Alarm bells banged the walls of his brain. But he had to stay cool. So he made a big show of examining the stone, already knowing its quality, but took his time to make it fun for them. "Oh, it's a good one, a really good one, but you're right, it's pyrite."

"Told you." Kaleisha threw the last corner of her sandwich into the air, a hovering gull snapping it up before the others could get to it.

She and Donovan laughed as the bird flew off, then Gabriel offered back the pyrite. But Donovan told him to keep it. "Like you said, it's a good one."

Gabriel rolled the stone in his palm to make it glitter. "Thanks, buddy, but you must want it."

"No, mon, I want *you* to have it."

Donovan must have really liked the stone, since he'd kept it in his pocket, yet the kid was giving it to him. Gabriel blinked hard and shook his shoulders, trying to ward off the unexpected shivers caused by Donovan's kind gesture. "Okay, yeh, mon. Thank you." Hammer was giving him the evil eye—he needed to wrap this up. "Likkle more," he told the twosome, squeezing his hand over the rock. Then he and Hammer strolled over to the yellow boat.

Kaleisha yelled, "Trust me, you don't want to rent *that* boat."

Gabriel gave a short salute, then could hardly get his phone out of his pocket fast enough.

What the hell was going on? The boy at the cove said "a man." But that might have been because of the baseball cap. That was probably why his friend had mistaken her for a guy! But she wasn't any posse girl. No way. No way.

Gabriel's call went to Deja's voice mail.

Once out of earshot of the kids, Hammer grilled, "You want to tell me what di hell a gwan?"

Excellent question. What di hell a gwan? "Remember the girl at the party . . . ?"

Deja, Friday, 1:00 p.m.

Her phone buzzed. Gabriel. Funny, she'd thought of him just yesterday. Still, this would be so awkward. And this was no time to chat. She let it go to voice mail.

Deja roamed the bus park with swivel-headed caution. It was busy with tourists and Jamaicans getting off and on buses and minivans parked in diagonal slots. Vendors, not taking "no" for an answer, kept beckoning to tourists to come buy T-shirts, phones, star apples, jackfruit, or coconut drops—and every kind of ganja imaginable. There was that mustached man who had been talking to her.

Her phone buzzed again.

Straleen this time. "Hey, so how did it go?"

Deja hesitated. "I kept the bag."

"Kiss me neck!" Then Deja heard Straleen repeat her favorite non-curse curse word to someone else.

Lila.

Then Lila got on the phone. "Deja . . . do *not* tell me you kept that bag!"

"I did—"

"Deja . . . I know you mussi think on this hard, so me not going go preach 'bout how dangerous this is, but you bloody know how dangerous this is?"

"Listen, I'm not an idiot. I talked to the guy, Webber. I'm like ninety-nine percent sure he's an agent, so I think I can trust him."

Lila repeated everything to Straleen. Then Straleen, back on the phone, said, "Deja. This is what you're going to do. Deja Reynolds, you fi make haste and gwan home. Now. We going to leave school, meet you there, and we make a big fire and burn it all off."

Someone tapped Deja on the shoulder. She jumped, almost stumbled.

"Hey, you taking this bus?" It was the mustached man again. What the heck!

"I'm on the phone."

"Yeah, mon. Okay, talk to you later." He grinned strangely and stepped back.

Deja moved away fast.

"What's going on?" Straleen sounded panicked.

Deliberately avoiding eye contact with the mustached man, Deja said, "Nothing, it's cool. Just some weird guy."

"Girl—"

"Don't worry. I'll call." She hung up and checked for the bus. Mr. Mustache waved. *Wonderful.* He was going to be a pain until she left. But for once luck was with her—the bus to Montego Bay, barely late for once, pulled up. Normally, she'd stand outside until it was ready to head out again rather than sit in fumes, but this time she was prepared to knock people over to claim a seat where she couldn't be seen.

As she waited impatiently to board—how were there so many people going to Mobay?—it struck her, a revelation. A twisted one. She almost laughed out loud. Her mother would probably—no, definitely!—tell her not to do this. But now Deja could somehow see from her mother's shoes. That going to work in Brooklyn was as desperate and calculated an undertaking as Deja's was now. They were both leaving *their* children to try to make life better for the whole family. Deja'd never thought of it that way. She suddenly understood her mother's decision in a way she never had before. At the same time, it was her mother's choice, for *family*, that put all of them in jeopardy this very minute!

Deja's head started spinning.

A car horn blared, which didn't help, but it did remind her to keep her guard up. At the edge of the bus park, near coconut-drop vendors, stood a row of drivers leaning against their minivans, waiting for tourists. And—hold on, she knew one of the drivers! Trenton. She used to help him with history and English before he graduated. She hadn't seen him in months! He'd dropped out of university when he got a job driving for Sparrow Cove Resort in Ocho Rios. He was really good at math, but the driving job paid more than he'd ever earn as a math teacher, he'd told her.

As she joined the long line of people waiting to get on the bus, she noticed the mustachioed man standing nearby, and then something even worse. Past him, down the street, was a guy who looked shockingly like Gabriel, with some other guy on a motorcycle, headed this way! Was this real? Was she really seeing this? It was like her brain slowed down, thoughts starting and stopping like she was glitching.

Why had he called?

Oh my God. Could they be "them"? If it was, they'd probably check the bus. Her heart froze midbeat.

He said he was in a posse.

Bumboclot! Could he *really* be "them"? Knowing it wasn't safe to just stand out in the open on this long line, her eyes swept tourists—all decked out in sun hats—across the park in search of another way. Trenton! He was waving some onto the Sparrow Cove minivan. She'd be safe among them. And—oh—if he was taking them back to Ocho Rios, he'd have to drive past Mobay first! She had helped him with all those history papers. He'd better remember. She wove her way through the crowd.

Trenton saw her coming and made a pretend jump shot, showing her *how* he remembered her—not for her school skills but as a netball player. He looked happy to see her. Skinny as ever, but his hair was short now—more presentable for the job.

"Hi, Trenton," she called out as she reached him.

"Wha' gwan, Deja?" He took another pretend jump shot. "You not in di NBA with LeBron yet?"

"NBA? Is what you talking about?"

"Mon, your jump shot is sweet. All net every time."

"Well, it should be. There's no backboards in netball, Trenton."

"Exactly, but you woulda had one in basketball. So you would be that much better."

He could always make her laugh. But this was no time for fun. "Any seats left?"

His face fell. "I'm really sorry. Don't know if I can take you today, you know?"

She thought about offering to pay him, even though her meager supply of cash was dwindling down to critical. "Don't worry, I have money." She reached into her pocket, fished out an American ten.

"No, me mean—" He leaned closer as she eyed a motor-cycle parking at the edge of the bus park. "Me have no problem giving you a ride, but me working for a charter tour company today. And they have a strict policy about giving rides to non-tourists."

She edged closer to the van, angling herself so she couldn't be seen—at least that was the hope. "Trenton, I *really* need a ride."

He held up his hands in a *what can I do* sort of way. "The charter company manager is an A-hole, mon."

She got it, she did. His kind of job was hard to get. There were probably thirty other people lined up who would cut off both arms for his job if they didn't need one to drive. "Trenton, if there's one day to make an exception, it's today. I have to get to Mobay, and I can't take the bus."

He narrowed his eyes. "Wha' gwan?"

She fought the urge to check behind her. "I have a problem I need to deal with, and you're literally my last hope."

He licked his lips nervously. "I took this group to Negril, and . . . I don't know how they'd react now if you got on."

"What's wrong with them?"

"Some groups are cool, you know? This one, well, all they do is complain and ask questions."

She put the note in Trenton's palm. "Trenton—"

"I'm really sorry. Can't risk it, Deja." He pushed the money back toward her.

Then she viewed a tourist talking to a vendor, pointing to the mountains. She was probably asking a question. "Gimme one sec—I know what I can do."

"Deja—"

She couldn't take no for an answer. "Wait—hear me out. They have questions. I can answer them. I can pretend the tour manager sent me."

Trenton rolled his head back as if to blame the heavens. "Deja—"

But Deja was already following a blond woman in a peasant dress stepping up and into the cool air of the vehicle.

Trenton scrambled after her, forehead furrowed, eyes wide. "Deja," he hissed.

Deja wouldn't let him get in trouble. But at the same time, there was no way she could let him make her get off the van. "Ladies and gentlemen, my name is Deja. And I'll be your *tourist guide* for the bus ride back to Chicago."

The passengers laughed. She remembered how her mother had told her that a joke didn't have to be *that* good to make people laugh when you were in a position of authority. Deja would have to tell her it worked . . . when she saw her again.

Trenton stared daggers at her, but he started the engine and pulled away all the same. The tension drained so quickly Deja expected to see a puddle. Then she dared to glance out the window—no sign of Gabriel. She smiled wide. Showtime!

Gabriel, Friday, 1:20 p.m.

He stood in disbelief by a vendor selling drops, enveloped in the smell of sweet coconut. Deja. She was in that minivan, the one that had just pulled out of the bus park. Shit. What kind of twisted luck had brought him here, to hunt down the one girl he'd ever connected to in his life?

Whirling around, he ran through the throng of people back to Hammer, who was talking on his phone.

Gabriel hesitated. Should he just let her go? If he did, what would happen to her? There had to be some good reason why she was doing this. Because no *way* was she a posse girl!

Hammer stashed his phone in his pocket. "Wha' gwan?"

"I saw her."

"Good, where?"

"On a minivan. It just left on the A1."

"Great. Let's go." He started toward his bike.

Gabriel grabbed his arm. "Hold on, mon. Maybe we should think this over."

Hammer cocked his head. "Is what you saying?"

"I don't know if we should go after her."

Now Hammer's eyes got slitty. "G, that was Teago on the phone. Me tell him me hear she going Mobay."

Gabriel dropped his arm. "Backside. Why, mon?"

Hammer looked at him incredulously. "Di children tell us she was taking a bus, and since we no see her, me figure she did take an earlier bus. That no make sense to you?"

Gabriel got it, he did. But—

Then Hammer went on. "Anyway, Teago calling Melville fi tell him to set up roadblock."

"Bumboclot!" Gabriel blew out a stream of air, looked out toward the ocean. "The A1 is the only coast road from here to Mobay, so she'll definitely run into Melville . . . unless we can get to her first." Then he puzzled, "But maybe Melville won't check for her on a tourist van?"

Hammer's eyes were filled with disbelief. "Hold on, hold on, hold on! She de pon a *tourist* van? Is how she do that?"

"Don't know, mon." Gabriel rammed his hands into his pockets, wishing like hell he hadn't seen her.

"We can't stop no tourist van, mon! Mess with tourists and di government a come after we! Teago would be in deep shit. Him would prefer lose di package than have us stop a tourist van and make something happen to a tourist."

Maybe they could catch up at some point—those vans made scheduled stops along the way so the tourists could get out and spend their money. Still, Hammer was right. Messing with a tourist van was definitely the wrong move.

Deja jostled in the Sparrow Bay van, gripping the metal bar on the seat in front of her, pausing in the story she was telling. Out the window, a group of jerk chicken shacks let her know they were entering Windy Bay. They were making good time—only one stop, to let tourists buy fresh mangoes— and that meant she'd easily make the four thirty meeting with Webber. So far, so good.

When she saw the tourists were hooked and eager for the next part, she delivered the punch line. "Because the Springtown clock tower was delivered to Jamaica by mistake."

"Zis is true, yes?" a French woman now asked.

"Yes. It's like when an airline loses your luggage by putting it on the wrong plane. Except, a *tower*." Deja grinned. "But everyone liked it so much, they held a fundraiser to pay for it. And there wasn't any GoFundMe in 1817."

As the tourists chuckled, Deja glanced back out the window. Fifteen minutes and Trenton could drop her off at the big road to Long Hill. She could flag down a taxi van for a ride up to Anchovy from there. Relief that this was almost over and nerves about what would go down with Webber clashed within her. Then she gave her head a shake—she had to stay focused on the tourists.

"If you look to your right, you'll see the New Testament Church. Also, on your right, the Seventh-day Adventist Church, and coming up, next to the police station . . . the Baptist Church. You might say religion is a bit of a religion in Windy Bay."

"Rastafarianism is a religion, no?" someone with a thick French accent asked.

"And smoking *is* their religion," another joked.

It was funny enough, but Deja knew a couple of Rastas—not the rent-a-dreads kind the tourists usually met, who were as much part of the Jamaican "amusement park" as Mickey Mouse was at Disney World. The ones Deja knew were righteous, peace-loving people. "I'd say smoking is *part* of their religion," she said with a smile. She pressed her feet against the backpack, knowing it was still there but checking anyway, and went on. "The government actually treated them badly for years because of their beliefs." And what was it her mother had said? Oh yeah. "In fact, even the great Bob Marley wasn't always well treated by the government, at least not until he became 'the great Bob Marley.'"

"No way," a man with very cool American sunglasses on— Ray-Bans?—his mouth agog, said. "Why?"

"My mother said it was because they were different: long dreadlocks, prayed to Jah, smoking ganja. Of course, nowadays you can have two ounces of ganja and it's *no problem*. In fact, Rastas are now allowed to grow ganja plants on sacred grounds."

"That's right," an old lady with yellow-tinted sunglasses, in the back, called out. "Babylon backed down."

Deja had to laugh. Even Trenton was laughing. "Yes, star," Deja replied in a heavy patois.

"Yeh, mon," the old lady shot back in her own version of patois.

Grinning, Deja spoke to the group. "For those of you who might not know, Babylon is what Rastas call crooked politicians and police."

"Amen," the lady said.

Deja nodded. "That's right— Rastas care more about 'livity.'"

"Livity?" asked a woman whose shoulders were sunburned as pink as the floppy hat she was wearing. "That's a new one on me."

"It's about living your life with love in your heart."

"Amen," the other woman said again.

Trenton rolled his eyes, but he gave a quick thumbs-up, unable to keep from smirking.

Despite everything else, Deja still felt a zing of pride in her country. And in herself. She'd be good at this tourist thing, she *would*.

Her gaze lingered out the window as she wished she could block out everything else, just for a minute, and take in the insane beauty that was rushing by: the forests on the right, seemingly endless in their stretch, green and deeper green yet, sloping up the hills and exalted mountains, and on the left, the beaches, bleached white, caressing the wide, wide ocean shimmering turquoise beneath the cloudless sky.

Deja turned back to the passengers. "Oh, let me make sure of something," she said casually, so she could check her phone. There were texts from Straleen and Lila. Go gangsta girl. 💪 💪 Keep 1K fi me! 🧡 🧡 🧡 And one from Uncle Glen. Engine fixed. On the way soon. See you at the Hot Time Grill. Deja gave a long exhale and texted her girls, then Uncle . . .

See you in Mobay.

Okay. Replaying all the tourism courses she'd taken, Deja wondered what else a tourist guide would say. Just ahead stood an unfinished housing development—dozens of half-completed houses amid overgrown bushes. She remembered driving by the area years ago—bulldozers had been plowing the land. Now it was a swath of unpainted cinder-block houses, some with doors and windows, some boarded up, and some without any roofs. Ghost towns, her mother called them. That could be interesting to the tourists.

She made sure she had all the information in her head, then announced, "On the right you will see an unfinished housing development—you might have seen others during your trip." Several heads bobbed. "Here in Jamaica, because loans are so hard for most people to get, people build a little at a time, doing as much as they can until the money runs out. Some move into the only finished room of their house while they wait to save enough money to build the next part of the house."

A man with neatly cropped hair, clearly fascinated by the

information, exclaimed, "That's smart. Stay out of debt! Just build a little at a time, oui?"

"Exactly," Deja said, now pointing at the settlement. "And do you see the metal rods sticking out of the top of the first floor of some of the buildings?" Everyone leaned in that direction. "Those rods will eventually be used to help build the second floors. But the *main* reason they're left exposed like that is that they serve as proof to the tax collectors that the house isn't actually finished."

"Why's that?" the same man asked.

"Owners only pay taxes on a house when it's finished, even if they've already moved in." Now *everyone* bobbed their heads excitedly, as if they understood the intricacies of finance, even finance Jamaican-style. Floppy-hat lady exclaimed that it was the cleverest thing she'd ever heard.

The minivan suddenly slowed. If Deja hadn't been holding the rail, she would have lost her balance. The car in front of them had come to a full stop. Trenton stuck his head out the window and then sat up straight. "Hmm, roadblock. Must be checking fi somebody."

Deja's breath hitched. *What?* They *couldn't* be! But of course they could. She leaned over Trenton's shoulder, and sure enough, just ahead, a police jeep blocked the road. Oddly, the other lane heading back toward Springtown Harbour was fully open. She ever so casually slipped the backpack onto her shoulders. She couldn't let them check her bag. No way. "I have to go now," she whispered into Trenton's ear.

His eyes widened, then narrowed. "You in *this* kind of

trouble?"

"Please, don't mention me, okay?"

"No problem." He opened the door.

Deja put a hand on his arm. "I hope none of this gets *you* into trouble."

"I'll be all right, especially since you were great—Ms. Tourist Guide. I'm gonna tell the resort to hire you!" Then he put on his official driver's voice for the tourists. "This is our guide's stop, folks. Let's give her a big hand."

They clapped. Deja gave a quick wave and stepped down onto the road, trying to keep her nerves in check. She checked out the people in the car behind the minivan. A woman was driving with a toddler beside her in the front seat. Whoa, that wasn't safe. She peeked the other way. An officer with a machine gun crouched, talking to a driver several cars ahead. Telling herself to stay calm, she glanced back again. Bumboclot!

About ten cars away, a motorcycle had pulled to a stop.

And—oh dear God, no—she recognized the driver. He was the one who'd been with Gabriel back at the bus park. And the person sitting behind him . . . Gabriel.

Gabriel, Friday, moments later

Bumboclot! Like an apparition, there she was, standing between the shoulder and a minivan, just staring at him. Wearing a backpack that probably held the cash. Did she have the drugs, too? He blinked hard to make sure he wasn't imagining things, and when he opened his eyes, she was gone! But no, she was running into the bush.

"That's di girl, no?" Hammer yelped just as she disappeared into a stand of royal palms.

Gabriel was about to swing himself off the motorcycle when Hammer lurched forward.

"Mi feel she's heading fi di houses over there. There's a road up ahead that we can use fi head her off." Hammer drove slowly along the emergency stopping lane.

Halfway around the curve, Gabriel swore out loud. "Roadblock. Backside!" An officer, a machine gun strapped to his chest, was stopping vehicles up ahead. "I know him. One of Melville's guys. Melville must be up there too."

"You have to talk to Melville, mon," Hammer insisted. "Get him to let us by 'cause you know him going go have 'nuff question."

Gabriel chewed his lip, studied the area ahead. "No, mon, Melville's too dangerous. We haffi' just dodge him." The only road into that housing development was about thirty yards past Melville's roadblock. They'd have to go past him to get there. When it came to honesty, Melville was like traffic in Kingston—always a new detour. There were no straight roads when he was around. "No, mon," Gabriel said again. "We need a next plan."

"Okay, maybe me just speed through di roadblock."

"You want to commit *suicide*, mon?!"

Jeezum, dude was rational one second and Hammer the next. Gabriel assessed the bush Deja had run into. "That path, back there—think you can drive it?"

"Only one way fi know."

Hammer swung the motorcycle around.

Deja, Friday, 2:45 p.m.

Deja raced along the path, slapping away branches, straining to hear what was going on behind her but too scared to look. Just ahead stood that half-built community housing. Okay—okay—she could hide in one of the empty houses.

Pushing through the bushes, she hit what would have been the main road into the community; now, crabgrass had sprouted up through the cracks. A rooster crowed; otherwise it was eerily quiet. She headed left, searching for an unboarded-up building.

Then she heard it—an engine. A motorcycle engine, coming from behind. She ducked around a dumpster, waited, then broke into a sprint, passing a house that was little more than a frame. The next one had no front door, but one room seemed to have glass in the window. It'd have to do. If she kept running, they'd spot her.

Slipping through an opening that might one day be the front door, she continued to a room that might become a kitchen. A shaft of sunlight split the house in half. She still felt too exposed. She ran back to the front wall and crouched below the window—pressed her cheek against cool concrete. Tried to quiet her breath.

The motorcycle was close, the engine angry, like it wanted something—then closer still until it sounded like it was right out front! Deja pressed a hand on the wall, braced, ready to run. Then the engine roared. Carefully edging up to the window, she peeked outside. The motorcycle was heading down the street. She slid back down, rested her forehead against the wall in relief.

"Why you come here?"

Deja stumbled backward onto the floor.

A woman, short, powerful in her legs and shoulders, stood in the doorway of what would be the kitchen, holding a knife long enough to halve a cow. "You no know this capture?"

Capture? This was a captured house? Uncle Glen had just been complaining about this. He had a strip of land up in the mountains way above Springtown, pretty worthless, no roads or running water, but still, someone had built a shack on it. He'd had to go up there and run them off before they built a house. If he didn't and they built a concrete dwelling, those people could be entitled to own his land by law. Capture land.

"I'm . . . I'm sorry," Deja stammered. "No. I didn't know." She used her most polite voice, trying to read the woman's intensity.

"You know now," the woman said, her voice steely.

Deja glanced in the direction of the motorcycle, then back to the woman, then down at the knife. What was worse? Then she decided. "It's just—I can't let those guys see me. Would you mind . . . ? Could I please stay for just a minute?"

The woman followed Deja's gaze. "*One* minute."

"Thank you. Thank you so much." She couldn't tell if the woman knew she was in trouble, or if she was just leery of whoever was on the motorcycle—outsiders could be owners or officials, wanting their land back. The second the motorcycle was out of sight, Deja stood and gave the woman a bow and jogged back outside, heat rising off the pavement. She guessed that Gabriel and his friend would try to loop around the community instead of doubling back, so she ran in the same direction they'd gone in. Ahead was a mound of dry sand—probably for mixing concrete—piled up high against a boarded-up two-story house. She eyed the mound—if she of the house. Then she'd have a good vantage point.

She took a few steps backward, then ran forward, pushing off as hard as she could, and leaped. The sand gave way as if she were running on a treadmill, and she slid right back down.

C'mon, Deja! She scrambled to her feet. Listened for the motorcycle. She could hear the putter—but not close, not yet.

Across the street was a house with a door but no windows. If she could get in, she could hide there. But for how long? She couldn't miss the meeting with Webber—damn!

Plus, if the last house had been captured, this one might be too. The whole damn place might be captured. This duppy complex was giving her the creeps. But did she even have a choice? No, she did not.

Before she even got to the door, it swung open. A woman, curlers in her hair, nightgown on, a gun in her hand, blocked the entrance.

This time Deja didn't freak out. Almost eerily calm, she wondered why this woman was dressed like she was about to moisturize and go to bed.

Then she wondered, if she so much as flinched, would the woman pull the trigger?

The returning roar of the motorcycle engine pierced her ears.

"Them troubling you?" the woman said, speaking out of one side of her mouth with an air of disgust.

Deja swept a hand at the sweat rolling down her cheek. How she answered could bust open a whole beehive of trouble—as if she wasn't in enough already.

"Me say . . . them troubling you?" The woman tilted her head toward the sound.

Deja didn't want Gabriel shot! She didn't want *anyone* shot, but what to do? She couldn't let them find her! "Yes. Yes, they're troubling me."

"Okay." The woman stepped out of the doorway, around Deja. "Don't worry, I got you."

Was she . . . going to help her?

The motorcycle was in sight. Which meant *she* was in sight.

"Cedella!" the woman called out, loud.

A second woman, taller, also in curlers, holding a long kitchen knife, scowling big-time, pushed through the door and joined the first woman. A human blockade. Grateful tears sprang to Deja's eyes.

But no! This wasn't their issue. What if Gabriel, or the other guy, also had a gun! She couldn't put strangers at risk. She should intervene, say something. A John Crow bird screeched. Another called back. The motorcycle engine cut, and they came to a stop in front of the house. Gabriel got off the bike, locked eyes with Deja. She read danger. But what kind?

The first woman raised her gun and held it steady. She knew what she was doing.

In turn, Gabriel grinned, probably trying to put them at ease. "Hey, we're not here for you."

The woman motioned with her head toward the highway. "Then you should go."

"Hold on now, we just want fi talk to her," Gabriel's friend said, swinging a leg over the motorcycle.

The woman shifted her aim toward him. "You stay right effing there."

He narrowed his eyes. "Me know you not talking to me."

"Oh, you want my gun to do di talking, then?" The woman said, raising her chin.

Gabriel kept his eyes on Deja. "Deja, we just need to ask you about something, okay?"

The second woman waved the kitchen knife, slicing the air. "Leave the gyal alone."

Gabriel took a half step toward the woman. "Honest! I just need to talk to her. I'm not going to hurt her!" His voice was smooth, measured, like he'd practiced or something. Like back at the church party, handling that fight.

"Please don't shoot him," Deja begged the woman.

The woman with the knife glowered at her. "Bitch, you want help or you don't?"

Deja *did*. She *did* want help. But she also didn't want anyone hurt—or killed. She hated that she thought that way, but it was the only way to think. She should say yes, thank these women, and be *done* done with it.

But she couldn't. So she prayed they somehow understood as she backed away, eyes on the gun in the woman's hand. "Buy me some time . . . please. That's all. I just need a few minutes."

"Now you talking, girl," the woman said, voice low, keeping her gun trained on Gabriel. "Either one of you moves, I will blow your heads off," she bellowed.

Willing her legs into motion, Deja ran, her stomach in knots, the situation crazy, like a weightless free fall into a cursed rabbit hole.

She flew past two empty houses, metal bars protruding from the sides like crooked fingers squeezing the life out of the structures. She ran and ran. Then she heard a car—then a siren. Police? Police?! Were they looking for her too? The balls of her feet were raw.

She had to get off the road. There was an opening between the next set of houses, but it was filled with another mound of sand. This time she climbed it as if it were a sand dune, slower, gently, so she wouldn't sink in, wouldn't slide backward, crawling. It was crazy hot, scorching her already raw feet, and her palms and fingertips—stupid sandals in the way. Finally, the top! She took a quick view of the area, got her bearings.

The hills were a couple of miles away. But just beyond the development was forest: palms, lignum vitae trees, and large tangles of shrubs, not thick enough to hide her. She'd have to go deep inside, but at least she had somewhere to go.

Gabriel, Friday, 3:30 p.m.

They were in a standoff. These women were not putting on a show. The one with the gun had clearly used it before, her expression less menacing than the other one with her—colder, deadish eyes. Blood Moon had always said the second time you killed was a lot like the second time you had sex—you weren't anywhere close to being as nervous as the first time. Was this going to be the woman's first time?

The one with the gun shifted her weight. "Mi not playing, you know?"

Hammer's hand had drifted down to his waist, to his knife. "Bitch, you better put down that gun."

"Who you calling bitch, bitch?"

"You, bitch."

She wasn't the least bit intimidated. "Bitch, I'll cap your ass."

A siren. Gabriel dared a quick look. A police jeep was heading their way.

Melville. Bumboclot!

They'd been spotted driving into the bush after all.

"It might be a good idea to put down the gun," Gabriel warned the woman. She ignored him. "Don't you see who's coming?"

Melville was going to be wondering what the hell was going on. Gabriel would just tell him the truth; they were following Deja, as Teago requested. Then a thought crept in. Did *Melville* know about "switching up the stash house"? No—he couldn't think about that now.

The woman with the knife glared, all twitchy, and this time, even the one with the gun began to appear uneasy.

The jeep screeched to a stop.

Melville was out of the car first. His steps were nimble for a man so round. He swayed like he'd played sports way back, probably cricket, maybe a bowler who could spin the ball. He had that sort of trickery about him. He was always clean-shaven; his uniform pants were always creased. He took up position between Gabriel and Hammer and the women, as if he were some sort of referee.

He seemed almost lackadaisical—probably taking his time to figure out what was going on. In no hurry whatsoever. His cohort, who joined him, was holding the business end of his machine gun toward the ground, like he had no stake in this confrontation. That was promising, at least.

"Ladies." Melville quick-waved his hand, like greeting a neighbor he had no time for. "You two live here?"

The taller woman lowered her gun to her side. "Is hereso we live, yes."

"Hmm, and I suppose you don't pay taxes?"

The other woman tapped the flat of her blade against her thigh. "We capture it."

Melville assessed the building. "You have a title fi this land?"

"We pour di concrete to make the house," the gun woman said, unintimidated.

"And di landowner nah go step to us," the knife woman added.

"Well, I think you need to worry more about *me* stepping to you." He pursed his lips, then eyed Gabriel. "You didn't think my man saw you back up on the A1, did you?" He grinned.

Gabriel took a step toward Melville—he needed to reason with him—

But Melville's nostrils flared. "Stay right there." Then he started interrogating the women. "Did a girl come this way—sixteen, seventeen, thereabouts?"

Damn it. Why the backside had Hammer said anything about Deja in the first place? They could easily have handled this, and Melville wouldn't be here, about to spiral everything into a colossal mess.

Melville aimed his chin at the women's house. "If you tell me what you know, maybe I won't delve into who *really* owns this house."

The gun woman's face went stormy as her partner told Melville that Deja had just left.

"You saw her? And she just left? How long?"

"She went down the road. Five minutes."

"Describe her," Melville ordered.

The woman hesitated, edged closer to her friend.

Melville took a half step forward. "It would make things easier."

The woman with the gun exhaled, hard. "Short. Dark brown. Jeans . . . blue shirt."

"And . . . ?"

"A backpack."

"Color?"

"Black."

Melville put on the fakest smile ever. "Thank you. You can go now." He barked at the officer. "Send that description to Mobay and Springtown Harbour Police. Tell the men to ask around about the girl, who she might consort with."

"Yes, sir." The officer made for the jeep.

Gabriel felt nauseous.

The two women scratched their scalps at the same time and strolled—no big deal, happens all the time—back into their captured house.

Gabriel figured he better say something. "Melville—"

Melville raised one forefinger. "Shut your backside! Me no like it when I can smell the lies." His voice was low, foreboding.

Now Gabriel lifted a hand for *him* to stop and listen. "Melville, it no go so. We were just going after the girl. That's why we left the—"

"Youth, me no want fi hear it. Now, just go, and check these houses, one by one. And make me know if you find her, or else me will come find *you*," he said, walking away before even finishing his demand.

Hammer folded his arms. "Suppose you find her first?"

"Suppose I do?" As Melville neared the jeep, he shouted to the officer, "She's on foot, so she can't be too far ahead." He jumped in and sped off, spitting dirt and dust at them.

Hammer motioned for Gabriel to get on the bike. "Mi can't stand that man."

"Whatever, mon. We have to find her. First." He didn't want to think what might happen if they didn't. Not to *them*. To her.

Deja, Friday, 4:00 p.m.

eja's lungs were on fire. With each stride, doubt tried to bully her into thinking she should give up. No way she could outrun them. Just turn herself in, see what would happen.

That same voice used to whisper at her during netball training, when she was on the verge of exhaustion and needed to finish that last drill. *The coach isn't watching, so why don't you stop? It's okay if you take it easy.*

She had always fought off that voice, and she would do it again. So on she ran, avoiding slippery moss patches grown into the crabgrass, weaving between the thin-trunked ramon and long-branched wild ackee trees that arched toward each other, making a weblike canopy.

At last she was in the shadow of a tangle of ferns, flowering hibiscus, slanting young bamboo, and thorny macca plants. She peeled off the backpack and threw it on the ground. Five hundred thousand American was heavy! Too bad she couldn't unload the pressure it represented as easily. She leaned into a tree trunk, trying to catch her breath. Each pant brought a musty scent exactly like that of the forest around her house. If only she were there right now. If only she'd burned the damn money like Straleen and Lila had insisted! In a fit of rage, she glared at the backpack, then hauled off and kicked it. Took a quick step forward and kicked it again! Damn it! Damn it!

But she had to calm down. Sinking into the grass, she began to pray, but she couldn't focus. Words just jumbled up in her mind, until four words streaked through her brain. *What time is it?*

She checked her phone. Ten percent battery—but worse, 4:07 p.m. She was going to be late! And she couldn't risk sitting here any longer. She thought for a moment. There was an old road up in the hills that wound through the town of Reading to Anchovy. But it would take hours to walk. She needed some kind of ride.

Sudden voices nearly gave her heart failure. "Jim, could you put some more of the fifty on my back?"

"Sure thing, baby."

A couple? Suntanning? Had she heard right? Had she heard anything at all? She scooped up the backpack and made her way from tree to tree until the sound of water helped her realize exactly where she was. Stately guango trees stood guard along a wide river meandering at a siesta's pace. It was part of Great River. She was as far from Anchovy as she feared. She really had to call Webber, but she needed some directions first.

A stone's throw away, where several guangos reached high over the muddy banks, a raft drifted. The gondolier, a skinny

Jamaican man in shorts, held an oar. A blond couple in sunglasses sat in the front, the man rubbing suntan lotion on the woman's back. *That* was who she'd heard.

A police siren sounded.

She couldn't help it. She wondered if Gabriel was okay—posse and police didn't mix. As she skidded down to the riverbank, her feet sinking into the soft red mud, she wondered if she'd ever know. Now the tourists were taking a selfie. Deja called to the gondolier. "Mister, do you know where the old road to Reading is?"

The siren again. Deja willed herself to stay calm.

The gondolier pointed down the river. "Two miles down so." Then he glanced in the direction of the siren and back to Deja. "Up ahead, three hundred yards, when you see where di river forks, go left there. It no easy fi dem to follow you on dat side. Stay close to di bank."

She felt a pang at his thoughtfulness. "Thank you. Thank you so much."

"Yeh, mon." He put his fist up against his chest, grace and style. "Bless up."

As the gondolier had advised, upon hitting the fork in the river, she went left. A few hundred feet in, she checked the area, then ducked behind a thicket of cane stalks to call Webber.

After the third ring, thank God, thank God, he answered.

"Mr. Webber, I'm late."

"You in trouble?"

"Um . . . no."

"What's your ETA?"

"I'm not sure. Three hours, maybe two and a half."

Silence.

He couldn't be backing out. Not now. Not after all this. "Hello, you there?" She hated the pleading in her voice.

"I have something to take care of . . . but I can meet you at seven o'clock, same place. Can you do that, Deja?"

She almost dropped her phone in shock. How did he know her name? How?! She'd used *67!

"Does seven at the same location work for you?" he repeated, sounding like the director at Donovan and Kaleisha's school. Which, of course, reminded her of the money.

"Do you have the money?" She used her haggle-over-fish no-nonsense tone.

"I do."

Okay. Three hours. That was doable even if she couldn't get a ride. "Yes. Seven o'clock. Same place."

"Good. Call me if there's trouble."

"Okay."

He hung up. She stayed there crouching, replaying the conversation in her head, puzzling over how he knew her name, fearing that meeting him was a mistake, fearing that she'd be late. Something rattled beside her, and she almost toppled over. No—it was just a big dewlap lizard. Man, was she freaked out.

But there was no time to freak out—she had to move. Had to and would.

A few hundred yards away, on the opposite side of the river, she spotted a small house set back in the woods, across the river. A cheerful orange cottage, a bicycle outside, a big basket on the front. A bird sang out. Was she in a Disney movie? This was almost too good to be true. A bike! Maybe she could borrow the bike! Deja thought about what the gondolier had said about sticking to the side of the river, but she couldn't take her eyes off that bike.

She tucked her phone, sandals, and her last Jamaican note and her last American twenty in the backpack, just in case. Holding it over her head, she waded carefully into the water—yikes, it was cold! At least this side branch seemed shallower than the larger tributary. She could make it across.

A jagged rock pitched her to the left, but she caught herself. For the most part, the riverbed was soft, mushy, her feet sinking an inch in. Then she went from waist high to neck high in a couple of steps. Not even halfway across! She wasn't tall enough. So much for changing luck. She'd have to swim. She was glad her mother had always insisted on weatherproof backpacks—the cash should be okay for a little while. Using it like a paddleboard, she pumped her legs and kicked hard.

Once across, clothes clinging like a second skin, Deja crouch-ran for the bicycle on the shady side of that perfectly kept cottage. The windows were tiny, like portholes on cruise ships, only square. Dainty hibiscus, roselle, and sandalwood flowers bordered most of the house. What a fairy-tale place!

She gave the bike a shake. Its paint-chipped frame seemed sturdy enough. The basket in the front, woven of plastic bands, seemed to be in good shape too. She squeezed the sides of the tires. Full. The grooves were worn, but all in all, she could ride this to Anchovy. Would twenty American do the trick?

"Is that somebody interested in stealing a bicycle?"

The singsong voice—even the cute laugh that ended her sentence—was nearly identical to her grandmother's. A voice she hadn't heard in eight years. Through a partially opened window, Deja saw a woman's face, lips pursed like a heart, one eye arched and the other practically closed, maybe even unusable.

"I . . . I . . . was actually hoping to rent it," Deja stuttered, flustered.

"Oh, my dear girl! You are wetter than a fish. We can talk about my bike after you come inside and dry yourself off. You'll catch your death out there." There was that laugh again, and a moment later the door opened.

The woman was shorter than Deja, with a hunch to her back, just like Deja's grandmother. Her dress, cornflower blue, from another era, was perfectly kept, as was the lace-trimmed apron around her waist. Deja blinked repeatedly. It was as if her grandmother had transported herself to this little house. "Come in, come in. Don't be shy."

Past the door, Deja was greeted by the leafy scent of pimento. The house seemed larger on the inside than on the outside. A cast-iron stove from way back sat majestically in the corner. By an oval table were two thick seats shaped almost like toadstools. The plank floors were covered with throw rugs intricately patterned with flowers and fruit trees.

Blinking yet again, this time to adjust to the dim light, Deja felt safe for the first time all day. She had a near-irresistible urge to curl up on the floor and nap like a cat.

The old woman angled her head, aiming her good eye at

Deja. "Come, come." Taking Deja's hand, her own supple and callus-free, she led her to the stove and the smell of fresh mint tea. She poured from an old kettle. "Here, this will do you good, dear."

"Thank you. I'm not that cold, though." But Deja smiled in gratitude, set the backpack on the floor, took the cup, and sipped the freshest mint tea she'd ever tasted.

"That's what you young people always say." The old woman next offered Deja a towel, as plush as any she'd ever felt.

"So, tell me all. Why are you swimming in my neck of the woods? There are only a handful of people who live out here, and I've never had the pleasure of meeting you before."

Deja felt a chill, probably from being soaked. "Um, I'm sorry. I'm dripping all over the place."

"Oh, don't worry about that. I was going to take a bucket and mop to the floor later on. You've just given me a head start."

The old woman put her at such ease, Deja almost started telling her the whole truth. But she knew better. "I'm on my way to Anchovy" was all she shared.

"And you're trying to swim there?" Her laugh was music.

"I . . . I have to meet someone, and I'm running late. And to be honest, I crossed the river to ask if I could borrow your bicycle. I—" Deja took another sip of tea. "I can pay for it. And I'll bring it back in a day or two."

"Money? Oh, I'm too old for that. What would I even buy?"

"It's no problem. Really, I can pay you."

The woman clasped her hands. "Oh, you're independently wealthy. Good for you."

Deja simply couldn't get over how similar this woman was to her grandmother. So she said so.

"Do you like the lady?"

Deja beamed. "Loved her."

"Oh, she's passed?" The woman made the sign of the cross. "I'm sure she's in the good place, waiting to give you some rum cake." Then she popped up with an "ohhh!" and was barely gone when she returned with a slice of rum cake on a plate with a rose design around the edges. "I don't like to brag, but I simply must when it comes to my rum cake."

Again, Deja wondered if she was in a fairy tale. Who just happened to have rum cake ready for guests? This woman, apparently. Deja was starving but felt she shouldn't impose. "I don't think so, but thank you."

The singing voice wouldn't be deterred. "Baby, you look like your belly a touch your back. Have some, and don't insult an old woman."

So Deja took the plate and a bite. The sugar, butter, rum, salt, and more rum were even more delicious than the tea. "This is fabulous, ma'am!" she exclaimed. "You should open up a bakery."

"I know." Her cheeks dimpled.

The cake was gone before Deja knew she'd even finished it, and somehow it left her feeling light, airy, unlike any rum cake she'd ever eaten. Had she stumbled into some kind of portal? How was any of this real? Again she wondered if this was a fairy tale. A magical cabin?

"Now, let me get you something so you can change out of those wet clothes."

"Oh, I couldn't possibly—"

"Oh, don't try to stop me. I can be a handful once I get going." The woman disappeared behind a door, only to return fairy-tale fast, holding up a beautiful green dress, belted around the middle. "It was my granddaughter's. I think you two are about the same size." Her other hand held a pair of shorts. "You might want to wear these underneath." She leaned closer. "For the draft." She laughed again.

"Really, I—"

"Yes, you can. I'll get you a bag for the wet clothes." She pointed. "The bathroom's right over there. Now, let's get you out of those wet things." She opened a creaky door, then closed it. "Oh, I'm so sorry. My unmentionables are in there drying."

Deja suppressed a smile. Her grandmother had also referred to her underwear as unmentionables. "I don't mind," she assured her.

"But I do." She swept a hand toward the door. "You can change in my bedroom."

Deja thanked her yet again, took a step toward the bedroom and stopped. "Oh, and the bicycle? May I borrow it?"

"Please, take it, young lady. I'd be glad for it to be useful."

"And I'll be glad to use it. But you *have* to let me pay you for it," Deja insisted.

"I might not have much time left in my life, so this may not sound like much of a threat . . . but over my dead body." That laugh again, so exactly like Deja's grandmother.

What was the point of arguing? She was just too damn cute. The dress? It was kinda cute too—about her size also. "Well, then, thank you again." Then Deja closed the door.

The bedroom had just one little window and barely enough room for a single bed and a dresser with a trifold mirror. She glanced at herself—whoa, she was a hot mess! She ran her hand along the wall to turn on a light to see better, but there was no switch, probably no electricity at all in this gnome house. But there was a half-burned candle and a box of oversize matches. Totally old-school.

"Um, ma'am, do you have a comb I can use?" Deja was asking, feeling the bureau top for one.

And that was when she heard a click.

Gabriel, Friday, 4:45 p.m.

G abriel trotted over a tuft of grass growing inside what had to be the tenth unfinished house, searching for Deja.

How the hell had she let herself get into a mess like this, anyway? They'd only hung out twice, but even so, nothing she'd said—not to mention how she doted on her siblings—pointed to *this* being her world. She might handle herself well, but no way was posse life her thing.

Finding nothing, Gabriel stepped back out onto the road and focused on the trail that led out of this creepy half-dead complex, the one Melville had just gone on a few minutes ago. He could still hear that crooked cop hitting the siren sporadically—each blare causing Gabriel's chest to tighten.

A motorcycle's rev announced Hammer's return. "Me no see hide nor hair, mon. Feel say, she well gone by now."

Gabriel veered toward the trail. "I have a feeling. Make we head for the trail. She's in trouble."

"*Trouble?* Damn it, mon. How yu can like di gyal so much? You no even know her."

Gabriel knew enough to know nothing would end well with Melville chasing her down. "Whatever. I'm going—"

"Bumboclot, G." Hammer fumed. "She's just another girl. And 'nuff a dem in Miami, you know?"

He didn't want 'nuff. He didn't want Miami or the hype of the Third Phase posse, either. Truth was, now he was crazy worried about Deja. The realization sent his brain shooting in every direction at once. It was so strange yet obvious, like after searching everywhere for your keys, you find them right in front of you. Deja had gotten under his skin.

"You done, Hammer?"

"Done? Me can talk fi days 'bout how you no know how fi be alone. Jeezum, you woulda bring home a skunk to keep yourself from lonely."

"Well, I have you, so I don't need a skunk."

"Me use deodorant, mon." But Hammer took a long sniff anyway, just to check.

Gabriel held up a hand—his phone was vibrating. Shit. *Teago*, he mouthed.

Hammer leaned back. "At least him no call *me* this time."

Gabriel forced himself to be upbeat—no telling what kind of mood the boss was in. "We're closing in on one person who might have the package," Gabriel immediately informed him.

"What the backside yu saying? Melville tell me you had the gyal who have my package and you let her get way."

Effing Melville! "It no go so, boss."

"How it go, then? Melville seem to be damn sure."

"He's assuming that, boss."

"Me take Melville's assuming over you not being sure eight days a week and five times on Sunday."

Damn, he was in a mood. Why the fuck hadn't he been this concerned over Jamal and Blood Moon? Gabriel suppressed a sigh. "We're on it, Boss. We're searching a housing complex now. It's cool."

"Cool? Me no even feel no breeze." Gabriel could literally hear him grind his teeth. "Now listen, Gabriel . . ."

Gabriel felt an instant chill. Teago never called him Gabriel, only *youth* or no name at all. *"Gabriel."*

"Once that package is found, me want yu to come back to Mobay. I need you to switch up the stash house."

Disbelief made Gabriel numb, unable to respond.

"Gabriel, yu listening?"

"Yeh, mon." Gabriel swallowed hard, spoke deliberately for Hammer to hear. "You want it switched up?"

Hammer's face turned to stone.

"It's this bloody state of emergency. A pain in my ass. But not to worry. It's just a precaution thing. If you find di package, give it to Melville, then call me when you're close to Mobay. I'll give you the details, okay?"

"Yeh, mon. No problem," Gabriel said, trying not to choke on his words.

"Good, good." Teago clicked off.

Hammer's eyes showed a mix of sympathy and fear. "Him ask yu to switch up the stash house?"

"He bumboclot did." The boss's voice was like his aunt's when she was drunk—*all nice* when she needed money to drink and score. *All nice.* Gabriel slumped back against a house as abandoned as he suddenly felt.

"We haffi' find dat package, mon." Hammer's voice went fierce. "And we haffi' tek Webber's offer."

Shit. Another country, another posse, another effing boss who could sell you out when it damn well pleased him? Gabriel slowly pushed off the wall, suddenly consumed by fury and disbelief. What the hell had he said or done to make Teago want to do this to him? He honestly couldn't come up with a single thing. What the hell!

"G . . . G . . . " Hammer got off the motorcycle, grasped Gabriel's shoulder.

Gabriel smacked his hand away.

"Come on, mon!" Now Hammer was shouting, shoving Gabriel square in the chest. Gabriel broke into a fighting stance, fists balled. But Hammer wasn't fazed. Maybe just . . . disappointed? Hammer'd *told* him, and he hadn't listened. Gabriel felt gravity coming for him, like everything inside his body was going faster than the outside world. Maybe he was even spinning in the opposite direction of the entire universe. It was *real*. Teago was setting him up. Shit.

"G, me going fi talk. Just listen, okay?" Hammer ran his hand over his head. "Listen hard, cuz then we need fi go after dat girl." This guy who didn't blink when gangbangers drew their guns, somehow knowing they wouldn't shoot, was now worried. He, no doubt, had Gabriel's back. The only person who did.

"Gabriel!" Hammer barked, getting him to focus. "Here's how

it's going to go. We going fi get di package, then call Webber to get us on a boat out of di country, zeen?"

Yes, Gabriel understood, just suddenly didn't have the energy to even nod.

"We going to Miami, mon," Hammer insisted.

Gabriel had only been to Kingston once and had never set foot out of the country. "Maybe."

"More than maybe. Listen, G, you know me. Me no mek no move unless me sure. We get in with Third Phase posse and we set. You know how di boss start you as ground soldier fi spy pon buyers and police, *then* you haffi' work up to overseer, and *then* region chief? Damn it, mon, we still not even region chiefs." He picked up a rock and chucked it. "No more *waiting*, mon. We need fi make this move even if Teago wasn't trying fi set you up."

Gabriel replayed their conversation with Webber from this morning. Right. "No more waiting," he said at last, once more eyeing the trail into the bush. He wasn't sure where it led. He wasn't sure about anything anymore. Except that Hammer was worried about him, and he was worried about Deja.

"Open the door! What are you doing! Open it!" Ramming her shoulder into the wood, Deja was too angry to care about the pain. She kept ramming. *They might carry two faces under one hat.* Her mother's warning, saying that some people were one thing while acting like another. Stupid, stupid, stupid. How could she have been taken in by this old woman? How could she have been so completely freaking duped? She knew better—she *knew*. And what did the woman plan on doing, anyway? She had to be sixty! Was she going to try to kidnap Deja? Hurt her? Deja stopped ramming and put an ear up to the door. Not a creak of a floorboard, not a squeak of the door, not a peep.

Calm down and think. Think. The window. Of course. Her knee slammed the side of the bed, a wood hard as concrete. Fury made her kick it. Desperation made her forget the instant pain and hobble over to the tiny porthole-like window, similar to the one in the front of the house. Donovan couldn't even wiggle through that. She peered through the clouded glass; no one was out there. She didn't want to yell for help—what if Gabriel or the police were around? Maybe the old bat had henchmen or even evil dwarves to do her bidding. Why the hell not!

Deja sank onto the edge of the bed, rubbing her big toe, then noticed again the matchbox and the half-burned candle. A moment later she had the candle lit and was eyeing the lock to the door—it was a simple one. She could pick it like the one on her bedroom door. Kaleisha, when she was little, would storm in there when she was mad about something and lock herself in. Deja just needed something long and thin and straight.

Searching the top of the bureau, she opened a tin box. It was filled with colorful ribbons, nothing else. She yanked open drawer after drawer filled with old clothes and linens. Then she saw a small drawer at the top right corner.

The handle was stuck. But with one huge pull, wood whined against wood and it opened. She felt through it, feeling frantic—a hair clip, a rag, and then a fingernail file. Ah! She pressed the tip against her palm. It was dullish, but it might do the trick.

Jiggling, twisting, and turning, nothing worked. Gah! She turned the file hard, and it snapped. Shit! She dug back into the drawer. There was a thin comb. Too flimsy. Tossing it on the ground, she glared at the lock.

Wait. Whoa! How was she only just remembering this? Back in an intro to hotel management class, they'd watched a long, boring video about security. The only interesting part was when they showed some of the different ways people had broken into rooms in hotels and guest houses. Maybe the video wasn't so useless after all. She snatched up the comb and sized up the lock's metal frame on the doorway opposite the lock. Buoyed by a slight hope, she slid the comb's needles between the doorjamb and the lock and pulled. The lock gave, just a little.

She took a slow breath and tried again, this time pulling up on the handle. As she did, the lock moved. Then *click. Oh my God.* Saying a quick prayer, she eased the door open, carefully, carefully. She listened. Nothing. So she crept out, pausing, listening. Still nothing.

The woman was gone. And so was Deja's backpack! The old hag! Deja scooped up her sandals and sprinted out the door. Squinting in the brightness, she spotted a path and ran to it, hugging to the river. Soon her legs were burning. But she pressed on, rounded a bend. And just ahead, pedaling with all she had, which didn't seem like much, was the old woman. Thank God it was uphill. Thank God!

Deja raced forward, driven by anger, as much at herself as toward the old woman. At the next curve, Deja lunged, grabbing the woman's skirt and pulling. The old woman screeched with fright, the bike pitched to the side, and the backpack rolled out of the basket.

Deja lunged once more, grabbing a strap of the backpack just as the old woman did. Deja yanked with all she had and tore it away from her. "This is mine!"

The woman's face was full of scorn. "I saw what was in it. Do *you* know what to do with all that money?"

"Me nah joke with you," Deja seethed.

The old woman narrowed her one good eye. "I know people, you know?"

Deja grunted. "*You* know people?" What did that even mean?

"Everybody in Jamdown knows people these days, girl." Then she added in a hush, "I can get you protection from whoever is after you for this."

"Protection? From *you*, maybe!" The old bat probably did know somebody, especially given how she herself was clearly criminally minded. "I can't believe you just locked me up in that room. What the hell!"

The woman now had a hand on her chest, her face flushed. Then she pulled out that nicey-nice voice again. "Hope you don't blame me. When I looked into your backpack to see what you were really up to, well—not too many chances like this left in my life. Who knows. I could have finally gone to Hawaii."

Deja slipped her backpack's straps over her shoulders, righted the bike, and wheeled it backward. "Sorry to mess with your travel plans." She reached into a side compartment of the backpack. Her last Jamaican bill, a thousand-dollar note, was still there. She slipped it out and flicked it to the ground. "Can't help you with Hawaii, but that's for the bike."

The old woman surveyed the bill, then Deja. "It's worth more than that."

This woman! "I took something off for the aggravation." Deja straddled the bike and started pedaling. Once she felt far enough away, she peeked over her shoulder.

And the old woman was busy tucking the bill into her bra.

Just like her grandma would have done.

Five minutes later, Deja's eyes were stinging with sweat. She'd always prided herself on being the non-perspiring type, even when doing suicide drills in netball practice, a trait she and her mother shared. But the incline here was ridiculous—she wasn't any Tour de France cyclist. It wasn't far to the top, but the strain was kicking her butt. Still, she pedaled and pedaled, hoping the path would empty onto a back road or something. And at last, it did. Thank God. She knew where she was now. An old pothole-filled route that led to the bird sanctuary that Kaleisha was obsessed with. In Anchovy.

Her phone read 5:45. She could still make it to see Webber. She just had to keep going.

Her eyes swept over the green valley hundreds of feet below, past the A1, all the way to the turquoise ocean, where three massive cruise ships sat like shiny new toys. Far away—and yet so inviting. They called to her, like they always did. Ships like those were what had led her to the micro cruise line idea. It could work. It could. She kept pumping, the road no easier to navigate than a dirt path because of all the potholes. Sweat beaded down her back. She kept glancing at the ships. Dark clouds were rolling in, and a stiff breeze carried a hint of rain, cooling, at least.

But her anger—at herself—was still hot. She should have been on guard, but she'd fallen for the old bat's lies. And damn, she was so tired. And another incline loomed before her. What if she couldn't make it up this one? What if she couldn't get this damn money to Webber?

Nope. She wasn't going to think that, nope, nope, nope. Head down, she pushed at the pedals as hard as she could, trying to center her mind. She stole another glance at the cruise ships. Had she heard a horn? A call? She peeked up. Holy shit! She squeezed the brakes as hard as she could, her heart slamming into her rib cage. Not ten feet in front of her was a sheer drop-off, the road jagging into a hairpin turn. And she was heading straight for it. Rocks and more rocks waiting below. *Please, please, please stop.* The brakes squealed. And at last . . . just as she was bracing to force the bike to the ground, it skidded to a halt. Shaking, Deja got off the bike, laid it on the dirt, and collapsed beside it. She could have died. And no one would know. No one would ever find her. What had she done? She looked up blearily and saw the three ships.

Everything happens for a reason, her mother always said. But this?

Hot tears began to roll down her cheeks. Straleen's and Lila's warnings were echoing in her head. What was she doing this for? What made her think for one minute that she could trust this Webber guy? She'd been duped by an *old lady*!

And was the guy on the boat even an agent? Was Webber? He knew her name! So he might know where she lived! How could she have put Kaleisha and Donovan in so much danger?

Just then a large flatbed truck bounced its way up the wiggly road, black smoke belching from the muffler, the back loaded with bricks. The driver puckered his lips and blew Deja a kiss as he eased the truck around the bend. Idiot. She hated how some men acted when nobody was watching them. What if Webber acted crazy too?

At the same time, she also hated giving up. She'd come this far, too damn far to turn back. Plus, Gabriel. She could hardly understand what he was doing! He must be after the drug money too. It had to all be posse business. She had to get to Webber. There was no other option.

She got back on the bike, laser-focused on the road this time. A plop of rain landed on the steamy pavement in front of her, and moments later fat drops pinged against her back. Curtains of rain drew across the horizon. She started to laugh, a nervous, exhausted laugh, a laugh she was afraid she might not be able to stop. Because, what next? She wouldn't have been surprised if a giant eagle swooped down singing Bob Marley's "Three Little Birds" while trying to slice her to ribbons with its talons. She kept pedaling.

At last she reached the top of the hill. Like a ribbon, the main road led straight to downtown Anchovy: a strip of stores, bars, a few of two-story office buildings, and the old train station. She allowed herself a thread of relief, then pushed off and glided down the hill, swerving only to avoid potholes. As abruptly as it had started, the rain stopped, and the temperature, sun, and humidity were starting to work their way again. But the wind was cool on her face as she sped downhill. She began to plan. She would hide the backpack before she reached town. That way, if Webber *did* pull something crazy, she could bargain for her life. It would be plain stupid to trust him. And no way was she going to be plain stupid twice in one day.

A half mile outside of town, Deja bumped the bike into a little opening in the bush, where a couple of mangy goats were grazing in a field surrounded by thick logwood and allspice trees. Under a ficus bush, beneath one of the allspice trees, she tucked the backpack and took out her phone to check the time. One percent charge left! The kids! Dang, she should have called a while ago!

And, of freakin' course, as she was punching in her uncle's number, the phone went dead. She gawked at the screen in disbelief.

One of the goats bleated. And suddenly both were bleating. Was someone coming? A van, dance-hall booming, sped by. But that was all.

Phone or no, she had to keep moving. Deja shoved the backpack deeper into the bush. "Third tree from the right," she chanted over and over as she got back on the road, already coming up with the next plan.

Gabriel, Friday, 6:00 p.m.

ammer's motorcycle was definitely not made for pot-hole-strewn dirt roads like Melville's jeep was. Gabriel could barely hang on as they pitched and bounced through the wood. He kept barking at Hammer to watch out for recesses and hollows. Hammer claimed to have seen them all but bumped over half of them anyway, all the while cursing the damage being done to his beloved bike. Winding deeper into the forest, Gabriel continually scoured the area for Melville. At one point they'd spotted his jeep on a trail near the river. Gabriel hoped with all his soul that Melville wouldn't find Deja back there. She had to be so scared! He at least had Hammer; he was lucky to have a friend like him. He'd stuck with him through so much. *Waiting for better to come.*

Hammer pulled to an unexpected standstill, yanking Gabriel out of his thoughts. "Wha' gwan?" he asked.

"Fork in di road, mon." Hammer nodded ahead. "Feel we should go right."

Gabriel gave the suggestion a chance, though he'd already decided against it. "No, mon, that lead back to the river, no?"

Hammer looked puzzled. "Wha' wrong with that?"

"She's not doubling back." Not a doubt in his mind.

"Why not? Is that *me* would do." Hammer revved the engine.

"She not you, mon. She's not no posse girl."

Something big thrashed through the leaves above them. They instantly covered their heads as it thumped to the ground and exploded. An overripe breadfruit. A cosmic hint that they should get moving?

But Hammer went on. "You no *know* that. She might just be some delivery girl."

"Nooo, mon."

"You no know fi sure." Hammer was sounding pissed.

"I do . . . ninety-nine percent . . . ," Gabriel insisted anyway.

Hammer twisted around. "You and your ninety-nine percent gonna make her get way."

"Come on, mon, try the left."

But Hammer resisted. "No, we going right, mon."

A bird squawked and . . . what? Clapping? Was he hearing clapping? Gabriel watched in disbelief as an old woman pushed through the trees, coming slowly toward them.

Hammer stood. "Bumboclot, what di hell is this?"

"Helloooo!" The old woman clapped her hands again to get their attention, like old people always did. Short, wearing a faded blue frock, one eye almost closed, she looked like she was somebody's grandmother who'd just baked a rum cake.

"You're searching for her, aren't you?"

Gabriel gaped. Could she be . . . Deja's grandmother? No way.

He and Hammer looked wildly in every direction. Was this some kind of setup?

"Hello! Did you hear me? You're looking for that girl, right?" She stopped, hand to her chest, a few feet away. "The one with the backpack?"

Gabriel studied the woman, the fierceness in her eye, the grandmotherly clothes she wore. "You seen her?"

She raised her chin imperiously. "Oh, I certainly did, young man."

"Okay, where she deh?" Hammer asked, his tone sharp, clearly not taken in by her harmless appearance.

"She went that way." The old woman pointed to the hills. "That road there. Said she was heading to Anchovy."

Hammer rubbed his chin. "Is what she look like?"

"You think I'm lying? Well, I am not lying." She propped a hand on her hip. "Short. pretty." She tilted her head. "But me know you want that backpack, no true?"

Gabriel believed her but wasn't taking any chances. "What do you know about the backpack?"

"Don't try to play me, young man."

Gabriel felt itchy. The old woman definitely knew Deja somehow, but still— "And why exactly are you telling us all this?" he had to ask.

She narrowed her eye. "Let's just call it payback."

Deja, Friday, 6:45 p.m.

The center of Anchovy was bathed in the hot pink of the setting sun. As Deja neared it, the hum of voices, car horns, and the lilt of reggae music grew—Sean Paul's hit, "Temperature," thumping from a car radio. Then she passed a store, then the open door of a butcher shop. She followed a minivan so packed with people, it sat low on its tires. Two schoolchildren still in their brown-and-white uniforms strolled into a supermarket, bringing thoughts of Kaleisha and Donovan, probably—hopefully—in Montego Bay at the Hot Time Grill restaurant or some other place, eating till their little bellies were full. But she was supposed to meet them at six! They must be getting worried. She gnawed at her lower lip. The minivan turned onto a side street, and Deja rode harder through its trail of smoke.

On the next block, her breath caught as she spotted a motorcycle coming from the other direction. But no—wrong color. Phew. She passed a money store. Three men in mesh marina shirts and fancy torn jeans talking with a policeman. She turned her head away as she pedaled fast. Then at the next corner . . . a cow. A skinny cow, just like the one she'd dreamed about, standing in the middle of the road, nobody paying any attention to it at all. Was she the only one who saw it? Was she . . . hallucinating? Straleen had said her cow dream was an omen. Shit.

She zagged around the cow, and minutes later she was near the edge of town, praying Webber would be waiting. The old train stop, a decaying boarded-up building, surrounded by grass grown wild, was just ahead. And, beyond that, the restaurant, a couple of SUVs parked nearby. Deja felt weak with relief. At a table out front, a man with a short, neat Afro, wearing sunglasses and a white linen shirt, leaned back in his chair, a bottle of Red Stripe sitting in front of him like he was on vacation. She was suddenly aware of how thirsty she was—her mouth thick with dust and exhaust fumes. The next table over was empty, but the bar door was open, a remix of Koffee's dance-hall song "Pull Up" pumping.

A flock of vireo birds squawked and took flight when Deja's bike tires crunched the sandy gravel. The guy—Webber, had to be; he resembled his picture—waved like they were old friends or something. His calm was a good thing, wasn't it? Even so, her hands trembled as she lowered the kickstand. *Play it cool. Stay alert. Keep your guard up.* She repeated this mantra over and over as she approached the table.

All chill, he extended his palm up to the chair opposite his like this was his house. "Deja, have a seat. Want something to drink?"

She'd never been this thirsty, but there was no way she was going to drink anything—not here, not now. "No. Thanks," she added, almost as an afterthought. She sat. Folded her hands on her lap. Then decided she should assert herself, so she scooted the chair closer to the table, propped up her elbows on the worn wood, and intertwined her fingers.

She figured he would ask why she hadn't brought the cash.

But "Why didn't you *take* the money?" was his question.

Whoa—she hadn't expected *that*. "It wasn't mine to take."

"Good answer," Webber said, as if genuinely pleased. "So, you ran into some trouble on the way?" He glanced at his watch. Who wore watches anymore? That was an old-man thing. Then she recalled that Minister Powell wore one too, and he wasn't that old.

"So, how does this work?" she countered in her best business voice.

He reached behind his head, cradled it like he was some sort of boss. "Tell me about Gonzalez."

The very question evoked the image of the blood on the deck, but she pushed it away. "Why?"

"Most people don't care . . . about others, I mean." He inhaled and made a show of doing it. "They would have taken my money and wouldn't have bothered to lift a finger to help the man."

A strange sensation came over her, a warning of bad things to come, so she spun around, looking up and down the street behind her.

"I'm not running any game here, Deja," he said evenly as she ascertained that there was no one, just mangy cows in the field across the street.

But when she turned back, he was holding a handgun, pointing the barrel to the sky. "And if anyone tries to steal your bike, I got you covered." He smiled and put the gun on the chair next to him. And huh—he had a neck tattoo—a barcode.

Instant alarm bells. Did agents have neck tattoos? Shouldn't he have had a holster? Wasn't that how agents carried weapons? Deja's heartbeat was running faster than any sprinter's. Why show her the gun? If he wanted to kill her, he could, so why the show of force? To threaten her? Chill, chill, she had to chill.

"Did you bring the money?" she asked.

"I did." He leaned forward. "Did *you* bring the money?"

Deja could only nod.

"And . . . you left it somewhere nearby to be safe, I'm guessing?"

Deja simply blinked, puzzling over her next move as *he* seemed to know them all.

"Here, I'll show mine first." He reached down, then laid a black plastic bag with handles, the thick kind she'd use sometimes to keep fish in, on the table and opened the top. Stacked inside were neat bundles of American bills, not nearly as many as she had in the backpack, but a lot. The second time she was seeing more money than she'd ever seen before.

Deja tried to control her breathing. "How do I know you won't take your gun and shoot me once I get you the backpack?"

He gave half a smile like it was a good question. "Deja, I don't need a gun to kill you—I mean, if I were here to do that."

He glanced toward downtown. "I appreciate how thoughtful you were about Gonzalez." His eyes expressed something, like he was tired or had seen a lot of shit. "Emergency services got in touch with my people when someone who I presume to be you, got in touch with them. It was you, wasn't it?"

Deja swallowed hard, wondering if her answer would get her in trouble. But at last, she gave up thinking and offered Webber a slight nod.

"Thought so." He became even more watchful. "If you hadn't done that, I couldn't have sent a team there to recover the body and the drugs."

Ears ringing, Deja could only picture Gonzales's pallid lips. That poor guy.

If she'd gotten to him earlier . . . Maybe if she'd checked the first time she'd seen his arm dangling over the side? Maybe? The guilt she'd felt leaving the boat came back in a rush.

Tree frogs—or was it crickets?—started up their sunset serenade. Webber's eyes searched hers. "All this had to be hard on you."

He didn't know the half of it . . . or maybe he did?

"But as I said, I appreciate it." He aimed his chin at the bag. "That's why I made sure to secure your cash." He paused for a moment as if making a note to himself. "Have to remember to write that up later."

"Write up? What?" What was he talking about? He was reading her eyes, which probably meant he was seeing her panic. Damn it.

"Oh, sorry. Department rules state that I can only give you

this cash in exchange for information. Now, what's really transpiring here is that I'm rewarding you for being a decent human being in regard to Gonzalez. Why? Because it's nice not to have to deal with scum for once." He poked at something on the table, then flicked it away. "So, for that and other reasons that I'm not at liberty to mention, I have your fifteen K like I promised you, and now I need that five hundred K that Gonzalez entrusted to you to bring to me."

She mouthed the number. It was really that much! Her eyes swept over the cash in the plastic bag. "How do I know *that's* not marked?"

"You're just going to have to trust me." Webber intertwined his long fingers, cracked his knuckles. "See, bills aren't really 'marked.' I mean they could be, but all we do is write down the serial numbers. Then we can trace them when they surface. If a criminal gets caught with the marked cash, we question him or *her* about the money to get more information. If the marked cash comes from a *legal* entity, like some store that never has any customers in it, we can question the owners—maybe they're part of a money-laundering scheme or maybe they just know who gave them the marked bills. Lots of ways to skin a snake."

"Thought the saying was skin a cat?"

"I like cats." He raised a shoulder. "No reason to skin *them*."

She wanted to laugh but forced herself to stay on point. "But how do I know they're not fake, then?" Deja remembered the fish women complaining when they'd gotten a fake bill now and again.

"Counterfeit? Still don't trust me, eh? Good. Makes me trust you more." He took a bill from a bundle. "Two ways. Now listen up. First way . . ." He took a slender flashlight out of his pocket. "I put this beam up to the bill, and you'll see a holograph of the face image on the bill." He clicked the light on.

Yep, she saw the face. The proof reminded her somehow of chem lab. The result of the experiment left no more questions. But she had to wrap this up. The kids were in Mobay. Somewhere.

"Want to know the second way?" Webber asked.

"No."

"No?" He actually seemed surprised.

"I wouldn't know if you were making this up, anyway," she said with a shrug.

"You could google it. You have a phone, don't you?"

"Battery's dead." She held his gaze.

"Well, with all this cash, you can get one with better battery life." He tapped the bag like a salesman. "So, want me to come with you and get the money?"

Her chest instantly tightened. "No, I'll get it."

"Thought you'd feel that way." The bag crunched as he folded it up and started to pull it back.

"Hold on. Can I look inside again?"

"Go right ahead." He pushed it back toward her.

Deja held the bag in her lap and sifted through the bands of money. She figured she should check the way the bills looked and how they felt. Each hundred-dollar bill seemed to be the same.

"Just so you know, that other way I was talking about? If you examine the bills through a light, you'll see a thin vertical strip with text that spells out the note's denomination." He flicked his hand. "Just so you know . . ."

Deja put the bag back on the table and stood. "I'll be back in about fifteen—no, maybe twenty—minutes."

He leaned close. "You shouldn't tell me or anyone else stuff like that in a deal like this. I could use that information to triangulate your whereabouts, maybe signal somebody I have waiting nearby to knock you off." Then he grinned, perfect white teeth gleaming.

That unbalanced feeling again. He was like one of those guys Lila liked to date: hot one minute and cold the next—borderline abusive, then showering her with adoration. Well, Webber had made a mistake here. She was over how he was playing with her. "You just drink your beer, and I'll be back soon."

"Oh, this?" With a sliver of a smile at the side of his mouth, he tapped a fingernail against the bottle, making a clinking sound. "Not mine. It was here when I got here. Didn't touch it, because somebody might come back for it. Like how I won't touch this cash till *you* come back for it." He raised his hand, a gesture for Deja to wait as he reached under the table for who knew what. Then he lifted . . . the leather briefcase and put it on the table, the one she'd ditched on the shore before transferring the money into the burlap bags she'd bought from Mrs. Waul. He laid it on the table.

"How?" The moment she asked, it struck her that she'd been watched, maybe all along.

"A tracker's built into it." He tapped the case. "Pretty smart of you to discard it. Made me suspicious of you at first."

"Why'd you trust me, then? Because of Gonzalez?"

"That, and my team asked around. Got your name pretty easily. Funny how people will talk when the person you're asking about isn't in a posse." He sighed. "Otherwise, it would take a crowbar to open their lips."

So that was how he knew her name. "Am I okay?"

He laid the case flat, leaned his elbows on it. "With me? Yes. We're the good guys. I wanted you to know, so when you ride off to go get the money, you won't get scared and do something crazy like run away."

After all she'd been through? "Run away?"

"Pressure does things to people in situations like this. Lord knows I've seen it." He looked her straight in the eye. "I'll be right here."

It wasn't that he was one step ahead. He could have been four paces to her right or high above in a tree. It was like she was playing a game of chess only he knew how to win. This guy was something else.

She rode as quickly as she could; if she couldn't beat the dark, she'd never find the backpack. Back at the grove of allspice trees, with crickets and frogs in full chorus, the smell of pimento reminding her of that nasty old woman's cottage, Deja trembled as she ran for the bush. *Please be there. Please be there!* The goats were gone, but thankfully the backpack was not.

Riding back through the thickness of the humidity and night's onset, the dance-hall reggae from the stores and cars, fewer now, seemed like echoes. The motorcycle she'd seen was now parked; she felt even more relief that it wasn't the one that Gabriel had been on. And the cow wasn't in the middle of the road and hadn't been when she'd ridden back out to the allspice grove. Had it even been there in the first place? Pressure did this to people, Webber had said. Like make them see imaginary cows? Maybe??

The trip back to the restaurant seemed so much shorter this time, over practically in a blink, maybe because she knew more of what to expect. But time quickly expanded when she exchanged the bag of $500,000 American for the one with her reward of $15,000. The cash might be marked or fake—or worse, not even in there, replaced with blank sheets of paper. But if the cash turned out to be real, there'd be other problems; where could she hide it all? She didn't have a bank account. Her mother did, but the teller would have major questions. Also, Webber probably already knew where she lived and maybe would come wanting the money back.

Webber instructed her to lower the bag under the table and check it. As he did likewise, relief came to Deja in a trickle, the tension leaving her arms when she saw that her cash was all there, hopefully unmarked and real. Sitting up straight, the bag now in her lap, she watched Webber closing the backpack. Fifteen thousand dollars! Fifteen thousand American dollars! She fought the urge to scream for joy, as well as the one to make another examination of the $15,000. Checking it again would be only paranoia. Then again, Uncle liked to joke that just because you're paranoid, it doesn't mean they're not out to get you.

Webber hooked a backpack strap over his shoulder. "Again, thanks for what you've done. You probably don't know it, but you've done a lot for your country."

Was he calling her a hero? No way. She felt more like a fugitive. And, reaching for her phone, she thought she was also a terrible big sister since she hadn't called her uncle, who must be out of his tree sick about where she was.

Webber stood, took out a set of keys, and clicked. The lights of an SUV parked nearby blinked. "Can I drop you somewhere?"

Her heart started thumping. "No." She remembered to be kind. "Thank you."

"Still don't trust me. Understandable." He pursed his lips, then asked, "What're you going to do from here? It's nearly dark."

As if she needed any urging to think about her uncle and the kids. "I'll be okay," she said, now desperate to get to Montego Bay and her family.

"Be careful." He made to say more but stopped.

She watched the SUV leave, and once she could no longer see the taillights, she yanked out her phone. Damn it. She'd forgotten it was dead. Tucking the bag tightly under her arm, she walked her bike over to the entrance of the restaurant and peeked inside. Empty, except for a man and woman talking at a table near the bar. A short, stocky woman wearing an apron marched out of the kitchen and toward her.

Deja glanced over her shoulder, then walked inside. "Hello. Is there somewhere I could charge my phone?"

The woman spoke in a monotone. "You not eating anything?"

She should leave as soon as her phone was charged, but she

was starving. As Donovan would say, her belly was touching her back. "Yes, you have oxtail?"

"The dinner or side order?"

"Dinner."

"Mashed or rice 'n' peas?"

She was getting hungrier with each word. "Rice 'n' peas."

"Green beans or lemon broccoli?"

"Green beans." Deja gestured to the bike. "I don't want to leave it outside."

The woman jutted her chin, motioning to the wall near the window. "You can lean it over thereso."

Deja held up her phone. "And can I charge my phone?"

The woman widened her eyes as if tired of all the things Deja was asking for.

Deja started nodding. "It's been a long day."

The woman's expression didn't change as she extended her hand. "Me can charge it behind di counter."

As Deja handed it over, the woman asked crankily, "Is what else you want?"

Deja almost laughed. "Nothing, thank you."

"Soon come." Slippers swishing across the floor, she made her way toward the kitchen.

Deja wheeled the bike to the wall, hoping the woman would be quick, especially because "soon come" rarely meant *soon*.

Gabriel, Friday, 8:00 p.m.

They rode at a crab's pace toward the old train station, following up on what a man had told them about seeing a girl on a bicycle that fit Deja's description. They'd covered just about every part of town, stopping at stores, houses, and farms, and if this last search wasn't successful, he didn't know what to do.

Hammer turned his head. "Me wonder if that old woman back in di woods was lying to us."

Gabriel didn't think so. Her voice was too steady, and she didn't do that too-long-stare thing people do when trying to convince someone of something. "Maybe, but maybe not. So let's check di restaurant down the road there. Last place, mon."

"What? Me no see no bike."

There wasn't much at this end of town, anyway. "Yeah, maybe you're right."

"You know what, though?" Hammer's voice turned pleading. "Me well hungry. You must be hungry too."

"Hammer, it's nearly dark—we need to find her."

"Mon, if me dead fi hungry, me can't find nobody."

Gabriel had to admit, he was pretty hungry too. Still, he had to find her. "Okay, let's check out this place, circle around town one last time, and if we don't find her, we come back and get something to eat."

Hammer grumbled but parked across the street from the restaurant. Gabriel hopped off the bike and walked over to a man with a salt-and-pepper beard sitting outside at a table drinking a Dragon Stout beer.

"Excuse. Me wonder if you've seen a girl on a bike?" He held out his hand to approximate Deja's height. "About this tall."

The man pursed his lips, bobbed his head as if trying to remember. "No, mon."

"You sure?"

The man nodded.

"Okay. Thank you." Gabriel turned to leave, but Hammer had suddenly joined him.

Hammer spoke quickly, before Gabriel could object. "Hungry have me, mon." He strode right past Gabriel into the restaurant.

Well, hungry definitely had *him*, too. Maybe it was all a lost cause anyway. But once inside, Gabriel looked, then looked again—no way. No. Way. There was a blue bicycle leaning against the wall by a window. Slowly, he gave the restaurant the once-over. There was a couple eating at a table by the bar. Then . . . dazed in a way that made him unsure of what he was seeing, he started toward the table in the corner where a girl sat, her back to him. The closer he got, the surer he was. She had just finished

spooning rice into her mouth when she must have sensed someone behind her, because she turned and stopped chewing.

Alarmed by the fright in her eyes, he quickly said, "Deja,
I just want to talk." He hoped she could see how real he was
being with her.

As he eased himself into the seat across from her, she jerked
away. Her eyes flicked toward something on the floor, maybe the
backpack, then back up to him.

Gabriel repeated, "Talk. That's all."

Hammer pulled a chair away from the table across from
them, the legs scraping the floor. When he sat, Gabriel could see
him mouth, *Bumboclot!*

"Just talk, Deja," Gabriel said once more.

At last she swallowed her food. "You keep saying that!" Her
voice was angry. "What the hell do you want?"

Hammer motioned for calm. "Look, you haffi' keep you voice
down."

Deja folded both arms. "No! I want to know what you two
are doing! Why are you stalking me?"

"Deja—" Gabriel paused. He got it. He'd be pissed too. "Just
give me a minute. One minute, please?"

She blinked hard. But she didn't say no. Good enough.

But then a short woman wearing an apron marched out of
the kitchen and stopped at the table. "Everything all right?"

Gabriel leaned closer to Deja, held up one finger, and
mouthed, *One minute.*

Deja's lips went tight, deciding, then to Gabriel's utter relief,
said, "No problem."

As the woman continued to eyeball them, a pot in the kitchen clanked, and the couple by the bar laughed at something. Gabriel wondered what to do if this became a scene.

At last the woman asked Hammer, "You eating?"

"Yes, yes. Is what you have tonight?"

She pointed at the chalkboard behind the register, where the dishes and their prices were handwritten. Hammer looked from it to Deja's plate, then to the woman. "Make me have di oxtail."

She turned to Gabriel, raised an eyebrow expectantly.

He'd lost his appetite. "I'm good."

"No, mon, you haffi' eat," Hammer insisted.

"Hammer, I'm good. I'm good," he said in a voice as irritated-sounding as he felt.

Hammer wouldn't back down. "You going fi hungry later on."

Okay, fine. He was probably right. And he'd just keep nagging otherwise. "You have jerk chicken?" Gabriel asked.

"Yes. Rice or mashed?" she asked next, boredom apparent.

"Rice."

"Lemon broccoli or green bean?"

"Green bean."

Seemingly finished, the woman stood for a moment, clearly trying to figure out what was going on . . . then left.

Deja was glaring at him with a fury that was piercing. "Okay, then. Spit it out. You get one minute."

The girl was fierce. "Um, I'm wondering what you're doing with that package."

She hesitated like she was confused. It sure didn't seem like she knew what a package was.

Hammer must have noticed the hesitation as well, because he said to Deja, "You're not in no posse, are you?"

Her shoulders hiked. "Posse? What? No. Are you crazy?"

Gabriel sucked in a deep breath. This was so fucked up. "Deja, so here's the truth: the drugs inside that backpack are part of a drop, um, a deal, one that went bad—" He pictured Blood Moon and Jamal lying on the beach. He and Hammer could easily end up the same way. Deja too! "Some people were killed, and—"

"Wait? What?" She gaped at him like she couldn't believe what he'd just said. "Drugs? There weren't any drugs."

"Is what you saying?" Hammer's turn to be confused.

Gabriel scratched at his locs. "Deja, is what you mean, there's no drugs?"

"There weren't." She started to say more but stopped herself, probably afraid to tell them what there *was*.

Hammer narrowed his eyes. "You no haffi' make this so hard, mon."

"Hammer, chill," Gabriel hushed him. To Deja, as calmly as he could, he asked, "Deja, what do you mean 'weren't'?"

She avoided his eyes, didn't answer. His brain churned into overdrive. If there *weren't* any drugs . . . then did she have the drop money? And there was only one way he could think of that led to her having that money. "Deja, do you have the drop money?"

She shook her head hard, then whispered furiously, "Why did you kill him?"

What the hell was she talking about? "Kill who?"

"Stop with the games, Gabriel. You told me yourself—you're in a posse. Isn't that what you do? Kill people?"

Hammer lurched forward, hissed, "We no kill nobody."

"Oh?" Deja kept nodding as if mocking him. "And the man on the boat. He just killed himself, then?"

Gabriel had this warped feeling that everyone was talking about something different—none of this made sense. "Deja, we're a little bit confused. There wasn't anybody on the boat when we got there."

"But you saw him? The pilot of the boat?" Hammer's questions tumbled over Gabriel's.

Deja shut her eyes and let out a low breath. Now Gabriel was sure that she knew more than she was letting on. Much more. "Deja, I don't know how you got mixed up in this, but you're going to have to talk to us. And we need that backpack." He swallowed. "If not . . . *we're* dead."

"G, me no see no backpack," Hammer said uneasily.

In a flash, Gabriel was off his chair and in a squat, looking under the table.

Just as quickly, Deja snatched up a plastic bag, too small to hold the drugs or drop cash, from the floor. She cradled it in her lap. "This isn't yours."

"What's in it?" Hammer demanded.

"It's not any of your business."

"Deja," Gabriel urged, reaching for her arm. But Hammer made a grab for the bag.

Deja whipped it away from him and sprang back, chin set as if she was ready to fight. "I gave the backpack to the agent. And you better not try anything. . . . He's . . . he's coming back soon. Any minute. And he has people with him."

Gabriel shot Hammer a look. In an instant, Hammer was at the door, head on a swivel. After a moment, he gestured that it was all clear.

Gabriel rested his hand on his gun in case, regardless. "What agent, Deja?"

She glanced from the door to Gabriel, to Hammer, who came back, confirming, "No see nobody."

"Deja? Who is this agent? And why did you give him the backpack?" Desperation soared. "Deja, you don't get how important this is." Brushing sweat off his forehead, he prayed for her to understand. "We . . . we're in a trouble. A lot. My boss . . . he's going to kill us. And we need that backpack. We need it to save our lives. I'm not lying to you. I swear. We're . . . dead without it."

Deja's eyes roamed his face, searching.

"Please."

At last Deja said, "I gave it to a man named Webber. That's all I know." Her eyes practically shot fire. "And you better not try anything. He'll be back."

Deja knew Webber? Gabriel's brain was officially exploding. Was *she* an agent? No way. She couldn't be. "Deja, how do you know Webber?"

She eyed them both as if deciding whether she'd tell them, then licked her lips. "He's who the agent on the boat asked me to deliver the money to."

Hammer flat-out gaped at her. "Wait deh, mon. The boat pilot was an agent too?"

This time she didn't hesitate. "Yes. DEA."

"Deja, can you describe Webber?"

And now she shrugged. "Thin, a little taller than you, short Afro, white shirt, real particular . . ." She paused, maybe picturing Webber, then looked up. "Kind of unnerving—a little like you don't know what he'll say next."

Hammer pointed to his neck. "Tattoo?"

Her mouth opened, then closed, as they *all* realized that they were talking about the same Webber. "Barcode?"

Hammer tapped his fist against his forehead. "Bumbo-freaking-clot!"

Gabriel felt something winding, winding, winding inside. "Deja, when exactly were you on the boat?"

"Yesterday morning. I was fishing. Saw . . ." She paused.

Gabriel remembered talking to her siblings earlier today. Kaleisha had said Deja had taken out that small yellow boat *yesterday morning*. Shit! *Webber!* He felt sick. All the pieces started fitting together. And on top of it all was a massive relief—Deja wasn't involved in any of this, not on purpose, anyway! "So . . . you found this guy, the one on the boat, an agent, who asked you to bring the cash to Webber . . . who is also an agent?"

"Yes!" As Deja said that, the waitress came with plates, setting the first down in front of Hammer.

"Is wha wrong with you?" the waitress asked Hammer, who was palming his head, probably trying to puzzle some way out of all this.

He looked up and mustered a faint smile. "Me all right." But there was something resigned about his tone.

The waitress shrugged and landed the jerk chicken in front of Gabriel. "What you drinking?"

"Just water, thanks." But his appetite was long gone.

"Me too," Hammer added.

The woman glanced at Deja, then at Hammer, and back to Gabriel. "Is what wrong with unu? You no want di food no more?"

Gabriel shrugged. "No, just thinking about things, that's all."

Her attitude livened up when she heard their mood wasn't about the food. "Well, eat it up. You will feel better." She sashayed away to the counter.

Hammer stood. "Me going go check outside fi Webber."

Suddenly, two men walked in. The one with a short Afro, wearing a white shirt, zeroed in on Gabriel.

Webber on his mind, Gabriel stood and pulled his gun. Both men threw their hands out in front of them as they yelled for calm.

Realizing that neither one was, in fact, Webber, Gabriel tucked the gun away with an apology.

Nervous smiles on their faces, the men backed away slowly. The waitress, desperate to keep them, asked if they wanted a table, at which time Hammer mused, "Can't wait fi see what dem post pon Tripadvisor."

After the men left, the waitress stormed right over. She was probably also the owner.

Gabriel quickly apologized, but he could see that the waitress meant business, as in the *business* she was losing on account of him being all jumpy.

In a cold tone, she said, "Please finish up your food, and leave yahso. Me no condone that deh kind of slackness inna mi restaurant." Before Gabriel could say anything else, she spun on her heel and headed for the kitchen.

Hammer said, "Make me go outside and check fi Webber."

Deja bit her lip, then blurted out, "He's not coming."

"What?" Gabriel asked.

A sheepish expression came over her face. "I . . . only said it to scare you. I was afraid you might try something. He's not coming."

"Where him deh?" Hammer asked.

She shrugged. "Don't know. He left after I gave him the back-pack."

Made sense, though Gabriel wished she hadn't made him go through all that and pull his gun. Then again, he hadn't exactly made her life a walk on the beach. "But all the other stuff you said is true?"

"Yep." Not a hint of hesitation.

Gabriel pressed. "Including the part about Webber being an agent?"

"Yes."

Hammer sank slowly back into his chair as if he'd lost a battle with fatigue. "We are so screwed."

Deja, Friday, 8:45 p.m.

Deja squeezed the bag in her lap, the plastic crunching under her clench. *They* were so screwed? Huh. What about her? That Webber guy knew her name and probably where she lived. What if he decided to do something to her so she wouldn't talk about this? What kind of agent was he anyway? "How do *you* know Webber?" she demanded.

Gabriel and Hammer glanced at each other. When Hammer gave a slight nod, Gabriel explained. "*We* were supposed to bring the drugs to *him*."

"To *him*? But—but—then he might not be an agent. . . ." A range of emotions cascaded through her.

Looking down at his food, Gabriel shook his head. "No, mon, dem agents deal in drugs, money, every damn thing they can fi trap you. Him must be an agent fi true."

"You sure?" She hoped he was, for her and her family's sake. Still, there was so much she didn't know and a lot more she didn't trust. "So why were you bringing drugs to Webber, anyway?"

Gabriel pushed his plate away. "It was part of an exchange. If we brought him the drugs, he'd get us off the island."

Deja opened her mouth, closed it, opened it again. "That because your boss is trying to kill you?"

He side-eyed the waitress, probably to make sure she was out of earshot, before saying, "That or set me up, so soldiers can arrest me. Pretty much the same thing. When you dead, you can't talk."

Why would his boss want him arrested? Had he done something? So she asked.

"Good question." But he offered nothing more.

Webber *was* a bad guy, then? "So Webber was helping you?"

Gabriel picked up his fork and started moving the rice into a pile. "Well, seeing how he probably is an agent, I think he wanted to set up Hammer and me—"

Hammer jumped in. "Him was pretending to help us. It was a setup thing. But him would arrest us as soon as we brought him the drugs." He mumbled under his breath, then said, "Probably make us rat out Teago, too."

Okay, could this possibly be more confusing? "Teago?" she asked.

"Our boss," Hammer explained.

Deja cocked her head. "Let me get this straight. Your boss was setting you up, *and* Webber was setting you up at the same time?"

Hammer, unemotional, nodded. "That's how it is."

"That's crazy," Deja exclaimed, still not even sure she understood.

Gabriel put his fork down. "A so it go in our world, mon."

"I think you need a new world."

"Funny, I was thinking the same thing," Gabriel said.

Maybe Gabriel regretted being in the posse or something? Did Hammer?

Then Gabriel surprised her, totally. "Look, for us, it's whatever. But for *you*—well, I want you to know I'm sorry."

She paused. She *thought* he meant it, but still. "You should be."

He reached for her hand. "I am."

She pulled it away.

Hammer arched one eyebrow. "Me no know if it help, but me sorry too. Never mean to do you nothing. It was just circumstances, if you know what me mean?"

The waitress returned wearing a big fat frown, holding out Deja's phone and two glasses of water. "It charge up."

Deja took the phone. "Oh, thank you so much."

The woman didn't say Deja was "welcome" or anything. Just casually put down the glasses, then slapped the bill on the table.

As Gabriel watched her walk away, he said, "She really wants us out of here."

Hammer quipped, "You bad fi business, mon."

"Ha ha."

Deja clicked on her phone. There was a text from Uncle.

Police are arresting us. Be careful. I think they're searching for you

And suddenly the room went out of focus, and she couldn't feel anything, not even the phone in her hand.

"What is it?" Gabriel asked from what seemed like two towns away.

Then, through the fog of it all, Deja scrolled to the next message. Maybe there had been some mistake.

Ms. Reynolds your uncle and siblings are in police custody at the Springtown Harbour station. Call back immediately on this number.

This second thunderclap of news had brought her mind to a near standstill. The phone wasn't in her hand anymore. Somehow Gabriel had it. His face registered shock. And now he was showing the phone to Hammer.

Gabriel said, "I'm sorry about this." His voice was breathy, desperate. "Serious. Sorry."

Hammer added, "Me too."

Then she had the vague feeling that the ceiling could be falling or that she was rising up to it, getting closer to the slowly spinning ceiling fan.

"Deja . . . Deja. Sit down, mon." Gabriel still had her phone. "Sit down, mon. Sit."

She blinked, realized she was standing and the bag of cash was on the floor below her. She sat, reached for the bag, rested it on her lap.

The waitress came back and put down some to-go boxes for them to pack their food in. A silent and clear sign that she wanted them to get out, as if they needed one.

Then Deja took back her phone. Reread the messages. This was real. "Why? What do the police want with them?"

Gabriel said, "It's probably Melville—"

Names kept swarming around her. "Is he going to hurt them?"

Gabriel looked down at the table. Did he know? Was he just afraid to say?

Deja couldn't stand the wait. "Is he?"

Hammer scooted his chair closer. "Melville is crooked police, but him not going go do nothing crazy right now."

"Right now?!"

At last Gabriel looked up. "He works for our boss, Teago. He won't do anything without Teago saying so."

Teago again? "The one who wants to set you up?"

"A him, same one. Yes," Hammer said.

Frantic, Deja asked, "But suppose he *does* do something?"

"He won't." Gabriel sounded sure. "Both of them probably think you still have the backpack—"

Deja interrupted. "I told you there were no drugs."

Gabriel exhaled. "I know. But he . . . he doesn't know that."

Her eyes drifted to her plastic bag, heart thudding against her ribs as she debated trusting them entirely. "So, here's the truth—I have cash from Webber," she blurted out, seeing no other choice.

Now *their* eyes drifted to the bag.

"What if—what if I pay him, this Melville guy?" Her thoughts were in a frenzy.

"How much you have?" Hammer asked, not a hint of emotion.

Seized with fear, she said, "Fifteen thousand, but you can't take it. *Please.* You can't."

"Deja, it's okay," Gabriel said. "I swear we won't. We won't, okay?"

Hammer mused aloud. "Couldn't even buy us a kilo anyway."

Gabriel shot him a look.

"Just saying, mon," Hammer went on, motioning to Deja. "We won't take it. Serious thing."

Pressing both hands over the bag, she asked, "So, what do you think? If I give it to Melville, will he release Kaleisha and Donovan and my uncle?"

"Truth? He would want more, mon." Gabriel rubbed his eyes with the palms of his hands. "Probably would think you were just holding out on him."

Deja's stomach lurched. "So he only wants the drugs? What— what kind of police is that?"

"Like we said, crooked." Hammer leaned back, and his chair creaked. "Dem all over Jamaica, mon. Like sand at di beach."

The waitress, standing by the counter, cleared her throat. Loud. Then the door to the kitchen opened and a huge man, also wearing an apron, walked out and stood beside her. Both glared in their direction.

Gabriel drew closer. "Okay. We need a plan . . . yesterday. Last thing we need is for them to call the police."

Hammer looked down at his plate, still nearly untouched. "Yeh, mon. We need fi go."

But all Deja could think about were those text messages. "What'll he do with them? My family? This Melville guy?"

Gabriel's chest rose, then fell. Finally, he nodded. "He won't do anything. Not until he gets what he wants."

"Until?" Deja's voice went up an octave.

"Easy, easy, he wants the drugs, so . . ." Gabriel swallowed. "So we need to find a way to get him to let them go."

Maybe she could call this Melville guy, pleading her case, her innocence, that of her siblings and uncle. She picked up her phone as she deliberated. Maybe she had to be there in person. "You need to give me a ride to Springtown," she said out loud.

Hammer asked "Why?" just as Gabriel asked, "What are you going to do?"

It was a reasonable question, especially as she quite honestly did not know what she was going to do. She'd know when she got there, though she was sure of it. But Gabriel's eyes had gone wide, urging an answer. "I don't know yet, but that's where my family is." Tears pricked at her eyes. "I have to get to them, and . . ." She took a moment, composing herself. "And I need a ride there."

"Deja, listen," Hammer began. "Me wish we could help you, but things desperate fi Gabriel and me. We going go get arrested or dead if we go Springtown."

"My little brother and sister are in jail! My brother is only ten years old!" Fury radiated down to her fingertips. "You know what? You guys are total assholes!"

Gabriel grunted. "We are. We have to be, but . . . But not this time. We'll take you to Springtown."

Hammer grasped Gabriel's forearm. "G, you want fi dead?"

Gabriel shoved his hand into his pocket, yanked out a stone, and laid it on the table. As a light glinted off it, Deja remembered the pyrite stone from the beach. When Gabriel had given her a surprise visit. How he'd been so good with the kids. "Is that . . . ?"

"We saw them this morning, Kaleisha and Donovan, at the dock when we were checking for the drugs." He glanced at her, his eyes soft. "Donovan wanted to know if it was gold."

She picked it up. Sharp edges. A golden glisten. Some said it brought people luck. She hoped so. Prayed.

"Good kids," Gabriel told her. He gazed at the stone as if it were a crystal ball, maybe seeing what the future might be if he didn't help.

Deja fought to keep her fingers from trembling. They had to say yes, had to. "Please." Her voice was a whisper.

Hammer looked from the pyrite to Gabriel. "G—is that the rock-stone di boy did give you?"

"Yeh, mon."

Deja, the stone now in the middle of her palm, held her hand out to Hammer.

He took it, turned it around with his fingers, giving it a thorough review. "It look like gold fi true." When he handed it back, he raised a fist to his cheek, thinking.

Gabriel shrugged. "They're just kids, mon. Like the ones under the truck yesterday morning. The one at the cove . . ." He held out his hands, palms up. "*Us*."

Hammer seemed to be looking past him, past the restaurant walls.

Finally, Gabriel raised an eyebrow. "You down?"

Hammer didn't even blink. "Always down, D."

Deja felt like she could collapse from the relief. "Thank you."

The waitress, lips pursed, came over and eyed the bill. Gabriel placed some Jamaican bills on top of it, lots more than the food cost. The woman scooped it up. "Me coming back with your change."

"No problem. Keep it."

She stared for a moment. . . . A smile grew wide, and she said, voice suddenly happy, "Thank you, and come again."

As she left, Gabriel said, "We know somebody in Springtown—"

Hammer cut in, "You thinking Chops?"

Of course. They'd been at the church party too. "You mean Pastor Powell, right?"

Hammer shot her an *aha* look. "That's right. You know him too?"

"I . . . talked to him about what I found this morning. Should've let him help, but I—"

Gabriel squinted. "Why'd you go to him?"

"He's my minister, that's why. I trust him."

Hammer sat back. "I'll be damned, Chops *is* legit."

"Guess that makes you Pope Hammer the First." Gabriel grinned hard.

"*What* are you talking about?" Deja asked.

Gabriel couldn't stop smirking. "Inside joke. No worry 'bout it."

Deja began to nod, putting everything together. "The posse? You know Pastor Powell from your posse, no true?"

"Yes."

And . . . so . . . "Pastor Powell knows your boss too?"

Gabriel said, "Right again." Then he turned to Hammer. "You know, me feel him still have some influence over Teago."

"Chops? You just finish convince me that him is a true man of di cloth."

"He is." Deja thought about Pastor Powell's scars. His calm. His wisdom.

Gabriel stared at Hammer and lowered his voice. "You know the story about Chops?"

"How he fought off those dudes by himself? Wish me coulda seen that one."

"Well, the guy Chops saved was Teago."

Then Hammer cursed like Uncle did sometimes. "Kiss me neck!"

And with that, Gabriel began punching numbers into his phone. "Chops . . ."

aking the back roads that had been all but forgotten since the A1 had been built, they zipped through the dark on the motorcycle, Gabriel's hands at her waist, her own at Hammer's. But fast wasn't fast enough to escape her fears for her family.

Hammer leaned into the next corner, gravel shooting out from under the wheels. Gabriel's hands tightened around her waist, like when they'd driven up Cornwall Mountain, though this time he kept a tight grip even when they hit the straightaway. It was awkward with his body pressed against hers, but it wasn't horrible, either. Maybe if things were different . . . there could have been something more between them than a world of crazy.

At last the lights outlining the horseshoe bay of Springtown Harbour came into view, the ocean like a sheet of glittering fabric laid flat in the night. How was it that just hours ago, she'd been hoping, praying that she'd get the cash Webber had promised—and now she'd give it all up in a blink just to take her family back home and make them sandwiches.

Now the prospects of doing all that were slim, hard to envision. Yet still, she prayed.

After what seemed like two loops around the whole damn country—wow, these guys were careful—they finally reached the church. They were feet from the rectory door when someone bled out of the shadows.

Deja caught sight of him first—a stocky guy, most of his face hidden. She clutched the bag of cash to her chest just as Gabriel started to draw his gun. Not now, she begged the universe. God, not when they had come so far. And then, thankfully, the guy stepped into a beam from a security light, armed but not aiming at them.

It was one of the Fleming twins that Pastor Powell had met with this morning.

"I know him," Deja shout-whispered.

Gabriel kept his weapon raised.

"G. Chill!" Hammer barked. "She say she know him, mon."

She laid a warm hand over Gabriel's cold one, pulling down his weapon. "He's okay," she insisted.

Gabriel's adrenaline was probably still on max; he'd only lowered his gun halfway. Then raised it again when a second figure came from the shadows. It was Shamar, the twin with the shorter hair.

"I know him, too," Deja assured Gabriel, and finally . . . he lowered his gun all the way.

Shamar nodded to Deja in recognition, then beckoned them to the rectory's side entrance. Knocked four times.

Door open, Pastor Powell looked everywhere at once, his face tight, tense. One glance sent Deja praying that things hadn't gotten worse.

Shamar nodded at him, probably indicating that everything was okay. But the pastor's eyes swept over the parking lot anyway before saying what they most needed to know. "The police do have them. They're at the station downtown." He held Deja's frightened, hopeful gaze. "No one is harmed."

Deja let her head tip back in relief.

Gabriel tucked his gun back into his waistband. "Melville with them?"

"He had to do something back in Mobay, but he's coming to town in the morning."

Deja stepped closer. "But how did they even get captured?"

"Melville had local police ask around. Somebody identified them as people close to you." He shrugged. "And a police boat caught them just as they left the bay."

People close to you. It was her fault. *All* her fault.

"But we should get inside." The pastor waved everyone in, except Shamar and his brother, who stepped back into the shadows.

As soon as she was in the foyer, Deja could barely believe her eyes: Straleen and Lila were rushing her. What—what? "What are you two doing here?" she cried out.

"Minister call us," Lila practically shouted in total hyper mode.

"Come here, girl," Straleen said, yanking Deja into a hug.

Pastor Powell intertwined his fingers. "Straleen and Lila do a lot of work in the congregation, as do you, Deja, so when I came up with an idea on how to address this . . . situation, I thought they could help."

Lila gave Deja a look. "*If* she'll let us."

Deja wished she could laugh. "Don't start, not now, not after everything I've been through today."

Then *both* friends were hugging her ferociously. Tears welled in Deja's eyes; she buried her head in Straleen's shoulder and let her day-ones rock her back and forth.

Once Deja finally pushed free, Straleen eyed her over. "Girl, you look rrrrough!"

"Have mercy. Where have you been?" Lila added with a nose wrinkle.

Deja laughed, thought of that old bat, and the duppy housing complex, and almost tumbling down the mountainside, distracted by the cruise ships. "Trust me, you don't even want to know."

"Every day the bucket go well, one day the bottom must drop out," Lila said like an old grandma, letting her know that she shouldn't have pressed her luck.

Deja wagged a finger. "Don't start, girl. Just don't."

Straleen flung her arm around Deja's shoulder. "Bet you could use a shower and some new clothes."

Deja couldn't wait. "Yes and yes. I'll go get some clothes later."

Pastor Powell vetoed that immediately. "Absolutely not.

Melville's men are probably staking out your house this very minute. You're staying here tonight."

"No worry. I'll go get you some of my things," Straleen assured her. "Shorts, T-shirt, so it won't matter if them too big."

"It's okay, really. Don't bother—"

Lila rolled her eyes. "Knew that was coming."

"Let's not, okay?" The last thing Deja needed was a lecture about friends helping friends or some nonsense like that.

Hammer peeked through the blinds, then closed them again. "Chops, di boys out deh? Dem all right?"

"The ever-suspicious Hammer." But Pastor Powell looked at him as if he were a little brother. "Don't worry, they're good."

Deja wanted to hug Pastor Powell for all he was doing—but she wasn't sure if you could hug a priest. "Thank you. Thank you so much."

"Not a problem, Deja. We're all here for each other." His tone had the same measured calm as his Sunday homilies.

Gabriel glanced at her, then got right to it with the pastor. "You chat up Teago?"

The pastor traced over his tattoo—the Chops tattoo. "Yes, so . . . it was a tense discussion, but the mere mention of an undercover agent got Teago rattled."

"It should," Hammer said dismissively.

To Gabriel, Pastor Powell said, "And, as you suspected, he hinted that he still owed me, and after a while he agreed to my plan—"

Almost simultaneously, Deja and Gabriel asked, "What plan?"

"Actually, there are two plans. They're not quite set, but with the help of your friends, we'll have everything in place in time."

Gabriel asked, "In time for what?"

The pastor said calmly, "I'll let you know once Deja's friends figure it out."

Lila and Straleen? What were they up to? But that had to wait. "Pastor, what about the kids and my uncle?"

"That's the first plan. Tomorrow morning we go meet Melville at the beach by the wharf, and exchange the backpack for the release of your siblings and uncle. At first Teago wouldn't believe me when I told him the drugs had just disappeared, but with some urging, he came around and settled for getting the drop cash."

Was she hearing this right? "But . . . I gave the cash to Webber," she gasped. Did Gabriel *not* tell him?

Straleen grasped her shoulder. "Easy, girl."

Deja shook off her hand. "There's no money," she reiterated. "I gave it to Webber." Then she remembered the bag in her trembling hand and quickly held it up as if it were a sacrifice— one she would make a thousand times over. "I have some—the reward Webber gave me. But it's not enough—"

Panic in *his* voice, Gabriel said, "Chops, I told you there's no cash."

Pastor Powell, serene as ever, clasped his hands. "Not to worry, not to worry. Here's how it's going to play out, God willing. At dawn we'll meet Melville, and once we're there, we'll work everything out. And by that I mean, after the exchange—"

Deja started to talk about the cash again.

"I know, Deja. I know." The pastor gentled. "But here's the thing—and this does *not* leave this room—"

Deja's breath caught. Gabriel shifted from foot to foot, in opposition to Hammer, who couldn't be more still if he were rooted to the tile floor.

Satisfied, the pastor told them. "We're going to bluff." He nodded slowly. "I'm going to tell Melville that he'll get the cash *after* all of you leave."

"Leave?" The moment she asked, the logic of it all started to become clear.

"I'm sure you realize that it's not safe for you here in Springtown." The pastor's voice took an even more serious tone. "Even if we *had* the money, we couldn't turn it over and trust men like these to just forgive and forget. So, after the exchange, you, your siblings, and your uncle will leave on his boat."

"No such thing as too careful right now, Deja, zeen," Hammer confirmed.

Deja paused . . . thought about how she'd "cautiously" left the cash behind for her first meeting with Webber. "Okayyyy." Maybe it would work? No maybes. It had to. There really wasn't any other choice, since they didn't actually have what Melville wanted. Then her heart started hammering. "What about you, Pastor?"

A smile blossomed on his lips. "Thank you for your concern, but I'll be okay."

She didn't buy that. "How?"

"Leave that to me. Let's just focus on getting you and your family out of town first."

Lila took Deja's hand. "You have family on the South Coast, don't you?"

She was right. Pastor Powell was right. Hammer was right. She and the kids would have to leave Springtown. "Yes. My aunt has a place in Saint Elizabeth, up in Santa Cruz."

"Good. That's out of the way." Pastor Powell wasn't sugar-coating it. "You'll need to lie low there for a while, but then you might want to think about leaving the island."

"Leave . . . Jamaica?" Her voice went shuddery. She couldn't begin to think of how they'd do that!

"No problem, mon." There was no shudder in Gabriel's voice.

Straleen pulled Deja close. "You have people, girl."

Deja liked hearing that, wanted to hear that. But the enormity of what she'd set into motion was starting to tidal-wave over her. She was already putting them in harm's way—and they'd told her not to do any of this, not to take the freaking cash in the first place.

And . . . leave Jamaica? Her *country*? Everyone she knew? And her whole family having to do the same?

"What about me and Gabriel?" Hammer's question broke through Deja's thoughts. There was an edge of concern, maybe even fear, in his voice—something Deja had never detected in him before. "You talk to Teago about us?"

Pastor Powell hesitated.

Gabriel seemed like he could guess the answer in the hesitation. "You joking?"

The pastor turned to Hammer. "In talking to him, I got a sense it wasn't a good idea to bring the two of you into the negotiation." The pastor blinked hard, the first sign of any sort of worry. "*But* there are a lot of fishermen here. I'm going to work on getting you and Gabriel out of town on one of their boats. You probably already guessed that the roads won't be safe for you after this. Melville and Teago will have men out there looking for you."

"What about my bike?" Hammer's fists were clenching.

Gabriel looked at him in disbelief. "What about our asses, Hammer? You no hear what Chops just say?"

Hammer gazed toward the back window. "Is a nice bike, mon."

And for the first time Deja felt a pang for him, for Gabriel. Until that moment, she had never really considered how truly desperate things were for them. Her family's problems had taken up all her brain space. This Webber and Melville shit was their world, after all. Somehow she'd thought things would work out for them. And then another tidal wave hit her. They'd known the risk of coming here . . . and yet they'd taken it anyway. "Come with us!" she blurted out.

Gabriel raised an eyebrow. "What?"

"Come with us."

Lila squeezed her hand. "Deja, think this through."

Deja squeezed back. "It's okay. Really." And to Gabriel, she said it once more. "Come with us. On the boat. To Santa Cruz." She was surprised over how sure she was about it.

"No, mon." Gabriel started to smile, then stopped. "You all in enough trouble. If we come with you, we're just going to bring *more* trouble." He gestured to the pastor. "There's a reason Chops didn't want to talk to our boss about us. Teago . . . that man him just want bad things for us."

Deja let go of Lila's hand. "*I* think it's okay. We can do it. We can."

Gabriel stared at Hammer for what seemed like an eternity, perhaps waiting for him to back up what he'd said. But Hammer kept his face steely. Did *he* think it was a good idea to come along?

The answer came as he finally agreed with Gabriel. "We just can't."

All the longing in his voice broke Deja's heart. "Yes, you *can*," she insisted. She couldn't let them get in trouble for helping her, helping her family. She couldn't bear it. Because she knew it in her heart—it was for *her*, for Kaleisha and Donovan and her. That was why they'd come back to Springtown with her.

Outside, two dogs barked, one after the other.

"It's *stupid* not to come," she added in frustration. "Why are you being so stubborn?"

Gabriel's face had that wistful look. "Thank you, Deja. We going go try another way like Chops—sorry, the pastor—said. But thank you, mon."

Gabriel was so stupid. Hammer too. She dashed at stupid tears.

"Um . . ." Pastor Powell's brown eyes, so warm, were moving across Deja's face. "I think Gabriel . . . and Hammer have chosen their path. But . . . there's something else we have to discuss." Then he motioned to Straleen. Raised both eyebrows.

Deja stiffened. Were they going to be stupid too? "What now?"

Straleen gave Lila a nudge.

Lila cleared her throat. "We worked out a backup plan with Pastor Powell, but we no want you to feel no way about it—"

"Like don't be thinking the main plan won't work or anything," Straleen clarified. They knew her so well.

"It might go smooth as silk—probably will!—but Pastor Powell wanted to be sure we had another way to go," Lila said.

Hammer coughed, watching warily. He might just be as tense as Deja. "Okay, okay, what the heck is this plan?"

"I would like to know myself." If they got hurt doing some crazy thing for her, Deja would just die.

Straleen's eyes lit up. "It's a big thing, but no worry, we plan it good. It no all set up yet, but we going work through the night fi get it so—"

Lila interrupted, a silly smile on her face. "Serious thing, we going figure it out. We just need to reach out to some more people."

"What for?" Deja's nerves felt tighter than piano wire. "I don't want *more* people mixed up in this. Backside, me no even want you two inna this."

"We in it, D," Straleen asserted.

Deja grabbed and shook Lila's forearm. "Girl, you better tell me what this plan is all about."

Lila stayed cool. "We going get di people to bear witness—"

Straleen added, "Shame that man, Melville, to do the right thing."

"He's got no shame," Gabriel broke in.

"Damn right," Hammer said.

"The way we're orchestrating things, he'll have to find some," Pastor Powell assured them.

"You haffi' trust us, D," Lila said.

"Look, I need to know what's going on." Then Deja warned, "Is my family's lives we dealing with—"

Straleen said, unblinking, "You no think we know that?"

"We going go make it work, D." Lila's voice broke as she said it. "If we tell you di things we're planning, you just going go make yourself crazy 'bout it. Just trust us . . . for once."

Straleen added, "Besides, me and Lila need to go. We have plenty to do tonight to get it all together."

Straleen. Lila. Gabriel. Hammer. The pastor. Even the Fleming twins outside. They were all at the ready. To help *her*. But what if it all went wrong? How could she live with all that guilt?

Deja, Saturday, 5:15 a.m.

Glad to be in a fresh pair of shorts and a T-shirt Straleen had gotten for her, Deja slipped on the big green backpack Straleen had gotten for her last night. It was packed to near bursting with clothes for the kids and Uncle and the $15,000 Webber had given her.

After a fitful night's sleep in the rectory, she stepped outside and into the dawning rose, praying hard that everything would work out. The Fleming boys, with their black tees, watchful eyes, and handguns, were still stationed outside; Gabriel and Hammer had joined them, eyes raking the empty street. A lone dog barked somewhere down the deserted block. When Gabriel motioned that everything was okay, Pastor Powell gave one last scour of the neighborhood, then banged the heavy door shut, rattling the key in the lock.

With Pastor Powell and the Fleming boys leading the way, Deja in the middle, and Hammer and Gabriel at the back, they marched off, careful to take side streets as they headed downtown, veering onto the same alley Deja had walked with Kaleisha and Donovan just—what, yesterday morning? Then, the stores had been awash in bright sunlight, and as desperate as she'd been, she'd held a ray of hope. Now, despite the plans and the convoy around her, hope felt like a long-ago memory. She rubbed a film of sweat from her face. Stink-filled trash cans, where food had had all day and night to fester, lined the alley. A porky rat scurried for shelter in front of them, tunneling through discarded wrappers.

Gabriel and Hammer had their game faces on. She didn't need any mirror to know that hers wasn't. She was so nervous, she felt nauseous.

But she couldn't be in this kind of head space! She smacked her thigh with her fist, like she used to do before a netball match. Opposing teams were taller, had intimidating uniforms with better logos and colors, all stuff to be *ignored. Be positive. Stay focused.*

As if he sensed a shift in her demeanor, Pastor Powell asked them to hold up for a sec. "So . . . we're getting close. And you all might feel the need to *do* something, but that's just pressure getting to you. Your job is to stay calm and let me do the talking, okay?"

Everyone nodded except Deja. No way could she agree to stay out of this if something went crazy.

"Deja, that means you, too."

How was he in her head? She dipped it as if agreeing—though she couldn't promise she could stand by the sidelines if things started to go sour.

❖❖❖

As they walked by the shuttered open-air bar that her uncle and the other fishermen haunted, Deja slowed up. This was odd. It was usually open by now. And where were they anyway, the fishermen? She couldn't see any of them. None on the dock or on the boats. Not even Mr. Wallace. Strange. And he wasn't out fishing already—the *Gregor* and the *Queen* bobbed beside each other. Which sent her thoughts cascading to how they were going to escape and whether the *Queen* was fully gassed up. Maybe she could grab a drum of gas from another boat . . . if they made it that far.

The muted wing whistle from the gulls flapping low over the water's edge emphasized the odd silence around them. Sand crunching beneath their feet was the only other sound. Her eyes darted toward anything that moved. Then she spotted a police jeep, which pulled up to the curb right next to the beach.

The doors opened, and out came a short, heavyset police-man and a tall, wiry one, a machine gun slung over his shoulder. But no one else. Then, then, a beat later—oh, thank God, thank God!—Kaleisha, Donovan, and Uncle stepped out. Oh, they had such blank expressions. Deja couldn't begin to imagine how scared they must be. It was all she could do to keep from breaking into a sprint.

Seemingly, at the short officer's command, the one with the machine gun led her family onto the beach and gestured for them to sit on the sand. The other policeman strode several feet away, as if he owned Springtown Harbour. Finally stopping, he folded his arms and tilted his head back. Had to be that Melville guy.

"Okay, this is it," Pastor Powell said, low-voiced. "I'm going over there alone. If everything's okay, I'll wave you over."

Deja forced herself to breathe steadily, steadily. Melville was going to freak when he heard he wasn't going to get the cash. No fish seller worth a damn would tolerate a buyer changing the deal at the last minute. Hopefully, Pastor Powell was a cool customer.

Deja told herself not to watch, not to try to interpret what might or might not be going down. But she couldn't resist. Melville's head started jerking side to side as he spoke—hard, fast, probably in anger. Deja felt like she was sinking into the very sand itself. What if this didn't work?

Then Pastor Powell was doing a lot of gesticulating, Melville doing the same, still nodding. It almost looked like a bizarre martial art. Melville suddenly stopped, pressed two fingers to his forehead, clearly thinking something through. Pastor Powell just kept on talking. What was he saying? Was it working? Deja swallowed down rising nausea.

Then the pastor was pulling out his phone. Gesturing frantically with his free hand. Handing the phone to Melville. Had he called Teago?

Finally, Melville tossed the phone back. He flicked a hand in the direction of the policeman standing guard. He in turn motioned for Deja's family to stand up. Kaleisha sprang instantly to her feet, as did Donovan. Uncle placed a hand on the ground, braced himself, and stood gingerly. She hadn't noticed this before. Was he hurt? Had they hurt him?

Now the pastor was waving for Deja and the rest just as planned—and so it began. As they started across the beach, Deja couldn't help it. Her pace got faster and faster, sandals gliding.

"Deja!" Hammer hissed.

"Must be cool, mon!" Gabriel whispered out the side of his mouth.

She slowed back to a walk, taking in every detail of her siblings. She saw how papery Donovan's skin looked. It aways got like that when he was dehydrated. Kaleisha was rocking from foot to foot, her eyes red. Uncle, however, despite his struggle to stand, now stood, chest out, chin up. Undaunted. Kaleisha took a step toward Deja, made to run toward her, but Uncle viper-fast took hold of her shoulder, stopping her. That was when Deja noticed Uncle's lip was busted. They *had* hurt him. Shit! But when he locked eyes with Deja, he seemed to be trying to beam strength *her* way.

Pastor Powell suddenly motioned for them to stop. They'd formed two opposing lines just five feet apart: theirs and Melville's. Deja's heart was twisting. Again, she wanted to dash over—to grab on to her family, hold them tight, keep them safe. Ached to smother them with hugs and kisses.

Eyes full of fury, Melville leered at Deja. "Where is it? Tell me!" he barked. Deja gaped at the pastor. What the hell had they been talking about the whole time?

Before she could say a word, he jumped in. "She doesn't know where it is. Only I do. And if you still have a bug up your butt about getting the backpack before they leave, I can call Teago again—see how loud he gets *this* time."

A tiny smile blossomed on Melville's face. "Was worth a try."

Wow, Melville was tricky. Now he gave Hammer and Gabriel the once-over. "And you two? You decided to bite the hand that feeds you, hmm?"

Gabriel held his gaze. "So, you rather I just go back and switch up the stash house?"

"Oh . . ." Melville laid a hand on his holster. "A little pissed, are we?"

Pastor Powell dispatched a look that clearly said *shut the hell up.* Deja pressed her shoulder into Gabriel's, willing him to calm down.

Melville gave a short, harsh laugh. "I see. You did it for the girl." Then he trained his vitriol on Hammer. "And what did you do it for . . . friendship?" Melville gave his head a slow shake, in a *you fool* sort of way. "The only friend you have is yourself, youth. You shoulda know dat by now."

The next moment the pastor flung his arms in the air. "Enough chitchat! We have a deal. Let's move on. The sooner they go, the sooner you get the backpack."

Instead of responding, Melville glanced at his watch, then over his shoulder. That small smile was back.

Weird.

What was he waiting for?

Gabriel, Saturday, 6:20 a.m.

abriel heard it before he saw it—the screech of a tires in the distance. Then a car roared down the street parallel to the beach, coming directly toward them. It bumped over the sidewalk, right up onto the sand, and skidded to a halt ten feet away. A wake of dust drifted over them all. Up went the machine gun, the police guard instantly primed. Uncle Glen drew Donovan and Kaleisha to his chest, shielding them. Deja gasped. Gabriel wanted to reach for her, but . . . Hammer slowly pushed his elbow into Gabriel's arm.

They knew that Audi. Teago. Bumboclot!

"Stand down. Stand down," Melville ordered his man. When the officer went slack-jawed at him, Melville's nostrils flared. "Stand down already. It's Teago, you damn fool."

Now Melville's sudden concern with his watch made sense. He'd been waiting for Teago. Shit! The smell of a double cross was in the air.

The Audi's driver's-side door flung open, and out came

Teago, dressed like he was heading to a club in red sunglasses, a flowing white shirt unbuttoned down to his navel, and layers of gold chains. Blocks, Teago's top enforcer, Gabriel's age but built like a refrigerator, heaved himself out of the other side of the car.

Hammer leaned close. "It going fi get ugly, mon."

Gabriel had already done the sad addition. The Fleming boys' handguns plus his Beretta didn't come anywhere close to equaling what was on the other side. The officer's machine gun was a game changer by itself, but there was also Melville's service revolver and whatever Blocks was carrying in his waistband. Not to mention that there were two little kids in the middle of it all.

Teago pinched his nose—allergies or too much blow? "Chops, me let you change up di deal, but me betta get that backpack." His tone was light, easygoing, exactly the one he used before he lashed out—Gabriel had seen it again and again.

"I gave you my word," Chops said, *his* tone one you'd use to calm a snarling dog.

"Talk cheap."

"Isn't that so true." Melville hooked a thumb in his belt. Snickered.

Gabriel's skin prickled as he went into hyperalert mode. Hammer elbowed him again. He'd sensed a hidden meaning in that snicker too. Melville was up to something. Gabriel glanced at Deja, who seemed to be trying to convey something to her brother and sister with her eyes.

Teago swaggered over to Gabriel and Hammer. "Is you two me come for. Time fi catch di rats."

"Rats?" Hammer scoffed.

Hot tears of fury pressed at Gabriel's eyes, surprising him. He forced them back, lifted his chin. "I know about 'switching up the stash house.' I know you were setting me up."

Teago's face blanched just for an instant, but Gabriel saw it.

"You know is why . . . ?" Teago waited, then spat it out. "Is because you too damn facety!"

What was so wrong about being feisty? How the hell do you survive in the posse world without attitude? "What are you talking about?"

"When people like you get facety with me, me can tell dem want fi leave di posse. And me nah go let dat happen." Teago pivoted to Chops, gestured toward Deja's uncle and siblings. "Dem can go. But me want dem two."

Now Deja couldn't stop herself. "No! They're coming with us."

"Ooh!" Teago shimmied his body, mocking Deja. "You're di one who come stick her ass inna my business."

And that was when Chops put two fingers in his mouth and whistled long and loud.

Deja, Saturday, 6:35 a.m.

Deja hardly knew where to look first. Out of the shadows at the dock end of the beach came the fishermen—dozens!— boots clacking over the stony part of the shore, Mr. Wallace and all the rest . . . with their phones held high. They were . . . filming this? Deja swiveled around to the east. Draped in the yellow morning light, walking toward them from the street, was Straleen, her phone raised high as well, and behind her were— what?! Mrs. Waul and all the women who sold fish, the chef at the patty shop, the butcher, the barber, a slew of girls from class, and more! And from the opposite direction came Lila with a parade of her own—the owner of the souvenir shop and her daughters, several women who worked at the new hotel, some teachers, a bunch of her mother's friends, and so many others— all converging to the same place. Here. All with phones held high.

Was this a mirage? A dream? Would she snap back to real life with Melville about to pull his gun if she so much as blinked?

Had she lost her mind? But Gabriel was gaping as well. It was real. And the grimace on Melville's face, on Teago's, confirmed it. Springtown Harbour had risen up, and they all had their phones out, filming.

On YouTube, people posted videos of criminals and police doing bad things—proof! *Oh my God. Oh my God. Straleen and Lila's plan! How . . . ? When?* Deja could hardly think.

Melville's face had gone ashen. His hand dropped away from his holster. Deja saw fear in his eyes, and surprise—and something else . . . embarrassment? The police's code was, after all, serve, protect, and reassure.

If he got caught on film doing something illegal, like helping a big-time criminal like Teago, threatening some little kids, he could lose his job, maybe go to jail.

Pastor Powell did a quick survey of the area, then focused on Teago. Ever so smoothly, he asked, "Can *they* go with them *now*?"

In those few seconds, Teago had regained his composure, planted a bored look on his face. Gave an *ain't no big thing* shrug. "Chops, me shoulda know you might try something *extra*."

"It's not me, Teago. . . . It's the people."

Deja broke into full-on tears. No stopping them. There was no need to hide her emotions. No need to pretend to be at the bottom of the ocean. She had people. Lots. People who stood for something. For her, too.

Teago muttered something under his breath, then waved them all away with a flick of his hand. "Fuck it. Get di whole lot of them out of here before me change me mind." He said this as if he had a choice.

"One more thing!" Teago wagged his finger at Gabriel and Hammer. "Don't think you safe. Di country no so big as you think." Spinning on his heel, he brushed past Melville, then got into the Audi with the big guy and left.

And Deja ran. Kaleisha ran, sand flying, knees flinging out to the sides, arms swinging left and right, as awkward as could be. Each stride seemed to take minutes. Deja grabbed her sister and pulled her close, smashing her face into Kaleisha's hair.

But when she looked up, Donovan had hung behind—his face was a twisted mask of fear. Her uncle was urging him to go to Deja.

"Donovan!" Deja called, and he snapped out of it and sprinted into her arms. She rocked them both, as they burst into sobs.

From the corner of her eye, she saw Gabriel walking over to Uncle, both with eyes narrowed, probably sizing each other up, some kind of testosterone thing. At last Uncle gave a grunt, extended his hand, and Gabriel shook it.

With her siblings still draped around her, Deja gestured to Gabriel. "You're coming, aren't you?" Then she took a step toward Hammer. "You too, right?!"

Gabriel tipped his head slightly in Hammer's direction.

"Can't stay here, that's fi sure." Hammer shrugged, as if *he* had a choice.

Gabriel gave Deja a sheepish grin. "We're in."

She smiled, a world of weight tumbling off her shoulders. She hugged Kaleisha and Donovan, harder, and harder still. "Shhh.

We're good. We're all good." Not wasting any more time, Deja lifted her siblings' chins. "Listen . . . listen . . . we're going to go. We're going to get on the *Queen*."

"Where are we going?" *Of course Kaleisha has to know.*

"To visit your aunt Gwen in Santa Cruz."

"Won't that be fun?" Uncle Glen asked as he walked over.

The kids' eyes brightened at the suggestion. That melted something in Deja's shoulders, and they seemed to lower back into their proper place. Then she grasped their hands and called to her uncle, "Can I pilot?"

He grinned. "Wouldn't have it any other way."

"Okay, then." But she hesitated, searching through the crowd until she saw them. Lila and Straleen. There. Both were still holding up their phones. Deja, wiping her tears, yearned to go hug them, too. Hopefully, one day she'd get to see them and tell them how much she loved them, and they could tease her for being so soppy. They were her friends . . . without exception. She raised her arm high in the air, and her girls waved hard goodbyes.

Hammer bumped fists with Pastor Powell. "Respect due . . . *Minister!*"

Jokingly, Pastor Powell ran the back of his hand across his forehead as if wiping away sweat. Deja could relate.

Digging into his pocket, Hammer fished out a set of keys. "You can take care of my bike till me come back?"

Pastor Powell took the keys, gave them a jangle. "My pleasure—might have to give it a spin now and again, just to keep it humming till you come back."

Hammer gave a firm nod. "Yeh, mon."

Gabriel stuck his fist out to bump Pastor Powell's as well. "Appreciate everything, Chops."

"Appreciate *you*, Gabriel. Took a lot to do what you did. Both you and Hammer."

"God's plan." Gabriel smiled for a moment and then, in a more serious tone, asked, "You cool?"

The pastor's eyes radiated confidence. "No problem, mon."

Deja felt a spike of pressure behind her eyes as she thought about what Gabriel had just asked the pastor. Because it hit her. The cash Melville and Teago wanted, the cash they didn't have—the pastor didn't have it either. Webber had it. In the frenzy of it all, she'd forgotten about what this all meant for Pastor Powell. As Gabriel and Hammer walked away, she whispered to him, "What are you going to do?"

He side-eyed Melville, then, still smiling, said, "Don't worry. God has a plan for me."

She could tell he believed this, so she wanted to. "Is it okay if I hug—"

But he stepped forward and hugged *her*. "God bless you and your family. If you need anything—anything at all—reach out."

He was risking so much for her, for them. She pulled away. "But seriously, will you be all right?"

"Don't worry. I'll be just fine."

"I'll be praying you are," she said with a grin.

He bowed ever so slightly. "Thank you, Deja. Godspeed."

Melville grunted. "You taking too much damn time. Unu need fi go before *me* change mi mind."

Gripping her siblings' hands once more, Deja led them to the dock, Hammer and Uncle behind her striking up a conversation about how fast the *Queen* could go. As the kids jumped from the dock onto their uncle's boat, Gabriel hesitated, surveying the beach.

"What is it?" Deja asked, a gust of wind sweeping across her face.

"I'm not sure. . . . Just, Melville . . . he looked . . . I don't know, sketchy. Like something's up."

She pivoted to check the beach as well. "How?"

"Not sure. Too . . . calm, maybe?" He bit his lip. "Just don't trust that guy."

He stood on the dock as everyone boarded, hand by his gun, gazing back to shore. Watching to see if Melville was going to try anything, Deja guessed. Uncle was checking the engines, directing Hammer to undo the lines on the port side of the boat.

Moments later Uncle joined Deja on the flybridge, wiping his hands clean on his jeans. Deja gestured to the gash on his lip. "That's pretty bad, Uncle."

He tapped his mouth with his fingertips. "This? No problem, mon. Just another beauty mark. So, where to, Captain?"

"Aunt Gwen's, but I haven't called yet." Her aunt had a huge house in the mountains—and there always seemed to be baby goats for them to play with, and lots of trees to climb, Deja thought with a smile. But she wasn't going to let herself think beyond what was next. If she could manage that, she could stay calm, focused, and fully alert for the journey that lay ahead.

"No worry. My sister always there, mon."

Deja turned the key, and the engines roared to life. She

motioned for Gabriel to come on board. He took a last glance at the shore and hopped on. As she backed the *Queen* out of its slip, Uncle put an arm over both Gabriel's and Hammer's shoulders. In a gruff voice that was only comical because Deja knew he was just playing tough, he announced, "Me can see you two no know boat, so make me school you 'bout it."

They both nodded like students on the first day of kindergarten. First Uncle opened a storage compartment, squirreled around, tugged out an armful of orange vests, and flipped them to Hammer and Gabriel. "Help the kids get dem on."

Deja had to stifle her laugh as she watched Gabriel and Hammer struggle to do the buckles on the kid's vests.

Uncle, an amused expression on his face, said, "How that going?"

Gabriel kept tinkering and finally finished buckling Donovan's vest. But Hammer was still struggling, not even done with one buckle.

Uncle gave a dismissive "pfft" and got the vests onto everyone, making a show of pulling the straps tight on Gabriel's and Hammer's.

Then Hammer pointed out to sea. "Mon, see how di ocean curve."

Uncle squinted in that direction and gestured nonchalantly. "Yeh, mon. That's the curvature of di earth."

"Huh!" Gabriel elbowed Hammer. "See, di earth *is* round."

Uncle cocked his head. "Is that even a question?"

Gabriel laughed, aimed his thumb at Hammer. "To him it is."

Uncle's brow furrowed. "Bwoy, you no go school?"

Hammer rubbed his chin, still staring at the sun sitting low but slowly rising. Then, at last, he said, "Maybe it's a disk? Di earth. You know, like a record?" He brightened as if he'd solved the riddle of the Sphinx.

Gabriel and Uncle made eye contact, shaking their heads in amazement.

Deja bit her cheek not to laugh out loud, then added more thrust. The boat evened out its keel, veered toward Negril. Her plan was to go around the island and eventually land on the South Coast. She inhaled the ocean wind, salty, fresh, and the tightness in her chest loosened for the first time in how long? Sun glint speckled the water. She felt grateful. Grateful to be behind the wheel again, charting a course, and for so many other things . . . including this gift of a calm sea.

Gabriel leaned over the side, a certain wonder in his eyes. "It's like we're flying over the water!" He did a double take when Hammer didn't respond. "Wha' wrong?"

Hammer, sitting upright, both hands on the bench, could barely nod. Probably already feeling some seasickness.

"Take some deep breaths, mon," Uncle bellowed, a huge smile on his face. Then he gestured out to sea. "Pick a point out pon di horizon and just keep staring at it. You'll be all right, mon."

Now even Kaleisha managed a sympathetic grin. But Donovan just sat there, staring down at the deck.

"Donny, Donny." Deja waved at her brother until she got his attention. "You know Aunt Gwen always bakes up a storm: sweet potato pudding, bulla . . . gizzada."

He didn't respond, a far-off look plastered to his face.

Deja tried again. "Which one is your favorite? Mine is gizzada—"

"Bulla," Kaleisha shouted.

"Festival," Gabriel said, bringing back the night they'd met at the church, an occasion that seemed like it took place a million years ago.

"She never makes *that*," Donovan said in a full-on cranky tone.

Deja looked from Gabriel and back to her brother. "We'll be okay, Donny, promise!" she called out, hoping she was right. She caught sight of a big airplane curving away from the island, a long contrail behind it. Leaving Jamaica. Departing from home, like they were.

Back in the storage compartment, Uncle rummaged around, then backed out with two handfuls of energy bars. He gave a couple to the kids, who ripped them open like it was Christmas morning. Then he flipped one to Gabriel; when Hammer frowned like he might heave, he jokingly kept offering anyway.

But with a slow turn of his head, his smile disappeared. "Deja!" he yelled, a hint of panic in his voice. "Starboard!"

Backside! Another vessel was coming toward them, fast. She couldn't make out what type.

Uncle scrambled to the hold, wiping the lenses of a pair of binoculars on his shirt. Pressing them to his eyes, he muttered, "Bumboclot."

It was a police boat. Headed their way.

Deja, Saturday, 7:50 a.m.

Gabriel smacked Uncle's arm for the binoculars. A moment later he handed them back, his face stormy. "*That's* why Melville didn't seem to go ballistic about what went down on the beach."

Hammer, face ashen, propped a hand on the gunwale and slowly stood. "Damn it! Him did have a backup plan too."

Deja shook the steering wheel, her frustration at a boil. Her eyes automatically locked onto the kids, their eyes wild, faces pinched.

Gabriel and Hammer, arms out wide for their balance, teetered over to her. "Dem must be coming fi us," Gabriel exclaimed.

Uncle had the binoculars back up. "Me feel it's di same boat that stopped me and di children yesterday."

Hammer, heaving forward like he might retch, strained to say, "Is a bloody double cross, mon."

Deja wasn't about to wait for any more talk. She went full throttle.

Kaleisha and Donovan made their way over to the flybridge. "What's happening?! What's happening?!" Kaleisha demanded.

Donovan, clutching his unopened protein bar, moaned, "I want to go *home*."

Uncle said, "Come, children. Make we go lie low pon di deck."

Donovan shook Deja's arm. "I want to go home!"

Uncle tried again. "Your aunt's will be fun, but first we need to just be a little careful." But they wouldn't budge.

Gabriel tried to guide them back. "Hey, mon. This is no joke!"

Donovan moved away.

"D—please listen to your uncle. . . . There could be a lot of bouncing, and I don't want you to get hurt," Deja tried in her most coddling tone.

And now Kaleisha was crying. "You said we'd be okay!"

She had. She had told them that. She *had to* tell them that.

Uncle got down on one knee and then lay down flat. "Well, *I'm* not going to get bounced out of the boat." He patted the deck, and at last the kids joined him.

Slam. Slam. Just in time, for the boat hit a set of waves. Water sprayed across the deck. Hammer fought for his balance, arms wheeling until Gabriel caught one. "Backside!"

"How far away are they now?" Deja asked, assessing the waters ahead.

Uncle glanced back. "Odd. Dem now keeping distance. No seem like dem want fi board us . . . yet, but—"

Gabriel cut in. "Just following us is bad enough, because then Melville will know where we land." Another wave, the biggest yet, jolted the boat, sent more spray flying. Gabriel wiped his face and added angrily, "And that means Teago will know."

"Yes. And him nah give out no second chance." The boat cut into another wave. Hammer clutched his stomach, leaned over the side, and puked.

"You okay?" Gabriel asked.

Hammer mumbled, "Don't know yet."

Uncle told the kids to stay down on the deck, got up, and walked over. Once there, he did a double take. "Backside! Look at *that* boat?"

This time Deja turned to look. There indeed was another vessel, a little more than a mile away, and it was much larger than the police boat. "Can't worry about that now; keep an eye on that police boat," she said, making some quick mental calculations. It would be hours before they could make land on the other side of the island. And even then, if the police boat followed them . . . "Uncle Glen—we can't put Auntie in any trouble. No way!"

Uncle pulled at his bottom lip. "Well, that's a mid-shore police vessel, and the *Queen* can't outrun it."

She knew, she knew. And then she had the craziest thought. . . .

No.

It was too crazy!

But . . . what if?

What if they used the go-fast boat? That one in the cove? It could outrun a patrol vessel. That was why drug dealers used them!

She said exactly that to her uncle. His eyes went wide. "Since when you have go-fast boat?"

"Long story—I'll tell you later." She tapped Gabriel, who was clinging on to the console—guy did *not* have any kind of sea legs. "What do you think?"

One eyebrow arched high. "I guess, if we can make it to the cove?"

"Which cove?" Uncle asked.

Before Deja could answer, Hammer, voice hoarse, asked, "How di hell we know if it still there?"

"How *you* know 'bout this?" Confusion seeped from Uncle's voice.

Gabriel talked over him. "But we don't know if it will start—"

"It can. I flooded it the other day, but I know what I did wrong, so this time I'll do it right."

"What last time?" Uncle's eyes became slits. "What boat? What cove?" Then his face looked betrayed as he yelped. "You flooded it. Me tell you never to do that, Deja!"

"Sorry, Uncle! All I can say is there's a go-fast at a cove near Green Island, and it might be there, and it might work." She shrugged. "That's all I know."

"That's not a lot, mon." He glanced back. "All the same, di water too shallow in a cove fi dem to get close, so we'll buy us some time, at least."

Hammer looked up blearily. "Is it me, or is that bigger boat getting closer?"

Deja peeked.

It was.

She turned the wheel hard left, angled for the cove, thinking, thinking. Webber said he'd had a team get the body of the agent, but they had left the boat. And Gabriel and Hammer had seen it. Bizarre. Why leave a $100,000 boat? Then it struck her. Was it bait? Webber was *fishing*, hoping to catch bad guys who came to the go-fast, or . . . at least *watch* them? Was he watching now? She suddenly had a ghastly vision of the agent on the go-fast. Like some deformed ghost. She shook it off, straightened the wheel.

"What if they catch us?" It was Kaleisha, back at the console. Deja immediately looked for Donovan. He was still lying stock-still on deck. This was scaring the hell out of the little guy. Shit. SHIT.

Uncle eased his arm across Deja's shoulder. "Oh, no worry 'bout that, Kaleisha. Deja is di second-best navigator in Springtown. She'll take care of us. But get back with your brother. He's a little scared, me thinks." He guided her to Donovan, planted a kiss on both their foreheads.

Deja wiped her sweaty palms one at a time on her jeans. Kaleisha's question played over and over in her mind. She wasn't going to let herself think about that now. She had to focus.

They roared ahead, bouncing over waves. The gulls following the boat mewed. Thankfully, *both* engines kept humming. Any malfunction now would be a disaster.

And finally, ahead . . . the cove . . . the go-fast boat. The shock of relief stung.

And the only important question leaked in.

Would it start?

Deja throttled down, called for her uncle who was kneeling next to the kids. As Uncle got up, Donovan started to cry.

"It's okay, Donny!" she began, when, with uneasy land-lubber steps, Gabriel switched places with Uncle. A moment later he'd fished the pyrite stone from his pocket. The one from that day on the beach?

As they closed the feet between them and the go-fast, Uncle whistled. "Backside! She's a beauty. Twin turbocharged thirteen fifties to boot. Wonder how fast she go."

"We're gonna find out." Deja motioned for her uncle to take the wheel. "Pull the *Queen* close. I'll go over and start her up."

"Can't flood it this time, you know, mon."

"Thanks for the vote of confidence," Deja hit back.

"Anytime, mon."

Hammer tapped her arm. "Look like them speed up."

Deja pivoted. The police boat had indeed speeded up. Only about half a mile away now. Still, they might just launch a smaller craft.

Gabriel said, "If they get close, they could start firing."

Kaleisha gasped. Uncle slapped Gabriel on the back, gesturing for him to be conscious of his words around the kids.

Deja wanted to say something soothing to the kids, but there was no time. Hand on the gunwale, she got ready to hop onto the go-fast when her breath quickened. The agent. The blood. Legs suddenly wobbly—stop! She couldn't let herself think about that. *Focus, Deja!*

"Close enough?" Uncle called.

Her leap over the side was her answer. The long swath of dried blood remained on the deck. Wasting no time, she lurched for the console, the keys on the panel. . . . *Please . . . please . . .*

please. She started her up. And . . . thank God, thank God, the go-fast roared to life. Deja spun, shot a thumbs-up to them all.

Gabriel and Hammer swung Kaleisha and Donovan onto the other boat, then leaped on themselves, crowding into the back. But her uncle remained on the *Queen*.

"Uncle!" Deja shouted frantically.

Gulls cawed.

Her uncle yelled back in a sheepish tone, "Maybe me should try and divert dem?" He waved out to the horizon. "Maybe drive di *Queen* over so?"

"What!" The police weren't stupid. "Uncle, we can outrun them! Get on!"

"Let's go, mon!" Hammer joined in.

But her uncle just stood there. Was he really going to try this stupid stunt?

"Uncle, please!" Kaleisha screeched.

A look—of sadness—passed over her uncle's face as he patted the *Queen*'s console as if saying goodbye . . . then eased himself on board the go-fast.

And now they had to *go*.

"Get low!" Gabriel warned as several loud pops sounded from the police boat.

"Hurry, dem a shoot," Hammer yelled, pulling the kids down beside him. Uncle joined them and said, eyes steely, "Do your thing, Deja."

She turned the wheel about thirty degrees. The go-fast pivoted. Then she swung the wheel back, getting ready. "Everybody hold on!" she cautioned, and punched the throttle. The engines roared, the boat jerked forward, and they jetted out of the cove. Donovan and Kaleisha screamed.

"Backside!" Uncle yelled, almost a cheer.

The boat was at 40 miles per hour . . . 50, 60, 70, 80, and she topped it out at 90! Not wanting to go to the full 105 . . . not yet. The power of this boat was like nothing she'd ever experienced. It was as if they were actually cutting through air. Larger rogue waves slammed the boat with jolting thuds. Deja gripped the wheel tightly; otherwise she'd go flying like the sea spray.

"Yeh, mon!" Uncle whooped.

Deja angled away from the police boat, which seemed dangerously close. Then, in almost no time, the distance between them and the police boat widened.

"Dem no have this kind of speed." Uncle's voice sounded almost drunk with the boat's power.

And then she saw it. Two flares, shooting across the sky.

Deja and Uncle eyed each other. Gabriel scrambled across the deck on all fours, then hauled himself up. "What di hell?!"

The boat they'd seen before was a massive Coast Guard cutter, closing in from the port side. It flashed its lights. Uncle tapped Deja's hand, motioned for her to throttle back.

She swallowed hard. "But—"

Uncle's voice was full of awe. "We no have no ship like that. Must be American, mon. We no want that kinda trouble."

She felt a pulsing in her ears. Should she do what Uncle said? The go-fast might be able to outrun the larger vessel—

But wait. The agent—could they be with the DEA? On a hunch, she checked on the Jamaican police boat. It was turning,

turning away! Then she knew for sure not to mess with the cutter bearing down on them.

Once she throttled back, Deja could hear Kaleisha and Donovan whimpering. She motioned for Uncle to take the wheel, then squatted down to pull them close. She hushed and hushed the kids. The thrum of the cutter's engine grew as it closed in, vibrating, it seemed, inside Deja's very body. Louder than that, however, was the voice from a loudspeaker on the ship.

"Stand down. Stand down. Put your hands in the air!"

Gabriel, Saturday, 11:30 a.m.

Gabriel hadn't seen a soul since the officer on the deck of the cutter had commanded, "Put that one in the brig. We'll interrogate him after this one."

Gabriel spent an hour at least in the bowels of the ship, sitting on a hard cot in a tiny cell with metal bars facing three other cells, all empty. He had the whole jail to himself, the only sounds a constant low grumble from the engine and occasional clanking from the network of pipes that ran along the ceiling. In some odd way, they reminded him of the noises he'd listened to during the long nights at the orphanage: the rooster's crow, the cats fighting, the loose pipes banging inside the walls—sounds that felt like company, proof he wasn't alone.

He lay back, wondering for the hundredth time where Hammer was, what that officer was asking him. And what about Deja and the kids? Her uncle? And what the hell was going to happen next? If they were all remanded to Melville, might as well kill them now, save Teago the trouble. . . .

A creaking sound.

The door to the "brig" was opening. Must be his turn for interrogation. He stood to see, in disbelief, the same coastguardsman who'd locked him up, along with Hammer—and Webber—walking in.

Gabriel pressed his head against the bars in defeat. Of all the people in the world, Webber? There was no doubt left in Gabriel's mind now—Webber was an undercover agent.

The coastguardsman, sunburned and blond, stopped in front of the cell. "Back away. Take a seat on the cot. Place your hands under your thighs."

It didn't register at first that they might consider him a threat. "Back away, *now*. . . ."

Gabriel did as the man demanded. Keys jangling, he unlocked Gabriel's cell door and ushered Hammer in. But as he moved to close it, Webber stuck out his arm to block him. He exchanged glances with the coastguardsman, who then took a step back.

Webber did the same, leaving a narrow opening. A sign? Or was Webber just messing with him? Gabriel looked to Hammer for clues—a secret twitch or nudge—but Hammer only frowned, revealing nothing. What had Webber said to him?

But what mattered more was "What are you going to do with the others?"

Webber folded his arms. "You . . . should probably be more concerned with what I'm going to do with *you*." His expression unreadable, he continued. "I'm going to ask you one question. Be careful how you answer, because it's the most important question of your life."

Gabriel tried to corral his breath. Give the barest minimum of a nod, barely a tilt, careful to appear calm, cool.

Webber's tone became more businesslike, more fitting the shipping agent he'd pretended to be and the undercover agent that he apparently was. "Two days ago, your friends—Jamal Jones and Fitzsimmons Roy, aka Blood Moon—were supposed to exchange approximately twelve kilos of cocaine that had come in from South America for half a million dollars. Instead, the jackasses tried to rip off the cash from the courier. Didn't know he was undercover DEA." He paused. "During the attempted theft, shots were fired. . . . DEA killed your friends." His stare was ice. "Did you know or have any part in this?"

Gabriel swallowed hard. "No . . . no . . . I didn't. Hammer didn't either."

Webber reached for the bars of the cell gate.

Webber didn't believe him! Bumboclot! But it was the truth! In desperation, Gabriel lunged forward, pushing on the gate. "No! I swear."

The coastguardsman had his pistol out as quickly as any posse member. "Back away. Now!"

Hammer grabbed Gabriel by the shoulder. "G—chill! Chill!"

But Gabriel held on, he and Webber in a staring contest, both pushing on the gate. No way was Gabriel going to let it close. No way were he and Hammer getting locked away, not for something they'd had no part in. Gabriel knew he wasn't just holding on to a cold bar on a cell gate. He was holding on to his and Hammer's lives.

The moment was fat with meaning somehow, like when

Chops had talked to him at the party, how they'd joked about *God's plan*. Then, Gabriel had dismissed it as just a *phrase*, a spiritual thing that you said when you were just talking stuff. But now, here he was, on an American Coast Guard cutter, away from Melville and Teago, and the words affected him like they never had before. Maybe God's plan was a kind of *leap of faith*.

And with that understanding, he stood there reassessing his entire life as the overhead pipes clanked. The ship's hull groaned. And at last, Gabriel let go over the cell bars like Webber had asked.

The air in the room tightened.

Webber's eyes narrowed. His lips twitched. Then, instead of closing the gate, he pulled it halfway, then . . . all the way open.

"Come with me," he ordered, a mysterious look on his face as he strode for the brig door.

Gabriel nearly sank to the floor, limbs subject to some greater gravity. "There's a lot I don't understand, still."

Webber wheeled around, a half smirk on his face. "Go ahead."

"Deja said there was a man on the boat—"

"A dead agent," Hammer added.

"Yeah." Gabriel thought of Jamal's and Blood Moon's twisted, lifeless bodies. "And when Hammer and me got there, there wasn't any agent."

"There was a shootout." Webber's stare went far off, like he was actually there on the beach. "The agent got them, barely got back to the boat."

Hammer ran a hand over his head. "So, why did you leave the boat there?"

"Why do you think?"

Hammer gave his head another rub. "A trap?"

Webber nodded. "There was a tracker on board. We figured somebody would come and we'd follow them, see where it took us."

Hammer asked the very question at the tip of Gabriel's tongue. "But what about the cocaine—"

"Company rules—my team is allowed to leave the cash, the boat, or anything like that to act as bait, but we don't leave drugs. Now let's—"

Gabriel held up a hand, gesturing for more. There was still too much he didn't know. "All this just to get Teago? There're a lot bigger dons in Jamaica."

Webber grinned . . . wider this time. "He's a start. Crime is out of control, gunmen are running the streets like wild dogs, and common decency is a fucking joke to them. And it's because there's an unholy connection between crooked law enforcement and organized crime that's murdering this country. . . . But I'm going to smash it apart." Webber said this as if it were a blood oath.

Hammer huffed. "Dat all good, but what about us?"

Deja, Saturday, 12:30 p.m.

eja rubbed her hands together, trying to warm them, waiting for Uncle to come back. They were freezing, even though it was way too hot in this "compartment," as the coastguardsman had called it. She could see out the porthole, the turquoise ocean glimmering. The compartment was twice the size of their living room back in Springtown, and this couch was a lot more comfortable. The kids had fallen asleep on it in seconds. But man, what she'd give to be back at the house now, to have had none of this happen. Shit.

At least they gave her back the money—a coastguardsman had checked and returned the green backpack Straleen had gotten her last night, and thank goodness, the $15,000 was still inside. More importantly, the kids were safe for the moment, fed and asleep. Deja envied their sweet heads, empty of the endless questions that were pummeling hers. What were these American Coast Guard people going to do with them? How was her mother doing? Was Pastor Powell okay? And what about

Gabriel and Hammer? They were probably in deep shit. And how long were they going to talk to Uncle? He'd been gone for nearly an hour! She glanced out the porthole. Where the hell was this ship going, anyway? Then the most ridiculous thought of all—fish she'd caught earlier in the week and frozen for the weekend were still in the fridge back home. Forty dollars US in snapper and parrotfish, going to rot. Damn.

Donovan scootched up against her, then fell back asleep. Kaleisha lay curled up against her other side, knocked out, and no wonder, after she put away two servings of mashed and a big fat chicken breast. Especially given what they'd gone through over the last horrible day. Despite everything, Deja felt a glimmer of thankfulness. At least they were okay. . . . At least that.

Footsteps. Deja raised her eyes warily. . . . Webber. Webber! Her mouth fell open. Did he think she was part of the posse? Drug running? She was about to tell him she could explain, when . . . more footsteps. A tall blond coastguardsman came into the compartment and behind him—Gabriel and Hammer.

The unexpectedness of it all gathered into a lump that lodged in her throat. Then she let out a low cry, about to jump up before remembering not to wake the children.

Gabriel's eyes were intense, mournful, as if he had cried or just gone through something sleep wouldn't help him forget, yet she saw it—they grew brighter as he saw her, the kids. Hammer's eyes, though clear as usual, focused, still betrayed apprehension.

Deja showed them both *What's going on?* looks, but Webber

was motioning impatiently to the couch on the other side of the compartment; Hammer and Gabriel took seats.

Deja pointed to the chairs next to the couch. "There's room over here."

Webber pressed his lips together. "This is fine."

Deja's thoughts ping-ponged. Why were they all here? Had he charged them with something crazy? They'd helped her. It wasn't fair!

Then Webber was in front of her, gazing down at the sleeping children. His eyes went soft for just a second. "I'll keep my voice down, but I need to talk to you."

Deja, bracing for whatever he was going to accuse *her* of, jumped in first. "Okay—but first, can I know . . . why . . . how . . . uh, why are *you* here?"

There was another momentary softness in his eyes. "I'll explain all that. But *you* tell me—um, when I left you in Anchovy, Gabriel and Hammer got to you. Am I right?"

She didn't want to sell either of them out, so she didn't respond. What answer might negatively influence their fate?

Webber glanced over his shoulder to the other couch, then back to Deja. "Don't worry about those two; I've got what I need to know from them."

"What is that?" It sounded desperate. She wished it hadn't.

"Please answer the question, Deja. They'd gotten to you after I left, yes?"

He seemed for real. Just as he had when she met him. From across the room, Gabriel caught her eye, nodded. "Okay—yes," she said at last. "I needed to charge my phone. So I went into the restaurant . . . got some food—I hadn't eaten all day—and . . ." She looked over to Gabriel and Hammer, then back to Webber. "Then they showed up. They were searching for me."

He nodded.

She rubbed her hands again—why were they so cold? She replayed the words she'd just said, too close to damning testimony. "But . . . but . . . they helped me! A lot! I mean, I wouldn't have gotten the kids back or anything without them—"

"I know, Deja. I know. Pastor Powell told me."

Deja's mouth fell open.

Hammer elbowed Gabriel. "Me tell you him wasn't no priest."

"He is. But he's also something else," Webber said to them matter-of-factly. "We've been monitoring the situation for a long time now."

Bumboclot! Was Pastor Powell really an *undercover* agent? Was Webber DEA? "Who's 'we'?" she dared to ask.

"Jamaican Intelligence SSB. Special Services Branch."

What?! She didn't even know they had such a thing! "But . . . there's an American flag on deck. This is a Coast Guard ship."

"Joint operation. It's why the US is authorized to operate in our waters." His eyes seemed to search hers. "We would have intervened on your behalf back there on the beach, but it would have jeopardized a years-long operation." He said this in what almost sounded like an apologetic tone.

Which made her think of—Uncle Glen. "My uncle, where is *he*? He didn't do *anything*."

Webber gestured upward. "Don't worry. He's up top with the master chief."

"Master chief? Who's that?"

"A coastguardsman in charge of security . . . It's nothing to worry about."

Her left leg started twitching. "And—and are we in trouble? I mean, we—"

"No. No, Deja, you're not." He let a half smile peek out. "Once we dock in Miami, we're going to meet with someone—"

Miami? Miami?! She was so stunned she could hardly get the words out. "Miami? We're going to *United States*?"

"Deja, I need to be honest here. It's probably best for you and your family to leave Jamaica. Teago has ties all over the island. And though he's in custody, we have to take all precautions, especially with children involved."

Shock lit up Gabriel's face. "You got him?"

"Damn right," Webber said, then turned back to Deja. "As I was starting to say, a case manager will come help you start your relocation process, if that's okay?"

"But my friends . . . There are others, too. . . . They all helped me. Will Teago want revenge on *them*?"

"And what about Melville?" Gabriel asked from across the room.

Webber motioned for Gabriel to wait. Folding his arms, he told Deja, "I wouldn't worry about the others so much. Teago would more likely be focused on you. Again, that's why we need to relocate you and your family." He swung around to Gabriel. "And we also have Melville in custody. And between him and Teago, we're going to squeeze out information about all the corrupt police who are working with the gangs. We already have Teago. More will fall." Webber said this like it was personal to him. He said this like he could hardly wait.

"Backside," Hammer muttered, clearly impressed but trying to hide it.

"You said it, mon. This is just the beginning. Crooked police, gangs, and even some politicians have been corrupting the soul of Jamaica for a long time now." Webber's jaw clenched, then unclenched. Determination practically emanated from him, Deja thought. "But it's all going to stop now." He paused. "And, um . . . another thing . . ." He reached into his pocket. "My men found it on the go-fast." He handed her the pin Donovan had made. "I can't give you a medal, but maybe this will suffice."

She ran her fingertips over the thin wood, then gazed at Donovan and Kaleisha. They were the real trophies. And though she'd tried her best, she'd put them through a lot. A whole lot. But as she closed her hand over the "medal," she vowed that from here on she was going to do her absolute best to protect them, whether they ended up in Miami or Timbuktu. Finally, she looked up at Webber. "Thank you."

"You're welcome—"

Gabriel cleared his throat. "And, um, what about us?"

Webber pursed his lips. "I've been wondering that myself. . . ."

Deja swallowed, then couldn't hold it in. "But they *helped* me. Melville had my *family*. Who knows what could have happened to them—" She broke off, blinking tears. "If they hadn't helped me, I just don't know—"

"I'm well aware, Deja." Webber gave his neck a crack in one direction, then the other, clearly intent on making Gabriel and

Hammer sweat. At last he cast his gaze on them. "I'm going to give you a chance. I'm going to investigate what it might take to relocate you both . . . because you did offer aid in a time of serious need to Deja, who was, in effect, working with the DEA."

Gabriel rubbed his hands over his knees as Webber's face went stern. "Given your criminal backgrounds, this is no slam dunk. But I will try to get you asylum in the US. And if it all works out, you'll have to do community service, lots of it." He aimed a finger at them. "And if I hear that either one of you so much as *jaywalks*, I'm going to have you deported right into Teago's jail cell. You understand?"

A second chance! With dread tingling up her spine, she sought Gabriel's eyes, willing him to look at her, willing him to agree. When at last she caught his gaze, she nodded. Hard.

Gabriel and Hammer exchanged glances.

Hammer jutted out his jaw. "I'm with it."

Gabriel shifted his attention to Webber. "Yeh, mon. Yes."

"I mean it—so much as a *jaywalking* ticket."

"I get it. We get it," Gabriel said. "And . . . thank you."

Hammer joined in, "Yeh, mon. Thank you."

Deja felt giddy with relief for them, almost delirious, not knowing whether to laugh or cry. Then Uncle and a stocky coastguardsman with massive forearms strolled into the compartment. The two men shook hands, the man left, and Uncle made a beeline for Deja. "Okay?"

She gripped his hand and squeezed. "Yeah . . . you?"

"Yeh, mon. No problem."

Webber glanced at his watch. "Deja, anything else I can do

for you? We still have about a day of travel in front of us."

She took out her phone, battery dead again. "Could I borrow a charger?" she asked. "My mom might call."

Webber tipped his head back, as if remembering. "Oh yes, I've been told about your mother. We'll get word to her. She'll need to be part of the relocation as well, given that you're all minors."

Mom! Deja could . . . not . . . wait to see her mom again. The kids were going to go crazy when they found out.

"As for the charger, I think I can scuffle one up for you."

Tears pressed at Deja's eyes as she ran her fingers over the grooves of the pin in her hand. Then she looked back up at Webber. "And . . . sorry, I have some more questions. A lot, actually."

Webber gave her a patient smile.

The relief of a moment ago had already shifted into a torrent of problems. "I mean, our house, all our things? How are we going to live? You know . . . school for the kids?" She laughed nervously. "I have the fifteen thousand, and thanks for that, but—"

"All good questions," Webber said soothingly. "We'll work all that out when we get to port in Miami." He held her gaze. "I promise you, okay?"

Deja nodded as she wiped at her tears. "Thank you."

As soon as Webber left with the blond coastguardsman to look for a charger, Gabriel and Hammer bounced up and over to Deja.

Gabriel squatted beside her, their eyes on the same level.

"Thanks for having our backs—"

"Yeh, mon, thank you," Hammer joined in.

"After all you did for *me*? I thank *you*. Both." Then she asked Uncle, "Sure you okay?"

Uncle waved a hand dismissively. "Oh, no worry, mon. Me and di master chief a good friend now. Him is a fisherman too, angler him say." Uncle shrugged, hope in his eyes. "Say he might be able to help me get some fishing work in Miami." He gave his ample belly a satisfied pat.

Kaleisha mumbled something. Deja ran her hand over her sister's hair until she settled back into sleep.

"Maybe we should talk more later, when dem wake," Uncle suggested.

He was right. Gabriel extended his warm hand. She took it with her cold one. They both squeezed. Deja could tell he was as reluctant to let go as she was.

But Uncle was looking at Gabriel and Hammer, nodding toward the other couch, as if to tell them they should give Deja some time alone.

As they walked away, she tipped her head back against the metal wall and closed her eyes, tired to the bone. Yet her brain wouldn't stop. How was her mother doing? Fifteen thousand would be good, but they'd obviously need a lot more than that to survive in America. Where would they end up living? Would they be accepted there? What kind of job would Deja be able to get? Would the kids like it there? And she'd never see Straleen and Lila again. . . .

When she finally opened her eyes, Gabriel and Hammer

were staring out one porthole, Uncle out another. For a second she wondered what they were all looking at. Then it became clear. Jamaica! And it came over her like sudden rain in October. They were *all* leaving Jamaica, *forever*. There was no way for any kind of safe return. Her lower lip trembled. Kaleisha and Donovan were losing the only home they had known. Her mother would never be able to go back and teach, the one job she truly loved. No going back.

Deja had lost track of time when Webber strode back into the room, tapping his phone and swiping a couple of times. "Found a cord, but, um, somebody wants to say hello." He handed the phone to her.

She looked, then looked again. It couldn't be—it was! The agent . . . Gonzalez. He. Was alive? He was alive! "Oh my God!" Deja slapped her hand over her mouth.

The man on the phone gave a half smile. "Good to see you under better circumstances," he said from what appeared to be a hospital bed. It seemed like somebody else was holding up a phone for him. Deja's mind went to the gaffer tape that she'd wrapped around his leg, smelled the metallic tang of blood as if she were right back on that boat.

"I owe you something . . . my life." His low-pitched voice went hoarse. "Deja, I hope to meet you one day." He smiled with closed lips. "But I'm a little tired right now. So, for now, just wanted to say thank you. See you around."

Then the screen went blank. But she kept on staring at the phone. Thank God he was alive!

Webber gently pried his phone away from Deja. "He's a tough

man," he said. "But as tough as he is, he'd never have made it if you hadn't stopped that bleeding and put in that phone call to 112. So I join him in saying thank you. I mean that." He gave her a slight bow and left.

Had that just happened? Had any of it? Everything was so surreal. The only thing she could be sure of was that she felt like there was a river running through her body, firm and strong. She studied Uncle, Gabriel, and Hammer, silently thanking them for all they'd done. Now, near-total exhaustion, she lifted her hand and placed a lock of her hair back into place. Then she gazed out a porthole across the room. With the glistening ocean so big and wide, the horizon seemed unreachable. But she thought about how she'd have to work hard, harder than ever before, harder than anyone else, day or night, whatever it took. She'd have to—no doubt about it—because, along with her mother, she'd have to make a new life for her siblings, and for herself, because better must come.

Acknowledgments

My agent, Faye Bender, has graced me and this undertaking with her extraordinary guidance and insight. I can't imagine a better agent. My editor, Caitlyn Dlouhy, is simply a great visionary who tirelessly pushes every page to be better and better. I can't thank her enough for her brilliant insight and the ever-encouraging way she conveys it. And thanks to all the great professionals at Atheneum and Simon & Schuster for all the awesome work you've put into this novel.

I have to thank Mark Mershon for the wisdom and experience he's lent to this project (and for his meritorious service to our country). To my writing group: Julia Rold, Tracey Palmer, Andrea Meyer, Bob Fernandes, Janet Edwards, Michele Ferrari, Elizabeth Chiles Shelburne, Bonnie Walsh, Rachel Barenbaum, Helen Browk, Louise Berliner, Jen Johnson—thanks for your early notes. Special thanks to Pamela Loring—thanks for all your great editorial insights. I must always thank Eve Bridburg, and the awesome writing center GrubStreet. Special thanks to the always fantastic Jenn De Leon. To my go-to aesthetes, Andrew Porter and Geoff Wilson, for our writerly talks and walks: thank you!

I'm so thankful for the ongoing support of Rob Swadosh, Michelle Hoover; the Brookline Public Library; the Brookline Public Library's Teen Librarian and comic expert, Robin Brenner; Victor Levin; Stephanie Julie Carrick Dalton; Adam Merfar; Rene Bastian; Joe Petito; Gayle Damon Ross; Oral Nurse; Piper Hickman; Hillary Spann; Rossen Ventzislovov; Jon and Lisa Gold; Cory Noonan; Esther Pedersen; Andy Salkin; Dr. Micki Fagin; Dr. Richard Balaban; Dr. Jose Trevejo; Dr. Alok Kapoor; Dr. Adam Keene; Daryl and Chris Andrews; Sana Haroon; Big Lou Kosokovalis; John Fitzgerald; Gunner Polacheck; Angus Lansing; John and Sheila Spezio; Helen Dimos; Linda Cutting; Ray and Susan Liu; Erik Blazer and Zsuzsa Kaldy; Shannon McDonough; Fabien and Christine Siegel; Sami Rasheed; Mikail Brincker; Tilde Westmark; Bozoma St. John; and matriarch Annie Bricker.

And I have to thank my dad for his counsel, and my uncle and cousins back-a-yard and inna foreign for their support.

Lastly, my brilliant wife, Maria, and amazing children, Oona and Babette, have given their insights and encouragement from day one. Thank you! You are everything.